WITHDRAWN
D0007524

Mother,
May I
Sleep with
Danger?

ALSO BY CLAIRE RAINWATER JACOBS

There Was a Little Boy

Mother, May I Sleep with Danger?

Claire Rainwater Jacobs

DONALD I. FINE BOOKS
NEW YORK

Donald I. Fine Books
Published by the Penguin Group
Penguin Books USA Inc., 375 Hudson Street,
New York, New York 10014, U.S.A.
Penguin Books Ltd, 27 Wrights Lane,
London W8 5TZ, England
Penguin Books Australia Ltd, Ringwood,
Victoria, Australia
Penguin Books Canada Ltd, 10 Alcorn Avenue,
Toronto, Ontario, Canada M4V 3B2
Penguin Books (N.Z.) Ltd, 182–190 Wairau Road,
Auckland 10, New Zealand

Penguin Books Ltd, Registered Offices:
Harmondsworth, Middlesex, England

First published by Donald I. Fine Books, an imprint of
Penguin Books USA Inc.

First Printing, August, 1997
10 9 8 7 6 5 4 3 2 1

LIBRARY OF CONGRESS CATALOGING-IN-PUBLICATION DATA:

Jacobs, Claire Rainwater.
Mother, may I sleep with danger? / Claire Rainwater Jacobs.
p. cm.
ISBN 1-55611-515-6
I. Title.
PS3560.A2495M68 1997
813′.54—dc21 97-12905
CIP

Printed in the United States of America
Set in Simoncini Garamond

PUBLISHER'S NOTE

This is a work of fiction. Names, characters, places, and incidents either are the products of the author's imagination or are used fictitiously, and any resemblance to actual persons, living or dead, events, or locales is entirely coincidental.

For Ronnie and Veronica,
and in memory of Rozsi

Many thanks to Caroll; Andrew; Stefan; Jo Ann Miller, my dear friend for her support and encouragement; Stacy Prince, for her friendship, advice, and for teaching me so much; Jennifer R. Walsh; Donald Fine; Carol Brennan; Anita Rich; Cherrill Colson; Lorraine Schimolar for her great kindness and insight; and to Nancy and Herb Katz for their help with the title.

Prologue

Spring 1990

BILLY OWENS SMILED into the mirror. He ran his fingers through his neatly combed, curly hair and adjusted his tie. He patted his newish jacket, posing first with it buttoned, then unbuttoned. It was all for April. Everything connected with April raised his gray life above the ordinary.

With April on his arm, all eyes were on him. Billy with the smartest, prettiest girl in town. Billy with the long and leggy blonde, the best catch in the school. He crumpled the letter he had written her the night before in a fit of anxiety and stuffed it in his pants pocket, grabbed his school books, and headed for the front door.

Thinking about April, he almost stumbled on a rock in the driveway and angrily kicked it aside. How would he get through the day until his date with her? Every day since he had met her a year ago, he had thought about doing it with her, being her first. He wondered if there would be blood.

He looked at his car. He was embarrassed by its age, its dents, its mismatched paint. But April didn't seem to mind, and that was all that counted. One day, though, he would buy a sports car.

BILLY HAD A feeling of dread as he looked up toward the open window for a sign of her. It was nothing, he thought, just those vague, shadowy fears that pursued him, fears he had to shake off at night so he could sleep. He hummed the tune he always hummed to help push the dark away, the tune about their small Indiana town.

Inhaling the perfume of the lilacs, he unconsciously clenched and unclenched his fist around the letter in his pocket as he walked along the stone path leading to April's white colonial house.

AT THE SHRILL of the doorbell, April glanced at the clock next to her bed. He's early, she thought in a panic, and hurriedly put the framed poem he had written for her back on the wall. Earlier she had almost succeeded in prying out the warped nail it had hung on. Feeling guilty now, she dropped the hammer she had been using onto the Stones poster that lay on her desk.

Why did she feel guilty? She had a right to change her life, to start fresh. She had dreams of a singing career and she had talent. Billy Owens had no goals, except her. Well, he just wasn't right for her anymore. And now that he was graduating it seemed the right time to split up. Oh, she may have been impressed by him at first—after all, he was older, a senior, and so good-looking and with good manners. But then he'd gotten to be too much, wanted to take over her life. Yes, time to end it.

When the bell rang insistently again, she ran downstairs to let him in, and when she opened the door and saw his face, she had a rush of second thoughts. Billy was on the slim side, handsome, and not much taller than she was. He looked younger than eighteen, and with his boyish freckled face, green eyes, and bright red hair, he was so attractive, her friends all envied her. Was she right to give up this guy?

Billy kissed her on the lips, flicking his tongue in her mouth. "I'm part of you, April." His voice was soft, nearly a whisper. He kissed her eyelids, put his tongue in her ear. "*You* are part of me," he said, his fears forgotten.

April's resolve was disappearing, replaced by a rush of . . . what? Confusion, desire. But when he grabbed hold of her, pressing her hard against him, she could push him away, remembering again why she had begun dreading their dates. He made her feel suffocated, always demanding they belonged together. For God's sake, she was only fourteen—until next week, anyway. He looked like a kid, but he was three years older. They were too different. He would be in college soon and—

"Are you alone?" he asked as he followed her upstairs to her room.

"Of *course* I'm alone."

He could have kicked himself for asking. Stupid. He didn't want her nervous, wanted her calm, reassured, willing.

"Who did you think would be here, Billy?"

He took in each corner of her room, as if she actually might have someone hidden there. He knew it was crazy; she would never *hide* anyone. Only a low-class type like him would ever even think of such a corny thing. His palms were sweating.

Her feminine bedroom calmed him. The canopied bed, the eyelet coverlet matching the dust ruffles, and the starched white curtains, her awards, neatly framed, somehow made him feel safe, almost comfortable.

"See, no one hiding anywhere."

"I cut gym just to see you. I . . . I couldn't wait to see you." He knew she didn't buy it, that she realized he had come early to spy on her. His comfort level was fast evaporating.

She seemed to be looking him over, the way she was taking in his corduroy jacket and his smartly fitting khaki trousers. He stood close to her, touched her hair with his fingers. Her hair—straight, blond, shoulder-length, the color of early Indiana corn, he thought.

"You're perfect, April," he whispered, scarcely hearing his own voice. He moved his hand along her neck, down the gold chain with the cross that hung on her throat, slipped his hand into her blouse. She nudged him away. "I . . . haven't finished practicing—"

He pushed her down on the bed and wrapped his legs around her. "Sing to *me,*" he whispered in her ear, pinning her to the bed, pressing on top of her, getting hard from the firmness of her young body, the feel of her breasts rising with her breathing. He put his hand between her legs, rubbing her. Sometimes she almost couldn't resist, but they had always stopped.

She was breathing hard, letting herself go for a minute. He lifted her skirt. Now, before she—

She pushed him aside and jumped up from beneath him. The telephone was ringing. She held tight to her cordless phone, backed away from the bed.

"I gotta go," she said into the phone after a minute. And then: "Billy, I'm sorry, but you are getting to be a . . . a pain in the ass." Yes, get it over with, she thought as she put the phone down. "And don't look at me like that, don't try to make me feel guilty about talking to Mark. He's just a guy in my music class. Why should I feel guilty . . . ?"

"Because I *love* you," he said, banging his fist on her night table. A glass figurine of a ballet dancer smashed to the floor.

"Look what you've done!"

"No one will love you the way I do."

"*Don't* love me."

He tried to force back his rage. "Okay, okay, I'm sorry."

"You're lying, you're not sorry."

But he *was* sorry—sorry to have her so upset with him, sorry he had lost his cool, shown his anger. Before they had never fought this way. He'd been able to smooth things over, to back off, even make her laugh.

"You make me feel guilty no matter who I'm with, Billy. You won't ever let me be with anyone else—even my friends—"

"I never told you not to see them!"

"I feel it anyway. It's the way you *act.*"

"You're crazy, you're lying."

The rage in his voice scared her, but she couldn't stop herself, not now. She held out the finger encircled by his amethyst school ring. "This ring doesn't mean you *own* me."

She saw the hurt and anger in his eyes and knew she shouldn't have said it, even before he grabbed her outstretched hand and tried to wrench the ring from her finger.

When his large fingers moved up to grip her wrist she jerked back, but he grasped her harder, burning her wrist.

"You're *hurting* me." As she raised her left hand to push him away his free hand swung up and slapped her hard across the face.

Stunned, she stared at him. No longer Billy, a stranger.

He knew it now. He was losing her. He opened his hand, brought her fingers to his lips. "Forgive me," he whispered, and tried to kiss her reddened cheek.

"Get *away* from me. I never want to see you again!"

"This is all . . . all a mistake. You know it, April. You know I love you, we love each other. I mean, what will people say? You're my girl, we're going to the prom together."

She pulled the ring off and pushed it into his hand. As she stepped back, a small piece of broken glass cut her bare heel. She ignored it and picked up the phone by her bed.

"Who are you calling?"

"My mother, okay? She told me to call after I finished practicing."

"You're calling to tell her about *this*—"

"No, really . . ."

Maybe she was telling the truth, he thought. Her mother always worried about her. It didn't change anything. He understood he had lost her, but he wouldn't accept it. He clicked the phone off with his finger and reached out for her. He grabbed her blouse and tore a piece of it.

Screams. He stared at what he had done, as though his hand had acted on its own. He lunged at her, clamped his right hand over her mouth. "Please *don't,*" he told her. His left hand clutched her throat. "The neighbors will hear," he said, squeezing her mouth shut. "Promise you won't scream." She could only nod.

She couldn't breathe. He was holding her too tight, his left hand still gripped her throat.

Abruptly he let go. But she was wedged between the bed and her desk. He was blocking her way to the door.

She collapsed onto the bed. He sat next to her, began patting her hair.

"I do love you, April. I do." He repeated the words like a mantra, as much to himself as to her as he caressed her face and body.

"Then let me go," she half sobbed, watching him trying to undress her. "I don't *want* to, please, please, Billy . . ."

"You're mine, April. I *need* you."

He kissed her wet face, and she felt his breath on her, his saliva. She could smell him through his sweat. Repulsed, she tensed every muscle and, with all her will and strength, shoved him away, snatched her cordless phone, jumped up and, almost tripping on the top step, ran downstairs.

She could hear him coming after her, his footsteps thumping down the carpeted stairs. She would never make it outside. . . . She ran into the kitchen, slammed the door shut, locked it, and dialed 911. Answer, *answer* . . . One . . . there was a crash at the door. Two . . . her chest constricted, her breath shorter with each ring.

The weak lock gave way, and he pushed the door open, hammer in hand. As he moved toward her, she dropped the phone on the counter, pulling her hand away an instant before he swung the hammer over his head and split the phone apart.

Huddled in the corner, fear strangling her voice, she kept her eyes fixed on the hammer. But, incredibly, what he thrust at her was his poem. "*Read it*," he ordered, the hammer raised.

"*Remember this?*" he asked. She nodded, unable to speak. "*What is this?*" he demanded, pushing the poem in her face.

"The . . . the poem you wrote me."

"For what?" He smashed the hammer on the butcher-block counter.

"My . . . birthday."

"Read it."

"I can't—"

He grabbed her neck, pushing her face closer to the poem.

" 'The passion of April,' " she read as the hammer pounded the rhythm on the counter.

" 'The poise of June/The poignance of October's tune.' " She stopped. He dug his fingers into her neck.

" 'From the sturdy rock of winter-hewn—' "

"*Louder, read the last line louder.*

" '*. . . is my love for you,*' " he intoned, swinging the hammer close to her, grazing her head.

She screamed, could feel blood running down her face.

And then she watched in disbelief as he got down on his knees in front of her. "I never meant to hurt you, don't leave me. *Don't . . .*"

She tried to run, but he was on his feet after her, grabbing at her. She backed into the doorway, legs wobbling beneath her.

The phone rang upstairs. For a split second her eyes moved in the direction of the ringing— Billy struck her in the chest with the hammer, knocking her to the floor. When she dared to raise her eyes, she saw him standing over her with the hammer. He raised it high, turning it as he struck her, the claw penetrating her throat.

He stepped back as blood gushed from her in an arced stream. No more songs for you, April, he thought as he brought the hammer up again. Gurgling sounds. She was trying to breathe, but it sounded like crying.

The phone rang. "Mommy," she mouthed, but there was no sound as the hammer came down again, this time cracking her skull.

Did he see her lips move? He bent over her blood-soaked body to listen. All he could hear was the breath that made her lips flutter as it passed between them. "I'm sorry, Mommy."

No sound now. He rammed his graduation ring back on her finger and watched as she shut her eyes to die.

He stepped over her and walked to the sink to wash the blood away. He knew he had to hold on to himself; he was shaking, and suddenly he was afraid. Sweat was on his forehead and in his armpits.

He peeked through the kitchen window. The sun shone. The lawn sprinkler sprayed innocently. A bird twittered in a treetop. The sky, still blue, covered the same world it had when he had entered April's house less than an hour ago. But nothing could ever be the same. When they found April, when they saw the blood, he would be hunted down. Even his father would join April's neighbors to track him. He could see the police, helicopters, troopers, dogs chasing him. They would show his face on national news, tell his story on *America's Most Wanted.* There would be no place for him to hide, no place someone couldn't ferret him out— He punched his thigh again and again. "Think! Think!" He squeezed the words out, wanting to hear human sounds if only from himself. Panic welled at the thought of the door opening, of being found with April. April . . . she was almost unrecognizable.

The sight of her exposed on the floor accused him. He had to cover her up, and with that thought his instinct to save his skin took over.

He thought of the patchwork blanket he and April had used when they had picnicked in their secret place by the abandoned quarry. The blanket, which he knew was stored upstairs in April's closet, and the old quarry loomed in his mind like signs, signs that told him the way to save himself.

He filled the stainless steel sink with hot water, adding green detergent from the cabinet, thinking that in an hour April's parents would be in the driveway. He pulled a towel from the rear of the linen closet, rolled up his shirtsleeves, dumped the towel into soapy water, and wrung it out. He bent down over April and meticulously scrubbed around her, under her. He kept fighting for control, fighting the impulse to run.

Going back to the sink, he spied a streak—a splash of her blood on his shirt—right in the middle of his chest. He looked at the clock. His heart resumed its unnatural banging. Squeezing the towel, he drained the rusty water and ran fresh cold water to scrub the spot from his plaid shirt.

The phone upstairs jangled in the silence, rang and rang. It had to be April's mother again. She knew something was wrong. . . . He stared at the mangled phone on the counter. He'd forgotten it completely. And then he saw the pieces of plastic that had been scattered around the room when he smashed it. On his hands and knees he collected the fragments. Too many details. Finally, mercifully, the phone stopped ringing. Hurry, hurry, April's mother is on her way.

He leaned hard into the speckled floor tile to erase every trace of the blood-tinged water, then scrubbed the sink with a clean towel, taking time to inspect the floor for shards that had ricocheted. He removed the broken telephone. The kitchen was perfect, not a sign, a speck, a hint. . . .

He looked at the clock. Four p.m.! He rummaged under the sink for a plastic bag that he stuffed with the phone, the towels, the shards, the hammer, and the framed poem, then placed the bag on April's chest. The hammer made it a bulky, incriminating sack. The sight of it made him sick. He rushed upstairs for the blanket, saw it on the top shelf of April's closet, folded neatly on her suitcase. Often left in his car, it would not be missed. He snatched it, eager to cover her bloody body. But he stopped short when he saw her suitcase. He yanked it from the shelf. He could throw the towels, the hammer, the whole bag of problems into it. . . .

And then he almost smiled at the brilliance of the idea that suddenly came into his head like a caress. He pulled open April's dresser drawer, flung a handful of underclothes into the case. He jerked skirts, blouses, jeans, and tops from their hangers and dropped them in. He snapped the suitcase shut. Now they would be searching for April, not for him!

Then he saw it, the broken figurine lying on the floor. He wet a pair of panties in the bathroom and gathered up the shattered glass, gingerly playing over the same spot for invisible slivers. He thrust them into the case. Thanks, Mom, he thought, remembering how his mother cleaned up with an old rag when she dropped a dish on her kitchen floor.

He grabbed the suitcase and was down the stairs. He stuffed the evidence into the soft suitcase, lay the blanket next to her, and rolled her onto it. Now, he thought, his mind speeding, there wouldn't be any blood on the floor or in his car. But there was her book bag, which was lying in the corner. He found her wallet and packed it away, then deposited her bookbag where she had first dropped it.

He decided he had thought of everything, had stepped on all the cracks. The adrenaline rush was bringing out the best in him. Even now he was thinking ahead, mind racing.

He went back to April. She was facedown on the blanket. Holding one end of the blanket against her back, he rolled her over, tucking in the ends of the fabric like an eggroll, his stomach suddenly queasy. He couldn't waste a minute. Any second her mother would drive up.

He lifted April up off the floor and heaved her onto his shoulder as he would a rug, almost toppling over with the weight of her. He lugged her to the door, managing to pick up her suitcase in his right hand. If someone saw him now. . . . He hesitated at the door, reached for the knob.

He opened the door. The fear of stepping off the porch, of exposing himself, was overwhelming. He almost tripped down the steps, and the body lurched from his hand, startling him into recovery, and he twisted his left foot to regain a firm hold of her. Ignoring pain in his ankle, he stumbled from the porch, jiggled the body to redistribute the weight. Only ten more yards to his car. Only two. He was never so happy to see his beat-up old Chevy. He could kiss its rusty, ugly body. It was his ticket out of here.

The body now out of sight, securely in the trunk, he backed away from the garage and headed for the back road. He felt light-headed, almost dizzy from the concentrated effort. He was traveling on empty roads, past cornfields, past the cemetery, past the Lutheran Church, when he heard the rumble of distant thunder. The wind ushered gray clouds overhead and the temperature dropped. Now a sharp right at the elementary school as he drove east past the dairy, then through the overgrown road leading to the quarry. Another ten miles. Soon it would be dark. Good.

It was raining lightly when he reached the quarry. He dragged her from the trunk, knowing he would have to carry her down, cover her with rocks. They would never find her.

He looked ahead into the deep pit, choosing his spot, on a ledge below—and suddenly slammed into the edge of a giant culvert at his feet. April's body bumped to the ground over the culvert.

"Stupid, stupid," he said aloud, and pounded the culvert with his fists. Hearing the hollow boom of the galvanized iron made him think of the steel plant where his father worked.

His left ankle throbbed painfully as he picked her up, afraid he had no strength left, no time to climb down and pile rocks over her. Then it came to him. The culvert was large enough for April's body.

The blanket would make it easy to slide her in, but there was a snag on the edge of the opening. He unhooked the cloth and pushed her feet-first into the conduit, then pulled his hands back quickly. A sharp, searing pain stunned him. The tiny twisted piece of protruding metal had sliced into his palm, into the mound of tissue beneath his thumb. Blood began pouring out, the pain making him nauseous.

Damn you, *April.* She had pushed him away, insulted him. Just like . . . he cut off the thought. Ungrateful bitch . . . Why did you do this to me? Then the rain fell on him like tears he couldn't shed. He saw lightning, heard the din of thunder. He jumped up, clutching the wound, pressing it together while he made a run to the car, forgetting to ease up on his ankle.

Miserable, in pain, he turned on the ignition and realized he had one more task before he could head home. He drove straight to the mall, the first place he could think of, to dump the suitcase. The rain was on his side; the mall was deserted. He parked behind a Chinese restaurant, opened a plastic bag of garbage in a dumpster, and added the suitcase, pushing it deep into the trash.

He sprang back into his car, refreshed by the rain. The danger and his own ingenuity had given him a high, and suddenly he realized he was famished. He had never known such a ravenous hunger as he drove to the Orange Julius stand at the opposite end of the mall. He had done it. He'd *made* it! He'd hit the winning home run in the last of the ninth. His mouth watered at the sight of the hot dogs rotating on the grill, beading with oil.

"Two dogs," he said, barely able to stop the saliva from dripping from his mouth. "And a large Coke."

He had never enjoyed dogs so much. Life was a high. He had a heightened sense of the people around him, the odors. Even the orangey smell from the juice machine and the sweetish smell of his soda were sharper. Night was falling. Smiling, Billy knew he would pull this off. He would go back home and act natural. *No way* anyone could connect him with April's death.

Still, he wished he could just blow out of this town like his mentor, his admired guide in life had done two years ago. He had skipped out on college, hit the ski slopes somewhere in Colorado. How Billy envied his old buddy, how he wished he were in his shoes.

And now, as he drove home through the rain, hearing the *swoosh* of traffic, seeing headlights poke their way through the netherworld between night and day, Billy's mind sped along with the highway sounds, and he realized that he too would have to leave town. And in deciding that, a perfect plan came to him. . . . One day very soon there would be no more Billy Owens. No. He would become the person he had always wanted to be. Then he would lose himself forever in someplace new, in his new identity.

He repeated his new name like a mantra . . . Kevin Glade, Kevin Glade.

Chapter One

Fall 1991

"MEET KEVIN, MAMA. Kevin Glade."

Laurie unclasped her hand from Kevin's as her mother kissed her cheek.

"Kevin, this is my mom, Jessica Lewisohn."

"What took you so long?" Jessica asked, smiling at Kevin as she looked him over.

"Getting by the new doorman was a bigger hassle than the trip from Cornell," Laurie told her.

Jessica smiled. "That's why we live in this building. It's safe." She looked directly into Kevin's face when he extended his hand. She could see his green eyes clearly through his round wire-rimmed glasses, and she inspected his hand as she held it firmly in hers. It was cool, she noticed, but attractively masculine. He had shapely fingers, long nails, apparently manicured—unusual in a college student, she thought—and short reddish hair on his wrists.

"Welcome, Kevin. I hear you're a Vermonter."

"Straight from the Green Mountain State," he said. He had an even smile and nice white teeth.

"I've been looking forward to meeting you, Mrs. Lewisohn," he said. "I've heard a lot about you."

"I shudder to think," Jessica said, taking in the uneasy expression on Laurie's face. She knew her daughter was embarrassed by their lavish apartment in their rather glitzy Manhattan building, its crew of doormen scurrying around in fancy uniforms with those epaulets that made them, Laurie said, look like characters in a Hungarian operetta.

"Well, I envy Laurie," he said with a note of sadness. His face was handsome, if ordinary, she decided, and his expression unreadable. But the round eyeglasses he wore did give him a gentle look. And the felt safari hat he sported, rakishly crushed down on the brown hair that fell on his neck, lent him an adventurous air. Smart move, Indiana Jones, and even smarter to have landed my terrific daughter, she thought, glancing at Laurie's pretty face. Then Kevin removed his hat, and she ushered Laurie and her first college beau into her living room.

"Wow. What a great view!" Kevin said.

The wall of windows in the living room practically hung over the Hudson River. A sailboat glided by as if by arrangement.

"It helps make life in the city bearable," Jessica said.

"I *love* the city," Kevin replied.

Try to be fair, Jessica told herself, feeling a wisp of doubt curl around her heart. She's not your baby anymore.

"I WISH YOUR father wasn't off on one of his wild goose chases," Jessica said as she sipped her espresso. Dinner was over, and she had her daughter to herself now. She sat on the black leather couch in her long nightgown, her bare feet tucked under her. Laurie was sprawled on the Victorian loveseat, which her mother noted was too small and delicate for her daughter.

"Daddy would really have freaked at the speech you made about naming me Laurel. So *corny.*"

"I'm the Jewish mother in the family, Laurie. It's my job, my right, to make speeches."

"Well, I can't *believe* what you said." Laurie hung her arms wide in exaggerated imitation as she repeated her mother's words: " 'My daughter is a New York flower. The mountain laurel, delicate yet hardy. A *miracle* of creation.' " Laurie took a breath. "Give me a *break*!"

Jessica pursed her lips. How like herself Laurel was. Sarcastic, rebellious, strong-minded. But like her father, she had the fair skin and blond hair from the Scotch-Irish branch of his family. Her daughter's imperfect features gave her face character, Jessica thought. She never did like girls who looked like spearmint-gum ads. She was also glad Laurie hadn't inherited her father's wide Cherokee nose. Nothing wrong with it, of course, but for a young girl it could have been a problem. Tom, she thought, why weren't you home to meet Laurie's beau? She needed her husband's help tonight. Maybe he could help her put her finger on her nearly instant reservations about this Kevin Glade. Of course, it could be that she was wrong, that her nagging feelings of unease were only suspicions of a jealous, possessive mother. It was an old joke, a contentious one, that no boy was good enough for her precious Laurie.

She recalled the day in August when she and Tom had prepared to drive their only child to college. Jessica had watched as Tom forlornly packed Laurie's last suitcase into the trunk of their station wagon, the realization finally hitting him that she might never live at home again.

"I feel like Polonius sending Laertes off into the world," Tom said. "And I feel every bit as foolish as he must have felt trying to say the right thing to protect his child."

"I'm only going to *Ithaca,* Dad," Laurie said. "Not Baghdad."

" 'To thine own self be true' isn't such bad advice," Jessica said to Tom later, seeing tears in his eyes just before they drove off, leaving their daughter behind at Cornell. She herself hugged her daughter tightly, feeling her young shoulders, kissing her soft cheek, seeing in her daughter's innocent face a vision of the future filled only with possibilities.

"Be careful," Jessica blurted out in spite of herself.

"I'm a street-smart kid, Mom. It's the yokels who have to be warned, not the other way around. This burg is duck soup for a city slicker like me." Then she smiled at her mother. "Remember our password? I had combat training in kindergarten. You don't have to worry about me."

Jessica pulled herself away from Laurie, holding back the tears, struggling not to imagine Laurie's empty room back home.

Remembering how she had released her daughter from her arms that day could still bring tears to her eyes. She *had* been a good mother. She hadn't burdened her child with the pain of freeing her. . . .

Jessica bit into the sliver of lemon peel she had plucked from the grounds in her cup. "Glade?" she asked her daughter. "What sort of name is that?"

"Oh, *Mom,"* Laurie replied, raising her eyes to the sky. "I forgot to ask him for his pedigree papers."

"I'm just curious, honey."

"Oh, sure."

"About his family," Jessica went on.

"Ease up, will you, Mom?"

Jessica bit her tongue. The last thing she wanted was to start a fight on Laurie's first weekend home.

"I like him, Mom. *I* trust him," Laurie said. "By the way, isn't he handsome?"

Jessica nodded. She took pleasure in her daughter's happiness. Don't spoil it, she instructed herself. She remembered her own first boyfriend and the fuss her domineering mother had made.

"He's so terrific, Mom." She fell onto the black leather couch next to her mother, her face flushed, radiant. Tenderness and sadness spread in Jessica's heart. Her daughter had slipped outside her domain. She was experiencing a life entirely apart from her mother. And she realized that although Laurie wanted her approval, she would have to watch her laser tongue. Now that Laurie was eighteen and still fluttering outside their safe little nest, she could well fly away and live her life any number of dangerous damned ways without her mother ever knowing.

LAURIE PULLED THE sheet up over her breasts. Everything felt silky after sex, she thought, stretching in her bed, happy that she had lucked out in the freshman lottery and didn't have to share her small room with anyone. The only glitch was that her room was on the ground floor right next to the building entrance and had a tall window that looked out on a grassy playing field; they had to be quiet when they made love or every student on campus would hear.

She felt the heat of Kevin's body next to her. " 'All's right with the world,' " she quoted to herself, knowing that Robert Browning hadn't had this in mind when he wrote the line.

"The morning's at twelve," she said aloud, waking Kevin.

"What?"

"The poem by Emily Dickinson. Doesn't it begin, 'The morning's at seven'?"

"Beats me," he said, lifting the sheet and nibbling on her nipple.

"It's almost twelve!" she said, trying to push him away. "My mom always calls at twelve on Sunday."

He ran his tongue over her left breast and sucked. "Mmm, tell her I need you, you're busy." He ran his hand down her belly. "Tell her you'll call her back," he said, feeling her body respond to his fingers. "Tell her you're mine now. Kevin Glade's on the case," he said, moving his mouth down her body, throwing off the sheet.

Five minutes later the phone rang, but neither of them was able to answer it.

"I'M RUNNING TO my sculpture class, Jessica."

"Sculpture class! What next, Anyuka?" Jessica asked her tiny but formidable eighty-year-old mother. *Anyuka* was the word for "mom" in Hungarian. Her mother, Rozsi Roth, pronounced the z's as Zsa Zsa Gabor pronounced the letters in her name, and with the same verve. Jessica spoke loudly into the phone to be sure Rozsi could hear her.

"What should I do, dahrrling, sit home? I'll be dead a long time," Rozsi said.

"I never knew you took sculpture class."

"Call and you'll find out. Now I'm in a rush. To what do I owe the honor?" Rozsi asked.

Jessica pictured her mother, her flowing white hair pulled away from her face and piled high on the back of her head in an elegantly knotted but soft French twist. Jessica and Laurie had inherited her long, interesting nose. Her bright blue, watery eyes staring through her fifties harlequin glasses would soon be peering out at the sights of the dangerous ghetto she refused to abandon. She always pictured her mother marching purposefully through the burned-out neighborhood carrying her familiar cloth shopping bag past boarded-up buildings where junkies squatted, stopping to chat with every neighbor she knew and, to Jessica's horror, those she didn't. Jessica had long ago stopped trying to talk her stubborn mother out of remaining in a neighborhood where juveniles practiced shooting real guns into the alleys between buildings. Her mother's apartment building had been vandalized so many times that nothing remained of the furniture, the mirrors, or the fake fireplace that had lent some elegance to the Art Deco lobby.

"It's Laurel. I just called her and she's not in her dorm."

"Ha! That's all? I picked up the phone on my way out. I have my heavy coat on."

"But I always call her on Sunday, exactly at twelve, and she's always still in bed."

"Maybe she's having a little company."

There was a pause. Naturally, her mother would think of that.

"What's the Hungarian expression for pumpkin head, Anyuka? Because that's what I have."

"Tok fey."

"Laurie has a boyfriend, Kevin Glade."

"What kind of name is Kevin Glade?"

Jessica laughed. "I guess the apple doesn't fall far from the tree, as you always say. I asked her the same question, and she thinks I'm a suspicious shrew."

"The last time my family trusted someone, they were thrown into ovens in Germany."

"Enjoy your sculpture class, Anyuka. I'll call you later."

Jessica hung up the phone. Even her eighty-year-old mother knew why her daughter hadn't answered the phone. Of course, being Hungarian it was the first thing she would think of. Her mother had quite a reputation, and several suitors were said to have threatened suicide when she finally married. Her own past hadn't been exactly dull, especially in the sixties, Jessica reminded herself, but she put the thought quickly out of her mind.

Tom would laugh at her *tok fey,* an appropriate image for the Halloween season, she thought. But what would he say about his precious daughter sleeping with this Kevin Glade? She wished Tom would call.

But she would go to the costume parade in Grenwich Village with her friend Ricky, watch the marathon in Central Park on the weekend, and try to stop worrying about her daughter's sex life. She wondered what part of the South American jungle her husband was slogging through at that very moment while she was trying to escape the poisons of civilization through nutrition. She turned on the blender to make herself some carrot juice to go with her giant muffin and her decaf coffee, which she realized, sadly, she would have to consume alone.

* * *

JESSICA STARED THROUGH her picture window at the strollers across the street twenty-four floors below on Riverside Drive. Dog walkers shuffled in the fallen leaves, and the sun set on the New Jersey horizon as she dialed her daughter's dorm once more. Dusk was her favorite time, but she wasn't enjoying the balmy evening or the turning leaves on the Palisades. Laurie's phone had gone unanswered for three straight days, and Jessica's heart beat rapidly at the endless array of disasters that could have befallen her. But why should her daughter be home at dinner hour? She remembered how on parents' weekend she and Laurie had run into her old friends from Science High School as they strolled on the campus. She tried to console herself by thinking of Laurie sitting in the wood-paneled medieval dining hall at Cornell, surrounded by her debate buddies, or competing at a debate round with her team, or studying in the impressive library. Cornell's magnificent campus, on a hill overlooking vast Lake Cayuga, was an inspiring setting. Could Laurie be enjoying a treat at one of the little slate tables on the terrace behind the student union, a book in hand, observing the stars twinkling and the lights of the town beginning to appear in the valley below?

It had been only a week since she had last seen Laurie—and Kevin. Kevin . . . She couldn't help it—her heart sank at the thought of Laurie's new boyfriend. She had pictured a very different young man for Laurie, someone more solid, like a young Tom. Kevin couldn't hold a candle to that Tom, who had been a brilliant, dashing activist in college, involved in the burning issues of the day, not clothes and rock. A scientist and a humanist, Tom had finally decided on law, to fight for Native Americans north and south. The matriarchal Cherokee influence had blended his soft-heartedness with his stubbornness. He was endlessly interesting, but he was also difficult to live with.

Now, after all their personal struggles, after his work was paying off, after she had worked her way up to head of social work at a well-known international agency, after all these years of doing her best to bring up a trouble-free child in a tough city, Jessica was hardly thrilled to see her accomplished daughter infatuated with a boy who, she felt, was not her equal. She and Tom had such high hopes for

Laurie in her freshman year. And as her friend Ricky might say, this Kevin Glade seemed to have a certain flair for mediocrity.

As she tried Laurie's number again, Jessica thought about the pumpkins and gourds and the basket of yellow mums set on the window ledge of Laurie's room. All presents from Tom. And she thought of the gifts that Kevin showered on Laurie—stuffed animals, boxes of candy, flowery cards—junk that, unfortunately, Laurie treasured. He was launching a campaign, with love letters and flattering attention, just when Laurie was most vulnerable—in her first months away from home. Was she with Kevin tonight? Jessica imagined the phone ringing in Laurie's room, the bed unmade probably, and of course, wet towels on the Laura Ashley sheets. CD's of Mozart would be piled up on the stereo equipment next to Sting and crazy groups like 10,000 Maniacs and the Smashing Pumpkins. Laurie's tastes were eclectic, like her father's; her book shelves were crammed with poetry as well as essays on science. On her wall, posters of the solar system circled various poses of a rumpled Albert Einstein, and above her bed bloomed a gigantic Georgia O'Keefe version of vivid flowers.

Jessica banged the phone down in frustration. Where *was* she! Then Tom's description of her anxiety, "Hungarian Hysteria," came to her. Don't be a damn fool, she thought, trying to ignore the tap of her heartbeat. In her mind's eye she glimpsed Tom's face admonishing her. And her daughter telling her to please back off, let her live her life.

So let go! she ordered herself. Your daughter is safe.

"KEVIN! I DIDN'T know you wrote poetry. There's so much I don't know about you," Laurie said.

The Delaware River lay in the arms of white sunlight, and Laurie soared with happiness as her little yellow VW bug rumbled across the bridge, the thought of playing hooky from her Ivy League life adding a piquance to her high spirits. Kevin sat beside her ignoring the sights and sounds of the town of Port Jervis as they crossed to the highway, his gaze fixed on Laurie's hair blowing in the breeze and the look of abandon on her face.

"Do you want to read it?" he asked, knowing her response.

"Of course," she said.

"The title is in French."

"Je parle Francaise," she said, glancing aside as she drove down the highway. His eyes had been riveted on her throughout the long trip, the look of adoration on his face making her a little self-conscious.

"It's about Vermont, how beautiful it is in the fall. All the seasons. It's the only thing I miss about it," he said mysteriously. "I'll write a poem just for you," he said, running his hand on her thigh, kissing her neck under her ear.

Laurie giggled, flooring the gas pedal, flying past woods and fields and farmhouses. They had just reached the foothills of the Catskill Mountains.

"What other surprises do you have for me?" she asked him.

THE OAK BRANCHES above closed over the road, blocking out the sunlight, and a fragrant pine scent emanated from tall, ancient trees as Kevin and Laurel drove up a dirt road and through a stone entrance that was almost hidden from view. Foxglove peeked out from patches of sunlit roadway, and mushrooms of all shapes, colors, and deadliness hid among the rusty ferns.

HARTEWOODS, PRIVATE CLUB was printed in faded letters on a wooden sign posted just inside the wall.

"This place attracts rain," Laurie said. "It could be sunny down the road, but clouds always hang over Hartewoods."

"It's beautiful," Kevin said, inhaling the piny, fresh air. "And chilly."

"Mountain air," Laurie said, stretching. "Sometimes, in the mist, it looks like headless-horseman country. Golf course on the left, lake coming up."

She drove past a rustic cabin and a shingled house that blended into the landscape. "Eighteen hundred acres and hardly any people. Don't you love the quiet?"

Laurie rounded the bend. The water reflected muted maples and lilac colors past their prime. "You should have brought your canvas," Laurie said. "Bring a painting back to class and make this trip legit."

"And ruin all the fun?"

"Lewisohn-Hunter estate coming up," Laurie announced, named for her mother's maiden name and her father's name. "It's just a big old summer house. We haven't closed it up for the winter yet. You can see the lake from the front," she said, pulling into the dirt road that led to their muddy driveway. "They don't pave here, to keep it primitive. Must have rained last night."

They picked their way over the flat stones and climbed up the rickety steps. Laurie felt for the key on the frame inside the screen door.

"Take lots of precautions, I see," Kevin said.

"No one steals here. It's a ghost town until spring, and the deer and the raccoons only steal food."

"Where is everyone?" Kevin could see no other house.

"The geriatrics go to Florida, and my parents go back to the city. If it wasn't for this wild Indian summer we wouldn't be here either." Laurie led him into a kitchen that had old-fashioned wooden cupboards and sixty-year-old appliances, then to an adjoining porch with a stone floor. A half cord of wood was stacked in a corner next to a picnic table. "The wealthy roughing it," she said, laughing awkwardly as they looked out through the rusty screens into thick trees and the lake beyond. The wooden floors in the living room were covered with threadbare orientals, and the walls were tongue-in-groove maple, the style of the thirties. An upright piano stood by the French windows, which opened to a small, weatherbeaten deck with a better view of the lake. The huge stone fireplace and the electric heaters, Kevin noticed, were the only sources of heat.

"It's colder than a witch's tit," he said. "It's warmer outdoors."

Laurie laughed. "This house has no insulation."

"I hate the cold," he said, shuddering.

"A Vermonter hating the cold?"

He gave her a look, quickly softened his gaze when he saw her surprise. "Well, I've got you to keep me warm." He moved toward her.

"It's getting dark," she said. "Throw some kindling into the fireplace, will you?" She lit a match and held it to the candles on the mantel. The shadows quivered against the bricks, and she peered at him to gauge his mood.

He saw her worried look and grabbed her waist. "It's Halloween," he said. "Let's make some mischief."

HE LOOKED DOWN at her lying next to him, naked on the bed. Her eyes were closed. I never thought there would be so much blood. . . .

He prodded her arm. Her eyes snapped open.

"You have a funny expression on your face," she said. "What are you thinking?"

"About our first time, I didn't expect so much blood."

"I had to throw the bedspread in the machine," she said.

"Did it hurt?"

"A little." She sat up and leaned on her elbow to look at him. "It's the price we have to pay."

"To keep beastly males like me away, I guess," Kevin said.

"You're probably right. The hymen protects us young females from getting pregnant before our bodies are ready to have healthy babies."

"Did you wear your diaphragm?" he asked nervously.

She nodded. "You know, some girls only have a drop of blood?"

"Girls talk about that sort of thing?"

Laurie laughed. "Why not?"

He grabbed her chin. She was no different from April, he thought for an instant. "You tell them about me?" he asked, forcing back his anger.

"Hey, what's wrong?" A beat of fear. "What do you think?" she asked softly, prying his fingers off. "Nothing intimate," she explained. "Nothing you wouldn't like."

"I'm sorry," he said. "I'm so dumb. I just . . . I just love you, Laurie." He took hold of her hands, kissed her nose and mouth softly. "Blame it on love," he said, kissing her fingertips.

"Do you forgive me?" he asked lightly.

"Read me your poem," she said.

He reached for his trousers on the chair by the bed and pulled a folded sheet from his wallet. "You read it," he said. "I want to hear your voice reading it."

She lay on her back, holding the poem up.

Vert Mont

Maple trees outlined in a Vermont moonlight
Sugar Bush sprouting into a midnight sky

(He stroked her thigh. She read on, not missing a beat)

Waiting for the Autumn moment when
the green leaf dies.

In orange tongued yellow flamed wind stippled
tumbling pride they hold out to November

Lavender gray.
Sap buckets bleed their barks in early March.

(He kissed her neck)

Snow burdened
they balance their slender weight

wind spilling
they scatter aloft their flakes

Sunned on, they glisten whispering life,
frozen inklings of emerald ice.

Budding along the milkweed way, chrysalis hung,
bejeweled with Monarch veins inside gold-throated jade

They also wait to emerge.

He licked her ear.

"My God, Kevin."

"Did you like it?"

"I love it," she whispered.

"Which do you like more?" he asked, kissing her. "I love you, Laurel. My flower," he said into her ear.

JESSICA PUT IN a call to her husband's hotel in Brazil before calling her daughter again, trying not to obsess over her absence. She pictured the ramshackle hotel Tom had described in his letter as she listened to the ringing, hoping the phones weren't down and the clerks weren't drunk or asleep. To her astonishment she was put through at once and the desk clerk spoke English.

"Señor Hunter? Yes, I know him well," he replied.

Jessica's heart thumped. He's dead!

"Just checked out. Headed home for U.S. of A.," he said.

KEVIN KISSED HER eyes. "What's the Hungarian word for eyes?"

"Szemek."

He kissed her mouth. "What's the Hungarian word?"

"Szaj."

"Funny language."

"It has the best curse words in the world. According to a study. Even beats the Arabs."

He kissed her breasts. *"Tszitszi,"* she said.

He laughed. "How do you say pussy?" he asked, moving his head along her belly.

"Punszi."

He laughed again, kissing her. "How do you say fuck?"

"Busz," she said.

He covered her mouth with his hand, pushing hard into her. She twisted her head back and forth on the pillow, but his fingers were still closed over her lips. "Are you *crazy*?" she managed to get out, tearing his hand away, gasping for breath. He was still inside her. "You almost choked me!"

"*Sorry*," he said, smiling, smoothing her damp face. And then: "I forgot you can scream all you want out here."

Chapter Two

TOSSING AND TURNING, he gave up trying to sleep and allowed himself to remember the day after April disappeared. He had known there would be a knock on the door, and so when it had come he was prepared for it. Staying in town had been a stroke of genius, but his body went rigid when he looked through the curtain and saw the police.

He had spent the whole night before in front of the mirror rehearsing, just as he would for a school play or a date with April. He could usually orchestrate a look, a gesture, a conversation, to get what he wanted. That day his performance had meant life or death. He had drawn his mouth down, digging deeply into the depths of his being, searching his psyche for emotion. And it had scared him. A feeling of horror had welled up inside him as he remembered the image of April's head rolled up in the blanket.

His heart had tumbled in his chest as he pulled the door open, the strain of his memories, of what he had suffered because of April, twisting his features into a mask of grief.

MARJORIE MEADOWS KICKED the burnt orange and bloodred leaves along the walkway, pulling her hand from her husband's. She barely saw the beautiful hundred-year-old elms, the picturesque Victorian houses blinded by shutters pulled closed against nightfall. She hated autumn, despised all beauty that once had given pleasure to her daughter April. Her husband, Gary, ran up the steps ahead of her to her sister's house, the only place she still felt welcome.

Her sister's friend Lara, a married woman with two daughters, stood on her porch next door and raised her hand in a guilty greeting, then turned around and went back inside to avoid them.

"Instead of feeling worried that April's still missing, they feel sorry for me that she's run away from home, or they blame me, and I feel ashamed!" Marjorie caught up with Gary.

"She *didn't* run away," he said.

"You're the only one who believes that," she murmured as he rang the doorbell. "I can't stand it anymore. Why don't they find her?"

Gary thought about the two birthdays that had passed without her. They were giving up hope. Gary put as much resolution as he could into his voice. "We'll have to do something about it," he said as the door opened.

At home later that evening, Marjorie sat on her bed and stared at the phone. Not an hour went by when she didn't think about calling the police for news. She had spoken to Detective McKenzie, who had come to the house the night April disappeared.

"Something terrible has happened to my daughter," she had tried to tell him that night. "Something's terribly wrong."

But he hadn't believed her. "It looks like she took a glass trinket and her phone," he had said. "Kidnappers don't pack a suitcase. It's Friday. She's off for the weekend."

"April would never do this to us!" she protested. "She would never leave, even for a few hours, without telling us. She would never run away."

Detective McKenzie, a nice-looking, kindly guy, tried not to be accusing, but his look said, That's what they all say.

"Only a teenager would take a cordless phone," he tried to explain. "Maybe she's visiting a friend, bringing the figurine as a present. Are you sure you haven't forgotten a date she had?"

"Of course not! We've called everyone. We're wasting time."

"Did you have a fight before you left for work?"

"No. I told you. She's not a runaway."

"No disagreements between you at all?" he asked.

She looked at Gary. "Over the phone bill, clothes. Nothing serious, believe me." She saw a flicker in McKenzie's eyes when she mentioned the phone bill.

"I do believe you. That's why I think she'll be back. Most kids reported missing are back within forty-eight hours."

"Not mine. She's not like the rest," Marjorie had explained. And then she had realized what she was saying.

Gary sat next to her on the bed, seeing the look on her face, knowing what was going through her mind. She had replayed the scene a thousand times since then, trying to believe her daughter was alive, trying to talk herself into having some hope.

"Maybe he's right," Gary had tried to tell his wife that night after looking into Brian McKenzie's care-worn face. But his thoughts belied his words. He had hoped against hope that this man of authority, who had more experience than he, knew the truth. He had tried to believe it for his own sake and for the sake of his terrified, heartbroken wife. But a father knew his own daughter better than any police detective did. And he knew what could happen to an innocent young girl like April. Even if there had been no signs of violence, even if the house had been just as they left it—he hadn't been able to stop the terrible thought from coming through. For an instant he had thought the unthinkable, and it had battered his insides. His daughter was dead. Some maniac had taken her and it was already too late.

SANDY UNGAR SAT at her desk in the cubicle that was her office in the police barracks. On the bulletin board were the Wanted composites, as well as pictures of runaways and homicides. Most upsetting was the picture of one April Meadows, pretty, smiling, appealing. Ungar had to keep pulling it from under the new notices to keep it up front. April's parents called and visited her instead of Brian McKenzie now that she had been promoted to detective. But most people didn't seek her out; she could be abrasive, short-tempered, characteristics she knew people didn't expect from someone small who wore a short, thick braid and had a youthful face. But despite her sharp tongue and brusque manner, April's parents sensed that she had never believed their daughter was a runaway. And she had fought with Brian McKenzie over it a year and a half ago when she was still a trooper and didn't have much authority.

"You mean, we're not going to do anything? Hunt for her?" she had said to Brian outside the Meadowses' house after they finished examining the premises and questioning April's parents.

"We *can't* do anything unless there are indications of foul play. There are no signs of a struggle, no forced entry. We'll have to follow the usual procedures. Make a blotter entry, send faxes to police departments around the country, and send out missing-person posters."

"What if I find something?"

"Then I'll send out the bloodhounds."

"Really?"

"If April's blood or clothing was found by a river, we would send German shepherds looking for her. You know that. You've been to the police academy. But without any visible evidence that she was harmed, there just isn't a whole lot we can do. And you know that as well as I do."

"The trouble with you, Brian, is you've seen too much. I can see this through the mother's eyes. Maybe because I'm a woman. Maybe because I'm not jaded."

"Like I said, if you come up with something I'll pull out all the stops. I *could* send April's dental records out with the missing-persons flyer. Do *you* want to ask April's mother for the kid's dental records at this point?"

"But this young girl isn't an airhead," she tried to tell McKenzie. "She's not the type to give her parents such grief."

"Remember that guy who reported his teenage daughter missing?" Brian asked. "We found the kid in California with her mother. The dude never told us his ex was living in L.A. People withhold information to avoid airing their dirty laundry."

"This is different. These parents are in major shock. You can see it in their eyes." But she knew she couldn't push too hard. She was a fledgling, and McKenzie was the detective showing her the ropes. Then a few months later, in August, when she got a call from a frantic mother reporting that her fourteen-year-old girl had never come home from the county fair, Brian immediately phoned the police in the next town. "Every summer a young girl runs off with a carnival worker on the last day of the fair," he said. And sure enough, it turned out the missing girl had run off with the lion tamer. Which was when Sandy Ungar had begun to doubt her hunch about April. But now she knew she'd been on the money all along. There was no news of April. And the longer there was no news, the more ominous it looked. Her mind kept turning back to the day they had questioned Billy Owens, April's cute, freckle-faced, redheaded boyfriend. April's parents swore by him, defended him.

"He would never harm her," April's mother had insisted. April's father agreed. "He's a perfect gentleman," he had said.

But Sandy didn't trust testosterone, especially in perfect gentlemen. Perfect people usually had more to hide. Maybe she was prejudiced, being emotional. Stick to the facts, trooper, she told herself.

Billy Owens's mother, she recalled, was tall and large-boned, with dark hair and hollow eyes. She had a haunted, tired look about her, but also a simple elegance. The house looked as if it had seen better days. The father was at work. They talked in the living room, the mother in the background, saying little. McKenzie took the lead in the questioning, but Sandy had been getting braver. She regarded Billy suspiciously as he told his story. He claimed he hadn't seen or spoken to April, that he had gone to the mall after school and that his mother was home when he got there. Later April's friend Mark corroborated Billy's story—he had seen Billy eating a hot dog at a fast-food stand.

"Did April get along with her mom?" McKenzie asked Billy.

"She loved her mom," Billy said.

"They *never* fought?"

"Well . . . sure, but normal fights."

"Did *you* ever fight with her?"

"Never! We . . . care for one another. She wouldn't run off . . ."

"Another boy? Any other boys in her life?"

"Mark. Mark Goldman. He's a sophomore, plays the guitar—is with her in her music class." Brian took the name down, closing his book.

"Do you mind if I look around?" Sandy remembered blurting the words out, not wanting to leave. She tried to ignore the disapproval in McKenzie's face as she addressed the air between mother and son as they led them through the house until they got to Billy's room, her real destination. The room was in perfect order except for a few notebooks and CD's scattered around. But then she noticed something as Billy rushed to gather the stray articles into a neat pile. There was a fresh cut under his thumb.

"Is Billy's room always this neat?" Sandy asked his mother.

"Almost always," she responded, smiling at Sandy.

"How come you didn't have a date on a Friday night?" she asked Billy.

"April always practices Friday afternoons. We were going to see a movie that night. But as soon as I got home I got a call from her mom."

"What did you buy at the mall?" Sandy asked casually, picking up a CD.

"Nothing. I didn't see anything I liked."

Believable, she had thought. Billy was a perfectionist. He was also a careful dresser. She could see why he was attractive to girls. "Is Billy a spendthrift, like April?" she suddenly asked his mother.

"Oh, no. He's very frugal," she answered defensively. Sandy remembered the look in Mrs. Owens's eyes when she realized she had given the right answer.

"What happened to your hand?" she asked Billy just as McKenzie headed for the front door, signaling that any more time with this family would be intrusive. But she didn't mind making Billy nervous even if her partner did, and even if McKenzie would give her hell later.

"I cut myself on an old license plate. In the trunk of my car. I fixed a flat the other day," Billy answered evenly as he followed her out. She knew he was watching the revolver bouncing on her uniformed hip as she walked. The weapon was larger than most and looked even more ominous because she was so small.

"What's with you?" Brian asked when they were back in his squad car. "You keep this up and you'll be up for a harassment charge. We have absolutely nothing on Billy Owens. He seems like a real nice kid."

"I don't trust anyone under twenty-one who doesn't have a messy room."

McKenzie laughed at that. He had seen the dregs of humanity, and this Billy Owens looked more like his own son.

"We don't know we have a crime," McKenzie told her. And they both agreed that Billy's demeanor, his body language, all the clues to deception they had been trained to detect were missing from his behavior. A polygraph test, even if she could convince McKenzie to give one to Billy, couldn't be used in court to convict him. It could only be used in his defense. Anyway, if he had fooled them he could probably deceive the polygraph.

Then, only three months later, April's mother had dropped her bombshell. Billy Owens had left town.

Did I make him nervous? Sandy had wondered. But Mrs. Meadows had only sobbed into the phone. "Now there's no one left to remember April. He's graduated, gone off somewhere." Sandy had had a sinking feeling as she listened, knowing there wasn't a damn thing she could do about it.

MARGE MEADOWS NOTED the condition of the dried flowers set high on the kitchen shelf next to her cookbooks. A thick layer of dust had settled on them over the past eighteen months. Until this moment she hadn't been able to bear touching anything that reminded her of her baby. She and April had driven down a country road one Sunday morning and stopped at a vegetable stand where they bought jams and honey and dried flowers, the ones that were fading now in the white vase. It had been one of those ordinary afternoons that became extraordinary in the memory of it—the sunshine, the colors, the steep hills and dramatic ravines near their small town—as vivid now in her mind as they had been on that autumn day.

She took the vase from the shelf, pulling the clump of flowers into the sink to dust them, to catch the broken branches. She looked down into the brown, spiny stems that held the craggy, stiff bones of the desiccated flowers. Suddenly she spied some familiar objects she couldn't place. They were tiny shards of pink plastic imbedded in the dried arms of the plant, and as she extracted them one by one, she wondered what they were. Then it descended on her—the plant suddenly began to resemble skeletal remains rather than a colorful collection of once pretty flowers. The pieces she had collected in her hand were shards from April's missing telephone! And the phone had to have been shattered by some terrific force for the pieces to have flown so far. It was at that moment that she knew she would never see her daughter again.

Chapter Three

"I WAS SO worried," Jessica said, almost in tears. "If you hadn't answered the phone just now, I would have called the police—"

"I'm sorry, Mom."

"How did I know you weren't—hadn't been in an accident?"

"I'll tell you the next time I go away."

"And I'm surprised you cut all your classes today."

"Please. I'm not in high school anymore. If I cut class it's *my* decision. If you or Dad want to stop paying tuition, that's your choice—"

"I never said anything like that."

"Well, maybe you feel if you're paying for me you have a right to control me—"

"No! Honey, that's not the point. The point is I'm interested in your welfare. Some others may not be."

"Kevin? You mean Kevin?"

"You never cut before. You always loved school."

"I knew it. You don't like Kevin. Admit it. I know you mean well, but nothing I do is right since I met Kevin. I don't call you enough, I don't ask you for advice about school, about clothes, about money. Mom, I want to make my own decisions. You've got to let me grow up."

"Okay, okay, hon." I just hope they're the right decisions, she added silently.

"I've gotta go, Mom. I have to start a paper that's due next week," she lied. Kevin would be at her door any minute, and she knew she wouldn't get a word of her paper written tonight. Life was becoming pretty complicated, she thought. She told her mother to let her make her own decisions, but she found herself asking Kevin for advice now on money and clothes and food. Was that being independent?

* * *

"DID YOU JUST talk to Jessica? Or Tom?" Kevin asked. Laurie laughed. It was the fad to call parents of friends by their first names.

"My mother," she admitted. "Why, do I look whipped?"

"I always know when you've talked to her. She doesn't like me, does she? But it's natural. I don't take it personally. She's just upset that someone is taking her place. I understand."

Laurie looked at him, surprised.

"But, Laurie, you've got to take a stand or she'll always be running your life. She means well, we know that, but do you want to have to report to her? You might as well be living at home if you do that."

"I don't know, Kevin. But . . . well, I'm all they've got."

"Exactly! You don't want to let that cripple you, deny you your freedom. I really don't blame her, but don't you see, your mother can't help it, she wants to control everything about you. It's time to break loose, Laurie."

"Let's talk about something else, Kevin. I can't handle this right now. How about some Chinese food, and then I've got to study for an exam."

"We'll go to the Veggie Villa," Kevin said. "It's closer and cheaper."

Laurie got her raincoat from her closet. It had started to come down hard.

ONE DAY HE would get used to the grass he was eating, he thought as he watched Laurie consume a pita filled with sprouts and other hairy inedibles. The glassed-in casual restaurant with its whitewashed walls, plants, watercolors, and classical music had an atmosphere Laurel thrived on. Hey, he was almost beginning to like it himself.

When the spiced apple juice arrived, Laurel watched his thoughtful expression and took his hand in hers. She stroked his palm affectionately as they looked at each other.

"What's this?" she asked, running her finger down the rough groove of the scar she found under his thumb.

"It's nothing."

"Come on, tell me," she pressed, trying to stop him from closing his hand over the scar.

His mind spun to conjure a story for her. "It happened years ago," he told her, stalling for time. Suddenly he was transported back to the quarry, his wound still spurting blood. His hand began to throb.

Laurel saw the look of pain on his face. He clenched his hand over hers. "You don't have to tell me if it's too painful," she said.

Then an incident from his childhood popped into his head. "It was an accident. When I was a kid," he said.

He pictured the pickup truck his dad drove and the day he had fallen out of the back as his father turned onto a road. His father stopped, heaved him up without a word, and deposited him in the truck. Hadn't even dusted him off.

"I fell out of a pickup when I was six," he said quietly. "But my dad was going slow," he added when he saw her shocked expression. "Cut myself on a rock. It bled a lot," he said. He pictured the sharp edge of the culvert, the clean slice through his flesh, the pain.

"Poor babe," Laurel said, pressing his palm to her cheek.

Elation poked through his fear as he appreciated his quick-witted reply. He couldn't keep from smiling.

Laurie smiled back at him.

Jessica looked at her husband lying on his stomach next to her in bed. She was still a little high from the wine they had drunk. She ran her hand down his spine.

"The only signs that you are a heathen, Tom darling, are your lack of body hair and that you're not circumcised. My mother would be shocked if she knew."

Tom didn't turn around when he spoke. "You mean you haven't discussed my penis with your mother yet?"

"Not yet." She kissed his back. "And I almost forgot your small *tushi.* So many Indians have small buns."

"How 'bout my face?"

"Yes. You look just like the Indian on the nickel. Except for your blond hair. And your red beard. A tall blond Indian is a bit weird."

"A rich Indian is even weirder. If Molly Running Deer had only known she was sitting on all that oil, that her son would be rich beyond her wildest dreams . . . and she didn't even have electricity!"

"All this sex is making me hungry," Jessica said. "Let's get up and eat."

"I'll make us a chicken sandwich. I've had no meat for a month. I can't wait to tell you about the tribe and the medicine men and the seeds from the herbs the team collected."

"I love the jewelry you collected," Jessica said, closing the door to her bathroom.

"I THINK YOU'VE lost weight," Jessica said as they sat together in the kitchen. She tightened her robe around her. Tom was in a pair of walking shorts. She looked at his long legs and his flat stomach. "The five pounds you lost are on my body. Is that the way it works?"

"You're just right," he said, taking her hands.

"Two months is too long!" she said suddenly.

"Oh, God. I came home early—for Thanksgiving. I thought you'd be happy."

"I am! I am! It just reminds me how much I miss you." She massaged the thin scar between her eyes.

"It's the kind of job I have. You know how much it means to me. I'm fighting against time. If I can help the Indians in the rain forest get their land back—"

"Please. No preserve-the-planet speeches."

"We're too old for this fight."

"We're never too old to fight. Don't you care that your daughter is sleeping with a Bluebeard?"

"Oh, Jess!"

"Forget I said it. I know you think I'm paranoid."

"Of course I care. Should I run out of the jungle because my daughter is having sex? She's eighteen, for God's sake."

"This isn't some primitive tribal ritual we're talking about, Tom. This is Laurie."

"What does Laurie think? He sounds okay to me."

"I don't think he's right for her."

"Who *is* right for her, Jess? If I allowed myself to think that way, I wouldn't let a male within a mile of her. You can't design a boyfriend for her."

Silence.

"Let it go, Jessie. Don't be so possessive. I'm surprised at you. You're a hip mom."

"I'm not possessive. I'm *caring.*"

"And I'm not."

"You're not . . . here."

"Let's not play Ring Around the Rosie, Jess. Are you really worried about this boyfriend? Or is this just to tell me I should stay home?"

"Tom, even my open-minded old mother says Laurie is too good, too trusting."

"Why does she say that?"

"Because she's afraid boys will take advantage of Laurie."

"Don't you trust this Kevin?"

"No."

"Why?"

"I don't *know.* It's nothing specific that I can point to. That's why I need you to help."

Tom stood up and collected the dishes, shaking his head. "Jess, you've got to give me something to go on. So far the way you describe him—"

"I want you to meet him."

"This sounds crazy." Tom looked at her. "Do you want Laurie to develop into a strong, independent woman?"

"Of course."

"I want her to be just like you."

"Oh, Tom . . ."

"But overprotecting her, even with the best of intentions, and doing her thinking for her is not the way."

"Is that what you think I'm doing?"

"It seems so."

"I don't want to hurt Laurie, you know that, Tom."

"Just think about what you're doing, Jess. She's got to find out about life for herself. Remember the article we once read in the *Times* by the shrink who treats young people? It said if a parent jumps in to take charge when a daughter is in a relationship it makes the child feel powerless."

"But Tom, this is different. Believe me. Kevin Glade is hiding something. I sense it, I smell it. When I'm near him I *know* it."

Tom paused before speaking. He couldn't tell her that he thought she hadn't really adjusted to Laurel's being away, that she was focusing too much of her energy on this Kevin. And maybe most of all, he felt guilty for leaving her alone so much.

"I give up," he finally said. "You know I trust your judgment." He shook his head. "Better you should pick on this kid than me," he said straight-faced, making Jessica want to scream.

RICKY SPREAD THE plastic sheets over the floor and removed the tissue paper from between them.

"Gorgeous," remarked Jessica, who sat cross-legged beside her in a sweatshirt and jeans. Ricky held an amber sheet up to the light. "The lead singer is black, and I can't use the same gel on him as I would on a white person. If I light him with yellow he'll look like a manila envelope."

Ricky had a boyish figure and crawled about nimbly on the floor, leafing through the gels she used for lighting Symphony Space, a theater just a block away from their apartment building. Jessica eyed her friend's flat tummy and small waist, her size-six model's figure, admiring her wiry strength. Ricky was five years younger, she reminded herself, and her body hadn't been stretched by a growing baby.

"Whites have pink in their skin, so yellow is okay," Ricky explained. She held up two sheets of magenta. "For the shin busters," she said, referring to the shin-high lights at the edge of the stage that imperiled the dancers.

"I'm so glad you live next door to me," Jessica said.

"Thanks to my dad," Ricky said with a wistful smile.

"When your father died and left you this apartment, Laurie was only eight, still bouncing balls in the hallway, driving the neighbors crazy. You were the only one who didn't complain. Remember when she crayoned a mural on the wallpaper in the hall?" They both smiled, thinking about the night they had scoured all traces of Laurie's artwork from the walls. "What would I have done without you all these years?" Jessica said. "I'd probably be divorced."

"Is the honeymoon over?" Ricky asked.

"Oh, we had breakfast early this morning, and he went back to the office for a few hours. He'll stay in New York long enough to raise some money and get some more legal support, and he'll be gone again in December. Then I'll be alone again."

Jessica noticed the papers on the drafting table near the window. Ricky's apartment had a view of the city with morning sun from the east. "Are you lighting a new show?"

"I have a production meeting for the *Mikado* at noon. The Gilbert and Sullivan Players are back from the grave," Ricky said, checking her watch. She held up two magenta gels to the light. "This one has more pink," she decided, looking up. Jessica couldn't tell the difference.

"I'm *under*whelmed by this Kevin character," Jessica announced. Ricky sipped her coffee and set her mug back on the rug, squinting at Jessica as she spoke. "He looks like a real granola type, but he doesn't feel like one."

"What do you mean?"

"Last week when Tom and I took him to dinner, he was so pleasant and charming. But, somehow, *empty.* He never said anything that showed any depth or . . . He's bright but . . ."

When she saw the look in Ricky's eyes, she put up her hands. "Please, please don't tell me I'm just a jealous, possessive mother who can't let go."

"Listen, I'm a lighting designer. I need to have details to build my lighting plot. Start with his background."

"Well, he's supposed to be well-to-do. Lost his parents when he was a small boy. Brought up by a mean aunt, went to the Putney School in Vermont. He paints, is an art major at Cornell but never seems to go to classes. He's supposedly trained as a pianist, but his fingernails are too long. And he writes poetry." She pulled a folded sheet from her pocket as she spoke. "He never took Latin—in a *private* school? And his birthday is *New Year's Day."* She thrust the page at Ricky. "Tell me what you think of this poem."

"First tell me what's wrong with being born on New Year's Day."

"It's so . . . so somehow theatrical," Jessica said. Ricky laughed as she smoothed the paper out on her lap.

Jessica helped herself to coffee and brought her mug back to the couch, where her friend was reading the poem.

"Well?"

"It's a very sophisticated poem."

"Too sophisticated for an eighteen-year-old? He looks older, and he acts older. Laurie's a baby compared to him."

Ricky gave her a look. "Why would he lie about his age?"

Jessica shrugged. "He always seems preoccupied, as if he had something on his mind. Where's that *joie de vivre* you're supposed to have when you're so young?"

"What else?"

"He doesn't have the polish of a prep-school kid. It's more the slickness of a con artist. And how come he never heard of the Sierra Club or Audubon Society? When Tom mentioned them he drew a blank, although he made a quick, facile recovery."

"Kids are pretty ignorant nowadays."

"He uses the right forks, says the right things, but I just get the feeling that he wants Laurie to think that he's something he's not."

"What do you think he's after?"

"Latching on to a rich girl? He knows I'm Jewish, and everyone thinks Jews have money." They both laughed. "Who knows?" Jessica said, shaking her head.

Ricky saw the genuine worry in her friend's face.

"Can I borrow this poem? I'll ask Marianne to read it. She's teaching a poetry course this term. Maybe she'll give us an opinion about Kevin's talent."

"Bless you, Ricky," Jessica said.

"Well, I'll always remember Arnie."

"Arnie?"

"Yeah, Arnie. I was so in love with him. And he turned out to be such a sleaze?"

"I remember now," Jessica said. "The director with the ponytail."

"Well, you never liked him."

Jessica exhaled in relief. She at last had found an ally.

Chapter Four

"TALK AROUND TOWN is that poor April Meadows was murdered," Patrick Sullivan told his daughter Kathleen as he finished his breakfast. Kathleen couldn't control her shock. "The cops are heating up their search. I wonder why, after all this time?" He looked into his daughter's face, noting her reaction. "You didn't know her, did you?"

"No. She wasn't in my class," she answered, collecting his plate to cover her emotion. "She was younger," she explained quickly. "I never knew her."

"Shocking," he said, grabbing his parka. The word made her feel guilty, even though it wasn't applied to her. "Give Brendan a kiss for me, will you," he said on his way out, "or I'll be late to the store again today." She could hear the sounds of Daffy Duck coming from the living room. Two-year-old Brendan was watching TV while he munched his dry cereal.

Kathleen collapsed in a kitchen chair when she heard the front door close. She reached for an imaginary cigarette, the habit returning after almost a year of not smoking. At first, when Billy had started dating April, Kathleen had envied her, thinking that April would be treated better by Billy, that she was a smarter, sharper, more popular girl who wouldn't get into the kind of trouble Kathleen had brought on herself through her own weakness and stupidity. But the day she heard that April was missing, she knew why April had run away; it was the same reason she had wanted to run away herself. She had felt sorry for April then, and for the first time felt compassion for herself instead of anger and shame. No one deserved the likes of Billy Owens.

Now, though, she was frightened for April, and stunned that the police were looking for a killer. After all, she had been the same age as April when her life was ruined by Billy. She'd been an innocent fool. She had tried to be a good girl. Now she was thinking maybe she wasn't to blame for wanting some fun that night. Taking care of her mother at fourteen while other girls were partying, knowing her mother wasn't long for this world, was too hard. So she had given in to temptation one night. When she heard that Billy had left town after his graduation, she had been so relieved. She wouldn't have to worry about running into him in town, in the supermarket, at a football game. After she dropped out of school, she had dropped off the face of the earth as far as he was concerned.

She heard Brendan moving about. It was time to help him out of his p.j.'s, to get him bathed and ready for his play group. She would pick him up later to go on the outing she had promised. What irony. Today was the day she was finally going to end the misery that began three years ago, the day she was going to gather up her courage and tie up the last loose end of the mess she had made of her life.

She peeked into the living room, where Brendan was sitting on the floor by his empty plate, hugging his blanket. God, how she loved him. Her dad loved him too. She waited until the program ended, looking around the room at her mother's favorite possessions, the lace curtains, the Irish crystal. She ran her finger over the dust on the bureau she had once kept highly polished for her mom when she became too sick to get out of bed.

"It's a good thing your mother didn't live to see this," she had always expected her father to say when he saw that the extra weight on her fifteen-year-old body wasn't from overeating, from consoling herself after her mother's funeral. But he had never uttered a syllable three years ago, nor had he since. She knew it would have killed her mother if she had known Kathleen was pregnant, but the C-disease had done it first. The cancer word was never spoken in the house, as if cancer didn't exist if you never said its name.

She stood before the bureau, where her high school diploma would sit. She was almost finished with night school now, and she planned to become a nurse, to make something of herself, to make Brendan and her dad proud of her; maybe her mother, too. And she was beginning to feel she had almost made up for all the losses, that she could move forward, finally even find some happiness. Maybe now she would be able to sleep at night, not wake up from a nightmare full of rage at the injustice, or with anxiety grinding in her chest. She caught herself in the mirror above the bureau, peered at her long blond hair, the gangly body that was filling out now, the blue eyes. Maybe she shouldn't go today, she thought, her resolve crumbling. No, she decided, she had put it off too long. It was time to face the fear.

She would go to the quarry.

BY NOON THE canine unit had searched the bushes around the Meadows house. No luck. The fire department came up with zero. Finally, Sandy Ungar thought, we did something, but they had let the trail grow cold. She banged her fist on her desk. Why hadn't she followed her instincts?

Even now McKenzie would say they had no real indication of a crime. Still, she had immediately sent out new posters of April, with dental charts this time, and the faxes now stated: "It appears the disappearance may be the result of foul play." But she couldn't tell Marge the truth. These measures didn't mean diddly; they wouldn't find her daughter. The police didn't have the manpower to launch an extensive hunt, and investigators in other states were busy solving their own crimes.

The call from April's mother this morning had caught her by surprise. It was a day early. And the timing was a bitch. Sandy had been on her way to a homicide scene when the phone rang, and she had blurted out, "There's no news, Marge." At the thought of the poor woman's response, Sandy's shirt instantly became damp. It was as if the sun's rays penetrated the squat little concrete barracks and her sterile, windowless office, and bored right into her chest.

"It doesn't matter anymore," April's mother had cried out. "My daughter is dead."

"HAVE YOU SEEN this young girl?" A year and a half ago April's face had beamed at him from the TV screen. And fear had flooded him as a skinny brunette, a local reporter, spoke earnestly into the camera. "April Meadows, just turned fifteen, has been missing for over three months under mysterious circumstances." A telephone number appeared beneath April's photo. "If you have any information, please call this number," a voice intoned.

Now at Cornell, whenever he prepared the messy dye and squeezed the plastic nozzle of Clairol hair color into his red roots, he would look up into the mirror of his dorm and remember those words. He had been staring into a different mirror in the lonely motel room where he made his first stop on the road to erasing Billy Owens from the planet. It wasn't fifty miles from where April . . .

He saw a flash of blood, April's body, brain matter. . . . He tried to squelch the recurrent image of April's head, split like a pumpkin. . . .

That awful night in the motel room he had been sure that one day they would find her body and *his* photo would be flashed on the screen. And his fright had made him dizzy and sent him scurrying in a sweat to a nearby mall to find some way to disguise himself. Even if they never found her body, he realized he couldn't take any stupid chances with that cop Sandy Ungar still alive. He scoured an immense supermarket, snatching items off the shelves, throwing them into his basket: first hair color, then mousse, a pair of barber's shears, a baseball cap, and finally sunglasses. It was surprisingly easy to shop unnoticed in the anonymous, empty aisles. He lingered just long enough at the rows of hair dyes to choose the right color. At the checkout he counted out his bills carefully. The money he'd taken from his savings account, and the bills his mother had tucked into his wallet, were running out fast. He tried not to think about what it had been like to say good-bye to his mother, but couldn't help it.

"I've been putting off telling you, Mom, but I'm leaving," he had said. "There's nothing here for me anymore."

There was a frightened look on her face that told of bad news she had always expected. "But where will you go?" she asked.

"I've got a job lined up in Michigan with a friend of mine. I'm too restless right now to settle down to school."

His father, standing in the living room doorway, had stared hard at him without wishing him well. Tears had welled in his mother's eyes, but she said nothing, as usual. She had lost the battle. He had known he could never go home or see his mother again. He thought she knew it too. And then he'd had an inspiration. He called April's mom to say good-bye, and she burst into tears. Nice touch, Billy.

His first dye job back at the motel spotted his T-shirt, the sink, and the bathroom tiles with brown ooze. But the results were worth it; they were astonishing. He recalled the children taunting him in elementary school, "Carrot top, carrot top. Chop chop carrot top. Rabbits munch on carrot tops."

He was glad he had blown that cow town. He remembered the stormy night he had left. He had headed for the highway, his head down, his suitcase in hand. He figured he would flag down a trucker and by the next day be a thousand miles away, before any cop even thought of searching for him. Now he marveled at his own cleverness in deciding on a random destination. He would hide wherever the trucker dropped him off. And the trucker who picked him up took him from the highway to Brattleboro, Vermont, a place they couldn't track him because it had been pure chance, a throw of the dice that he wound up there.

He was a different person these days, a college kid in Ithaca, looking at himself in the mirror. He remembered how he had first trimmed his brown curls, just after dyeing them, and discovered that cutting his hair short straightened the kinks. And when he combed it back with mousse, he was struck by the change. The contours of his face took on a new dimension. With his forehead visible, his face appeared longer, and his expression seemed to become much more mature and thoughtful. But the dramatic darkening of his bright red hair to an inconspicuous brown created the most amazing effect of all. He felt transformed emotionally when the fiery color of his hair, like flaming autumn leaves, was turned to winter brown.

He had a new self. A sense of peace came over him, similar, he imagined, to the serenity monks achieved through meditation. He fell under the spell of his new identity, and a momentary elation surged through him at the thought of shedding his past like a snake in a new season molting its papery skin.

A baseball cap had shaded his fair skin from freckling that summer, then a straw hat with a cloth band gave him refuge, and now a more urbane one of broad felt shielded him from the glare of prying eyes.

He stood up to assess himself in the mirror. Definitely more "studly," he decided, using his newly acquired college slang, and stretching himself before the mirror. He had grown more than an inch since he'd left Indiana. His bones were heavier and he had put on some weight. The curly, redheaded boy-next-door look just wouldn't cut it at Cornell, he thought. Eventually he had let his hair grow smooth and wavy down his neck. A touch of class. This was the Ivy

League, not the bush league, he reminded himself as he bent over a sink in the rarely used bathroom at the end of the hall. His roommate, a hotelie from the hotel school, was out catering some school banquet again. The door was locked, just in case, against a student's unlikely intrusion. Adept at applying the dye now, he put the finishing touches to the stray strands of red hair he had overlooked on the top of his head. He would clean up and discard the telltale container in a dumpster in College Town.

These college kids didn't know how lucky they were. They had money, parents. . . . He missed his mother. He hadn't dared to call her in over a year, but the other day he couldn't resist and had dialed her number when he knew his father would be working, just to hear her voice. He imagined that somehow she knew he was on the other end of the silence.

College was the ideal hiding place for a nineteen-year-old without family, friends, or means of support, he thought. And in Ithaca, with its huge Cornell campus and its colleges, he was lost in a sea of students. He adopted an old high school buddy's name and requested that his records be sent to Cornell. Kevin Glade, the ski bum, would never know Billy had appropriated his name; nor would he ever set eyes on the glowing letters of recommendation Billy had concocted. Billy had even enhanced the Glade family name by achieving a better score than Kevin himself could have made by studying like crazy for the SAT's. But, of course, the real Kevin would never know that either. The classier the school, he had discovered, the easier it was to scam it. He had turned Princeton down. And financial aid had flowed at Cornell when the owner of the crafts co-op in Putney, Vermont, wrote a letter attesting to "Kevin's sterling character," lamenting his tragic status as an orphan. The only hitch was money. His aid put food on the table and took care of the tuition, but it took some cash for clothes and a social life. Especially now that he had found the love of his life, the luscious female who had eclipsed April and then Betsy. He'd had to leave Betsy behind in Putney. Small towns were notorious for ferreting out secrets.

Laurie. He etched her name into the mirror with his dye-stained fingers. He would do anything for her. When he had arrived alone in Ithaca, he had been a shadow, disconnected from his family, his town, from any love. But now he was completely happy. Laurie was his lifeline out from the world of the dead.

LAURIE JOGGED HOME from her last class, singing along as "Watershed" boomed through the earphones of her portable CD. The Indigo Girls singing her favorite song made her think of Kevin. "He is cute, he is smart, he is charming," she sang to the rhythm of the song, memory of the scary moments at the summer house pushed into the back recesses of her mind.

The song reminded her of the windy afternoon at the lake the day she had first met Kevin. It was in August, her first week at school, the Sunday she had picnicked with the debate team at the water's edge. She had walked right into Kevin's game of Ultimate Frisbee, causing him to drop a point. He hadn't minded, he was so polite and sweet. She remembered looking into his eyes the moment he caught her with his glance—and her heart had flipped. It made her breathless just thinking of him. The longer she knew him, the more intense was her sense that there were lives stored up in him, that there was more to life than what we saw on the surface. It wasn't anything he said. It was a kind of silent expression, an undercurrent of emotion and layers of feeling that she had never experienced in a boy before. He exuded an aura. It attracted her, captured her, held her.

And he also had a vulnerable quality that made him all the more appealing. He had some secret hurt that she could see in his faraway look sometimes. She remembered the funny expression in his eyes when she had tried to drag him out on a sailboat that day they met, how he tried not to admit he couldn't sail—hell, couldn't swim—embarrassed by his fear. But she wouldn't let him out of it. And she knew he didn't want to lose her the minute he found her, that he was as dazzled by her as she was attracted to him.

"Come on, scaredy cat, don't you trust me?" she teased him.

"How good are you?" he asked her.

"Don't worry, you won't drown. Just hang onto the boat if it turtles. Or swim to shore."

"I have my new watch—"

"Just leave it in your shoe," she said, laughing at his excuse. "Your friends will guard it."

Then she had tugged his hand, pulling him along, feeling a tenderness for him, for his awkwardness, for his willingness to suffer to please her. But once out on the lake she had tacked abruptly and brought the sailboat back, not wanting to prolong his visible misery.

Now, after two months together, she and Kevin were like two bugs in a rug, two peas in a pod. They had the same tastes, the same interests, and Kevin even kept his cool about her mother.

Lost in thought, she didn't see Doug and Little Mini cross the quadrangle to meet her until it was too late. They were the very people she wanted to avoid. Tonight was the practice round for novices in the debate team. She intended to skip it and spend the evening with Kevin.

They hurried toward her, throwing their arms around her. She laughed at their dramatics, so unlike Kevin. Sweet, gentle, placid Kevin. Well, most of the time . . .

KEVIN UNLOCKED HIS desk drawer and pulled out his last letter to his idol, Lorna Barrett. Catching a glimpse of his altered image in the small mirror on the wall, he smiled. He would burn the letter. He rummaged through his roommate's drawer for a cigarette lighter. He held up the letter, and flipping on the lighter, he fed a corner at the top of the paper to the flame.

He thought about the first letter he had written to his favorite actress, and all the succeeding letters. He remembered the first time he had seen her, the pitch-black movie theater, how uneven his breath had become the minute she appeared on the screen. She was so young, so innocent in *Young Love,* yet sophisticated too—the same age he was. And he had written to her, poured his heart out in letter after letter, telling how he adored her.

When he saw her on the screen he imagined she was acting for him, that when she looked at the audience she was looking at him, that she was having a secret, silent conversation with him. This is you, Kevin, she was saying when she kissed an actor. Or, I'm just playacting this, Kevin, when she was making love to someone else. It's you I love, she would tell him without moving her lips. Sure, he knew it was a fantasy, even as he sat in the dark obscurity of his local movie house. He knew it, but that didn't change his feelings.

He pictured her pouting lips, her natural blond hair, her beautiful long legs, her knowing, sexy eyes. He had never stopped writing her, even after he left home, even though he knew he couldn't send the letters. He'd have to start calling instead. But now he didn't need any Lorna Barrett, the rejecting Ice Queen. He hadn't even seen her last movie. He read the words he wrote as the flame crept down to his fingers.

> Dear Lorna,
>
> I've found my own beautiful one. Her name is like yours, she even looks like you. She has your long blond hair, your bedroom eyes, your lean, willowy body, your gentle, ironic smile. Her eyes talk to me the way yours do. She's capable of loving me the way I always imagined you would love me. It was a hopeless love, the love I had for you. Well, you're nothing to me now. Laurel is my soul. She can fill the void in my heart.

The last thing he saw in the flame devouring his past were the letters of his real name, Billy Owens.

He dropped the charred residue into the ashtray and stirred the ashes, and then heard sounds in the hallway. Quickly, he reached for his glasses, cramming them onto his face, then relaxed as the footsteps and laughter receded, and he carefully adjusted the wire rims on his nose.

He remembered how nervous he had been just a few months ago when he decided to trade in his sunglasses, which he decided made him look too . . . too uncollegiate, for the politically correct round frames he wore now. He had walked up and down the busy streets of lower Manhattan near City Hall in the sweltering July sun, his back wet with perspiration. He had just taken care of his illegal enterprise—making a fast buck buying drugs in sin city to unload in Vermont for a profit—and he was hunting for just the right optical shop. It had to be a large, busy, assembly-line operation where customers were numbers, not names or faces. Easy to do in New York. He found one almost immediately among the seedy discount stores. Through the windows he could see clerks lined up at the counter and their clients waiting turns on plastic cushioned sofas. He strolled in, blending with the crowd. If you looked confident, he had learned, most people trusted you. It was the guilty look, the fearful tone of voice, the hesitation, that gave you away. Still, he wasn't sure how much attention he might draw by asking for clear glasses in a new frame. He needn't have worried.

"Got a summer job on Wall Street?" the optician had asked him. He was wearing his button-downs and Docks.

"Yeah."

"I get lots of young lawyers from around this area. The kids want to look older, more professional. They ask for clear glass."

"So it's not unusual."

"You'd be surprised. They come in all the time. The thicker frames go to the MBA's, the accountants, the businessmen. The brokerage houses go for the round ones," he informed Kevin, looking him over.

He still kept the extra pair in his desk drawer from the "buy one, get one free" deal.

Manhattan was filled with endless surprises, he thought, the least of which was Laurie. She was more wonderful than April. April was budding, Laurie was the full fruit. And what's more, she didn't think there was anything wrong with loving him. In the city, he thought, anything goes, and nobody knows. It still shocked him how the college girls from New York, from good families, talked. And acted. They weren't ashamed to use words that mothers in his Indiana hometown would wash their kids' mouths out for uttering. Laurie talked openly about sex. And more shocking than anything else, Laurie's parents *knew* they were sleeping together.

But Laurie was no slut. She was a jewel. A star. She was tall, with bright blue eyes, long blond hair down her back, and a full-throated laugh. In some ways, though, she was more innocent than the small-town girls who were always on their guard, worrying what their neighbors thought, the town thought, their parents thought. Laurie, wary of the outside world, trusted her inner circle completely, assumed every friend was as good as she was. She was untroubled and uncomplicated. He loved the way she walked—long, firm, confident strides. He was prouder of being with her than of anyone in his whole life. She was a radiating sun. And now he needed her to make him shine.

He buffed his cowboy boots on the back of his corduroy trousers, smoothed the brim of his hat, and headed for the quad to catch Laurie on her way home from class. He knew how it pleased her when he turned up unexpectedly. He was sure of it. It showed that he loved her. He hurried down the stairs, suddenly afraid he had missed her.

KEVIN HADN'T PREPARED for the drop in temperature, and his short leather jacket was inadequate for the chill. But climbing Libe Slope was more than enough exertion to warm him up. He scanned McGraw, the history building, looking for Laurie, then checked his watch. He was too late to run up to the third floor to meet her class. Then he saw her. She was standing right in front of the statue of Andrew Dixon White, and Doug, that bag of blubber, that creep from Mars, had his arm around Laurie's shoulder. He was out of breath from hurrying up the hill, but he bounded up the stairs to the stone benches on the terrace overlooking the statue. The terrace was deserted, and he had a clear view of the scene. He sat down, feeling the damp of the sweat under his jacket and the cold wind whipping him. He removed his glasses, staring intently. He had caught her. Fleeing from the police had sharpened his senses, honed his awareness.

It was twilight. He strained to make out Mini, Doug's midget sidekick, casually standing by. Evidently *she* didn't mind Doug pawing Laurie.

Laurie was laughing, poking Doug. Now he was grabbing her books. Laurie was still laughing in a tug-of-war that she won. She retreated and now they were all laughing. Finally Laurie threw Doug a kiss and headed for her dorm, and Mini and Doug walked in the other direction, right toward Kevin.

Kevin raced down the stairs, replacing his glasses as he stepped into their path.

"I hear you called Laurie last night," Kevin said, a steel edge in his voice.

"Hello, Kevin!" from Doug. "So *nice* to see you again."

Kevin glared.

"Yeah, I did," Doug said. "So what?"

"Here's what. Laurie doesn't want to see you anymore. She's just being polite. So stop bothering her."

Doug blinked in shock as Kevin grabbed the lapels of his overcoat.

"Hey, *get lost*," Doug said. But his voice was unsteady. He was no match for Kevin's strange burst of anger.

Abruptly Kevin released him, stalking away.

"Holy shit!" Mini whispered.

"I should've punched him," Doug said.

"He's not worth dirtying your hands on. What does she see in Count Dracula, anyway?"

"So that explains why she's been pushing us away," Doug said. "Why she's not coming to the practice round tonight. Two to one she quits the team."

"Okay with me," Mini said, shivering as she followed Kevin with her eyes.

Doug opened the door to Olin Library. Inside, the shuffle of books, interrupting the heavy silence, followed them to their tables.

KATHLEEN HOPED FOR rain, but the clouds just hung there, darkening the pit, the ledges casting shadows. If it rained she would have to run home with Brendan, she thought, inching forward, holding Brendan's hand. He thought it an adventure. And why shouldn't he?

She had done everything wrong that day, almost ensuring that she couldn't come. But at each obstacle, after each delay, she had forced herself forward, in spite of the hour. Something told her she had to come to the quarry, something as urgent as her need to see it to purge her dreams of it, to free herself of its hold on her. He was like a plague on her memory. She stood at the edge of the pit looking into the shadows, and suddenly she knew she had done the right thing. She sat down on a culvert, remembering the scene, an adult looking at her childhood.

It had all started with the school dance. That night her mom had told her that the shade of blue in her lace dress brought out the color of her eyes. Then her mother teased her, calling her a long drink of water, laughing at her height. In spite of her mom's derision she knew boys looked her over when they thought she wasn't aware of them. But she was rarely asked out or whirled around the dance floor because she had that sad face and ran right home after school. She was shy and awkward and wished she knew how to talk to boys the way other girls did. Then Billy, popular, handsome Billy Owens, picked her, Kathy the wallflower, and danced with her all night, and she was transformed into a rose. It was her night out, and she had been chosen by Billy for all to see.

When he drove her from the dance and added liquor to the punch in her cup, she should have refused. But she didn't want to be a nerdy, scared little girl. Her head spun, and she felt happy. When they reached his special, secret place, she was flattered, not afraid. She was acting out her fantasy. This couldn't be real, she thought through her haze when he kissed her. Oh, it felt so good what he did. More fantasy come true.

Oh yes, she knew it was wrong, she would stop soon. It was a sin to do it for real. Her mother would kill her! But before she could resist, it was too late. He had her pinned to the ground, and she had hated it, *hated* it. She couldn't cry out. She was too ashamed. The pain was awful, and she knew she was betrayed, and worse, that she had betrayed her dying mother.

Afterward, she kept it a secret. Now women were speaking up on TV, but not in her town. And she didn't have the guts to be the first. It was okay if you were a lawyer or a teacher or a respected married woman with a family. . . .

Her neck grew hot. She felt perspiration beading her brow even though a cool wind blew. This time it wasn't anger, humiliation. It was pure fear at the thought that Billy Owens got what he wanted, no matter how.

Brendan . . . where was he? Panic, then she spied him playing at the mouth of the culvert. Brendan had his father's orange-red hair, green eyes, and the freckled face she had been so taken with. Now she had only love for Brendan, he was her whole world. And, amazingly, the beauty of his loving gaze had almost erased the agony of the way he had been conceived. You will never know your father was Billy Owens, she swore. Brendan looked up at her when she stood and walked quickly toward him. The quarry was deserted, and the granite ledges were creepier than she'd remembered.

Brendan held his palms out to her. He had been playing with something that looked like a ball. "Mommy, Mommy, Halloween," he said. He toddled toward her, both hands still outstretched, offering her the toy. When she looked closer she saw what her child held in his plump little fingers.

A skull, a human skull, with tiny bits of flesh still clinging to it.

Kathleen's shrieks echoed in the quarry.

Chapter Five

JESSICA AND ROZSI were side by side at the butcher block counter in Jessica's sparkling new kitchen, paring cooked cabbage spines and rolling the stuffing of meat and rice into the leaves.

Rozsi held the salt shaker aloft. "Am I allowed?"

"No, absolutely *not.* Remember your heart—your blood pressure."

Rozsi added salt. "Just a pinch. I won't stay for dinner tonight, but it's a pleasure to cook in this kitchen, Miss Rich Lady."

"Are you sure you won't stay to dinner?" Jessica asked, ignoring her remark.

Rozsi shook her head.

"It's women only. Tom has a meeting, so I invited my friends over. They're all dying to meet you."

"Meet an old lady? Your fancy-shmantzy friends."

"Marianne Sweeney's a teacher, one of seven children whose father's a plumber. You know Ricky, she works in the theater. And Margo's a starving artist supporting her oddball husband, Stanley. They're all struggling."

Rozsi shook her head again. This time it meant, you don't know what struggling is.

Jessica lowered her voice. "Ricky gave Kevin's poem to Marianne. She's going to give us her verdict tonight."

"Mert shutogs?" Rozsi asked in Hungarian.

"I'm whispering because I don't want Tom to know. He'll be pissed—angry."

Rozsi tossed her hand in dismissal, a do-as-you-please gesture.

"What are you two whispering about?" Tom asked, suddenly appearing in the doorway. He was wearing a business suit, his overcoat slung over his arm.

Rozsi looked embarrassed, but before Jessica could shoot him a warning he cut her off.

"Cooking up plots together?"

"Very amusing," Jessica said.

"Don't forget the eye of the newt," he said, laughing.

Jessica waved him off as he left. "Go to your dinner meeting," she said to his back. "You're missing Rozsi's stuffed cabbage."

"There's plenty for tomorrow," Rozsi mumbled. Jessica wondered why her mother hadn't been as conciliatory with her own husband.

"I'd like to talk to Laurie," Rozsi said, trying to distract Jessica from her irritation. "I'll tell my Laurika to dump this Kevin."

Jessica shrugged. "Maybe she'll listen to you. But if I open my mouth it's the kiss of death. You know what happened with Tony when I was seventeen."

"I was only trying to save you pain, but it was no use."

"All mothers try. And daughters don't listen."

"Was I wrong?" Rozsi asked.

"No. But that isn't what I thought then."

Rozsi stacked the little cabbage rolls neatly in a large kettle and poured tomato sauce and pickled cabbage over them.

"You took it out on me," Rozsi said softly, still staring into the pot. Jessica dropped the lid on it and turned up the flame.

"So, should I stay out of her business, Anyuka? Should I let her get involved with someone I don't trust?"

Rozsi rubbed her hands decisively on a dish towel before looking at her daughter. "Be a mother," she said.

"YOU HAD THE balls to invite Marianne and Margo on the same night?" Ricky asked as they stepped out onto the terrace to see the view. She saw that the table was set in the dining room and dinner was ready on the stove. "You know what Marianne calls Margo? Carmen Miranda. She can't stand those big earrings and the makeup. 'All Margo needs is the fruit on her head,' Marianne told me the other day."

Jessica smiled. "Margo calls Marianne Hester Prynne."

"Hester who?"

"You know. *The Scarlet Letter.* Repressed sexuality. Margo can't stand Marianne's mother superior Catholic school attitude or her lace collars."

"Well, she's pushing fifty," Ricky observed.

They inhaled the fresh autumn breeze, hugging their arms to their bodies. "Quick, take a look at my new vegetation before we freeze," Jessica said. They stood on the wooden deck that crisscrossed the concrete terrace. The sun was descending. Gray clouds dimmed the sky as they peered over the rail. Even after fifteen years it still made Jessica a little queasy to look down. The rain had washed the streets, and the terrace, still wet, smelled woody and musty. A thin mist hung on the shiny plants and bushes newly set in round tubs. "I wanted greenery all winter, and I read that junipers, weeping crabapple, and azalea survive New York winters. One day after Laurie left, it looked so barren out here I just planted them."

"You're a woman of action, Jess. It looks terrific. I wish I had a terrace. But then I'd have to keep up with you."

"The deer eat everything in Hartewoods, so I have more of a garden in the city. Some people hunt the deer. But I don't see how people can kill them. I'd be more tempted to go for one of those big, ugly cows you see all over."

"I didn't even know you had a gun," Ricky said.

"Oh, Tom taught us how to use his rifle. It was actually kind of fun target shooting, but I can't imagine shooting anything else. Even Ed Polley."

"Ed Polley?"

"The psycho who socked me," Jessica said. Ed Polley was the mentally ill man who had attacked her six years earlier. She had just admitted him to the psych unit at the institute when, without warning, he had socked her so hard between the eyes that she had been lifted several feet off the floor and into a wall. Both of Jessica's eyes had swollen shut, and her headaches had persisted for a year. She had taken a week off, her first in five years. It was her last year at the institute.

A gust of wind hurried them into the dining room. She heard her plastic watering can rattling against one of the planters outside. "Has your bedroom begun to howl yet?" Jessica asked.

"The corner bedrooms sound like Boris Karloff movies," Ricky said. The wind raced the clouds, slowly clearing the sky. "Remember when Rozsi's kitten took a stroll on this railing when Rozsi was in the hospital?"

"How can I forget!" Jessica said. "I still have a nervous stomach thinking of it." The wind slammed the terrace door shut just as the doorbell rang.

THE MIRROR COVERING the dining room wall reflected the magnificent sunset over the Hudson River.

"Glory be to God for dappled things," Marianne recited, dreamily leaning her elbows on the window ledge and looking across at the Palisades. " 'For skies as couple-colored as a brindled cow.' " The wind whipped the waves on the river into little white lines of froth.

"The vivid colors are created by air pollution," Margo said.

"Gerard Manley Hopkins," Marianne announced, ignoring Margo.

Margo rolled her eyes.

"You'll meet him later, when we talk about Kevin's poem," Marianne promised.

This wasn't good news to Margo, Jessica thought. But Margo had an artist's intuition, and she might help dissect the poem. After supper, she thought, trying to be patient. She disappeared into the kitchen to get the stuffed cabbage.

"Look at the beautiful boat all strung with lights," Marianne remarked, sighing. "I wonder where it's going." The sky was plunged into a deep dark blue as the sun dropped below the horizon. "It's a scene right out of Venice," Marianne rhapsodized. Ricky and Margo were seated at the table, sampling their chablis.

"I hate to shatter your illusions," Margo said, "but it's a tugboat pushing a garbage scow."

Uh-oh, thought Ricky. It's beginning.

"You have a real poet's soul," Marianne shot back. Your paintings probably stink, she thought.

How would you know? You teach the stuff. You don't write it, Margo thought.

"Din-din!" Jessica sang, setting the crock in the center of the table next to the rye bread and the platter of chicken paprikash.

* * *

KEVIN PRESSED THE square button on the intercom, then let himself into the lobby with the key Laurie had given him and walked a few steps down the hall, then unlocked the door to her dorm room. She had probably stopped at Entrepot, a pricy shop, to pick up some dessert. Not the goodies he was accustomed to, the salty potato chips he adored, the snacks so filled with preservatives they lasted for months in his desk drawer if he forgot to eat them. Now it was Cape Cod chips, green spaghetti, and carrot cake. He'd been forced to make some lifestyle adjustments to woo his new love, to change his dress, his speech, his taste in music and art. He watched and listened and learned, and now he was looking for a way to ingratiate himself with her father. Tom would let him in, he felt. Tom had given him an opening.

Kevin's latest idea was to compile a dictionary of college slang. He'd been making notes all semester anyway to help him fit in with the college crowd. Maybe it was because he was a bit older than the others in his class; he just couldn't fall into the easy use of trendy words like tripindicular for stupendous. Laurie's dad would go for the dictionary. At dinner, that horrible dinner when he had been interrogated by Laurie's rapacious mother, the only points he had scored were with Laurie's father when he had explained, to Tom's amusement, that a "hot" guy who was really cool meant that the studly dude was really handsome.

Tom was definitely approachable, he thought as he eyed Laurie's room, not wanting to overlook any detail while he had the chance. But he stayed on the bed, resisting the temptation to hunt through her possessions for fear she would walk in. Yes, Tom, who appreciated his interest in words, his widening vocabulary, would soon be in his pocket. But the mother, Jessica, she was a whole different problem. He didn't even like her looks—her dark hair, brown, almond-shaped eyes, bony cheeks, sharp nose. He felt on solid ground with Tom, but Jessica was like a hawk circling him, keen-eyed and unpredictable. He had never met a Jew before, up close, anyway. He wondered how an Indian and a Jew could produce such an awesome creature as Laurie. Picturing Jessica's face, he suddenly remembered the extra makeup on her forehead right between her eyes. But then his heart quickened at a sound. He kicked off his boots, threw himself on the bed, and grabbed a book. Laurie's key was turning in the lock.

THE BEST PART at a dinner party was sitting around the table drinking coffee, Jessica thought, especially now that no one smoked.

"How did you get to be a lighting designer?" Margo asked Ricky. "It's an unusual specialty."

"I studied musical theater up at Fredonia. I can sing and act and play several instruments. But I'm also technically oriented. When I worked backstage and discovered the lighting board, I realized I could be creative and practical at the same time. Sometimes I think I'm too practical—my rational side doesn't go in for astrology or all the Eat-a-Pineapple-and-See-God types in the theater."

"Like Stanley!" Margo said, making everyone laugh. The women knew Margo's hubby was in his New Age phase.

"We need to know the technology, literally the nuts and bolts, behind creating the illusion."

"Like a magician," Margo said.

"Exactly. That's why The Amazing Randi—you know, the famous magician? He debunks ghosts and goblins and mind readers. He admits his illusions are art. He doesn't confuse it with reality. I think most people ignore facts because they *want* to believe in the supernatural. Even normal people, like Arthur Conan Doyle. He believed in *fairies.*"

"You are putting us on," Marianne said.

"It's documented. Even brilliant people can be duped, have weird illusions."

"Lots of smart people were fooled by Simone De Beauvoir," Margo said. "Thousands of women got themselves sterilized after reading *The Second Sex,* to follow her example of not having children. And now I read that she gave up a terrific affair with a novelist to scurry back to Sartre to devote herself to his work."

"Who's left to admire?" asked Marianne.

"My candidate for fallen idol of the year is Bruno Bettelheim," Jessica said, and unconsciously touched her fingers to the scar on her

forehead. "We talked about it all week at my social-work conference. Bettelheim blamed mothers for autistic kids when all along it was neurological. He created generations of guilty women."

"Speaking of women," Margo said, scraping the last remains of pastry and apricot from her plate and licking the fork, "I have a dilemma you can help me resolve."

Jessica was growing impatient with the small talk. She badly wanted to get to the poem. It looked as if it would be the last on the agenda.

"Should I dye my hair and perm it and look glamorous like Jess, or should I go *au naturelle*?"

"I *don't* dye my hair," Jessica protested. "See my gray," she said, bending her head toward the group. "And these corkscrew curls are mine. It's not a perm."

"Sure," said Margo.

"I'll show you pictures. When I was a kid I was the only one in elementary school with bushy ringlets." She collected the cups and saucers and dessert plates and brought them into the kitchen, craving the quiet, needing to clear her head. She touched her fingers to her hair with satisfaction, recalling Margo's remarks. Soon she would be wondering whether to color her own hair. Did she have the courage to wear it gray? Women were always dissatisfied with themselves no matter how attractive they were. Jessica realized at that moment why she enjoyed washing dishes. She daydreamed while she did it, and the soothing water, the semi-absorption in the task, somehow freed her mind.

Then as if in a dream a male hand appeared out of the sudsy pan, the knuckles and wrists covered with light red hair. It was the back of a hand arched over a keyboard, floating up to her from a memory she had stored. Kevin dyed his hair! Her hands dripping with soapy water, she ran into the living room.

"Kevin dyes his hair."

"My son Wolf dyes his hair *purple,*" Margo said, laughing at Jessica's announcement.

Marianne laughed to herself, remembering when Margo's eccentric husband, Stanley, who was then in his Mozart phase, had named their newborn Wolfgang. "My daughter Anne has a friend who changed her eye color," Marianne added. "She wears blue contacts."

"That's no biggie nowadays," Margo remarked. "It's like nose jobs."

"Or eye lifts or tummy tucks," Ricky said.

"Nothing's the same anymore," Marianne said wistfully. "Have you seen those ugly orthopedic shoes the girls wear?"

"You mean those black Doc Martens?" Margo asked. "They're the ultimate in women's lib 'cause they're as ugly and comfy as men's shoes. They look like shoes the prison guards wore in the forties."

"What about the poem?" Jessica finally asked in frustration. "Did Kevin plagiarize it or not?"

"Plagiarism is the kind of heresy that says more about the character of the thief than the seriousness of the crime," said Marianne.

"Wow! What a pronouncement," said Margo.

"I think it's an important question," Ricky said.

"Then you agree that if he plagiarized the poem, he's a person who has no morals or scruples," Jessica said.

"Wait a minute," Margo said. "Don't hang him yet. He's only eighteen. At least give him a fair trial. Let's hear the evidence."

Marianne took out the poem. "It's not that clear-cut. I can see the influence of Gerard Manley Hopkins here. Hopkins was a poet-priest who celebrated the glories of nature—just as this poem does. He's widely studied because he was one of the innovators in poetic rhythm and language. Kevin's poem imitates his alliteration and typical rhythmical stresses, and uses the Hopkins invention, sprung rhythm."

"Did he copy it?" asked Ricky.

"Not a line. I know all of Hopkins' poetry. He's simply imitated his style. This poem is so derivative, it's clearly an imitation. Listen to this." She took a small book from her purse. "It's 'Pied Beauty,' by Hopkins." She read the poem. "Now Kevin's poem." She read it aloud.

"It doesn't sound like a male's poem," Margo said.

Marianne gave her a dirty look. "In my opinion a very bright student, a male or female could have written it."

"It's so polished," Jessica protested.

"I get poetry from students that's far better than the stuff I read in *The New Yorker,*" Marianne said.

"But—"

"Give it up," Margo said. "Kevin's innocent."

* * *

CALLING LAURIE BEFORE it got too late had been in the back of Jessica's mind as the dinner party wound down. But she enjoyed the conversation as the women relaxed on the leather couches and upholstered chairs in her living room. The lights were dim and comfortable, and there was an air of confiding, of letting your hair down, that they all loved so much. They finished the last drops in their coffee cups, their eyes glancing at their watches from time to time, postponing the inevitable. It was a weekday, so it was almost time to leave.

"Girls like deep, dark, mysterious men," Margo was saying. "Men with layers, men with a past, like Bogey in *Casablanca.*"

Ricky agreed. "Girls like to have their imaginations stimulated. They think it's romantic to become attached to a troubled man, someone who needs to be saved."

"Saving souls is a disease women are prone to. Giving succor, restoring faith, resurrecting the fallen. We've learned it over the eons at our mothers' breasts," Marianne said.

"That's why so many women are nurses and teachers," Margo put in.

"Or social workers," Jessica added, thinking of her scar and thankful she was doing some good in a safe, civilized office in midtown.

"Does Kevin look thrillingly decadent?" Margo asked.

"Well dressed, clean-cut, stylish. Plastic," Jessica said. "Whatever happened to old sneakers and torn T-shirts?"

"Most mothers would be grateful he doesn't look homeless," Marianne insisted.

"But what's he trying to prove?" Jessica asked.

"I think if he wore ratty clothes you would hate him," Margo said. "This kid can't win with you. So he's a little phony, trying to make a statement. Didn't you?"

"I did wear all black in college," Jessica said and half smiled.

"That's not phony?" Marianne asked.

"What does Tom think?" Ricky asked.

"He likes him," Jessica admitted. "I think he's so afraid of being overly protective he talks himself into approving all her suitors. Maybe he's fighting some Oedipal feelings. I mean, it happens."

Marianne and Ricky moaned in unison. "You don't really believe that crap, do you?" Ricky asked as they got up to leave.

Jessica laughed as they straggled toward the door. It was nearly midnight, but she could still call Laurie. Cornellians burned the midnight oil. But she would hold her tongue about Kevin's dyed hair. She wouldn't start a fight the night before a big debating tournament.

"DON'T GO TO Boston." Kevin was pleading.

"I'm sort of their heavy hitter," Laurie said. "They'll have a pretty rough time without me," she said. She didn't want to brag, but it was true. The team didn't have a chance if she deserted them.

"What about me?" He looked sad and hurt, like an abandoned child, Laurie thought. "Next week I'll be in Brattleboro with my aunt . . ."

"You're invited for fall break," Laurie reminded him.

"No, thanks," he said, thinking of the dinner in New York with her parents, of how he had overheard Laurie whispering in her mother's ear: "You are such a snob. I won't have Kevin interrogated."

Laurie lowered her eyes. She was remembering the way her mother had quizzed him about debate, not knowing he had dropped out of the club after a couple of weeks, how she had made him feel the need to recite the debate resolution rapid-fire to prove he knew it. "Resolved that limiting freedom in art infringes on First Amendment rights." Her father had laughed, but her mother had just looked at him.

"They won't give you the third-degree, I promise you," she said, even though she knew it was futile to try to persuade him.

"Just don't go this weekend." His eyes were misting over. He thought of his own parents, his house back home, and the loneliness he felt became real. It wasn't his dull, mediocre parents sitting like statues in their dusty, overstuffed living room watching the boob tube that he cared about. But he was missing something, he always missed something. It was as if he had a hole in his psyche, a void that craved satisfaction. But he had no name for it. All he *knew* was that Laurie was surely what he needed now. When he saw her face, touched her petal-soft skin, it was like a freshet on a parched day, a cool draft of water down his dry throat. That was as close as he could come to understanding what the longing was. And its message went straight to Laurie's core, its appeal as compelling as a wounded bird's.

She took his hand, trying to imagine him at five years old, on the night he had learned that both of his parents had been killed. She thought of how his aunt had brought him up in wealth but without love. No, she decided. She wouldn't go. He needed her too much.

The phone rang.

Laurie grabbed the phone on the first ring, sensing it was her mother.

"I wanted to catch you before you left for Boston. I know you leave real early tomorrow. Just wanted to wish you good luck, sweetheart."

"Thanks, Mom."

Damn! Laurie thought. But how could she explain to her mother with Kevin breathing down her neck? And her mother would never understand. Debate had been her life in high school. She had been a national champ. Well, the Boston debate was only one competition, she rationalized. No point in upsetting her mother now. Besides, tomorrow she might change her mind and go to Boston, after all. Her resolve weakened as she heard her mother's voice.

Then the tightening muscles in her chest told her she was just plain lying, but she couldn't stop. And it was just like when she was a child, roller skating too fast downhill. She felt free and very scared.

Chapter Six

LAURIE PUT DOWN the phone, disgusted with herself. She had barely been able to hear her mother over the Frank Zappa CD Kevin was blasting, the one he had bought her. She didn't have the heart to tell him how much she hated it, but she had winced and irritably motioned him to lower it while she spoke to her mother.

"When you talk to your mother, you're a different person," he said.

"Yeah, right, a liar."

"She's like the FBI. She's probably got your phone tapped. She watches your every move."

"Like you, Kevin," she said, letting out the words she'd been afraid to say. "You're always showing up unexpectedly. I still don't know how you knew I met Doug, why you resent Doug."

"That pile of blubber? What does he want from you? Why doesn't he stick to his Indian bimbo, Mini?"

"She's not Indian and she's no bimbo. She's a nationally ranked debater, and Doug is my *friend."*

He began drumming his fingers on the table.

"Why do you put down all my friends? Doug is brilliant. I miss him. And I'm beginning to miss debate."

"You think I'm dumb, don't you? You didn't have to talk for me that night at dinner with your parents. I'm as smart as your asshole friends."

"I was only trying to spare you the rubber hose—trying to save you from my mother's inquisition—"

"I can talk for myself!"

Laurie felt her temper rise. *"Do* you know what the Sierra Club is?"

"You made me look like a moron."

"You didn't have a clue."

He drummed louder on the table. Snobs! Fucking snobs, trying to take her away, trying to make me look like a nothing. And now she was doing it.

"Do you know what the Audubon Society is?" She knew it was unfair, but his drumming was driving her crazy. She had lied to her mother, and her anger was building. "Well . . . ?"

He began humming the tune he always hummed to calm himself down. He turned away from her, humming louder, unable to stop, knowing it enraged her.

"Stop that stupid humming!"

He whirled around, tried to squelch his rage, but in Laurie's moment of panic she looked at him just the way April had, and he had the urge to beat her face into a pulp to obliterate those eyes that condemned him. He dug his fists into his eyeballs.

"You bitch, you bitch." His voice seemed to be coming from far away. Had he actually spoken? But he heard her voice clearly enough.

"Get out of my room, Kevin."

His hands dropped to his sides like lead weights. He was rooted to the spot, paralyzed.

When she saw his face, her voice failed her.

THE CRAFTS FAIR circling the Museum of Natural History was an annual event Jessica had attended with her daughter ever since she could walk. New Yorkers browsed through stalls of silk scarves, bonsai, pottery, jewelry, and every sort of amateur artwork. Jessica inhaled what felt like sharp, clear air and wondered how much of the traffic fumes were seeping into her lungs. She saw a young couple walking together, hand in hand, and felt a sense of her own youth. She could almost taste the carefree years, feel the healthy flesh, the blush of innocence. For a moment she looked out at the world through twenty-year-old eyes and was young again. And as soon as she experienced it, a memory struck it down. Marianne's daughter had read in the Columbia *Spectator* about a freshman who was missing, who had disappeared. Jessica imagined the distraught mother trying to grasp that there were more than two thousand people murdered every year in Jessica's beloved city. Just then she spotted the earrings she would buy for Laurie's Hanukkah present. Distracted from her morbid thoughts, Jessica realized she was grateful that her child was at least living on a campus in a small city like Ithaca. She refused to allow thoughts of Kevin to intrude.

The earrings were gold and of the latest design; they curved behind and around the ear and decorated the front of the lobe. She remembered the dangling earrings and leather sandals she herself had worn to parties in Greenwich Village during college, parties her mother had waited out in a sweat until she returned at dawn. Young people think they're invincible, she thought, recalling how she used to ride the subway—the subway!—home to the Bronx in the middle of the night. Her mind continued to wander as she thought about how she'd held little Laurie's hand while they stood in awe of the prehistoric bones in the grand dinosaur hall of the museum, about their picnics in Central Park afterward, their country weekends in Hartewoods. Nature had to be pursued and planned for in their urban lives. She was beginning to understand why Tom needed to escape to wilder habitats, to get the smell of the semi-desert plants in his nostrils, to experience, as he had after leaving Oklahoma, the drama of the Colorado mountains. New York skyscrapers, those grand but lifeless concrete mammoths that narrowed daylight on city streets, couldn't compete.

It was lonely searching through the crafts fair without Laurie or Tom to share her discoveries. Soon Tom would be gone. She missed Tom most on Sundays when they would breakfast late and read the *Times,* lingering over lox and bagels and almond espresso. She would have to remind Tom to bring Laurie a Christmas present from Brazil. A good excuse, she thought, for calling him and hearing his voice and . . . wasn't that Mini? She lived near here, across from the planetarium. She was a hyper little dynamo, born on an island off India, who thought nothing of zipping to New York from Ithaca for a weekend. Jessica tapped the pert young woman bending over the African tote bags.

"I haven't seen you since Sodikow cracked the whip over the team at Science," Jessica exclaimed after they embraced.

"I never thought I would miss him," Mini answered. They laughed together over the fanatical debate coach who had transformed scared freshmen from shaking piles of Jell-O into top debaters, many of whom had been recruited by Cornell.

Mini compared Laurie to her mother, who was dressed elegantly in a fashionably short wool suit, dark stockings, and patent-leather shoes. She noted the small diamonds sparkling on Jessica's ears. Laurie was good-looking too, bigger boned and taller, imposing in a different way. Mini had always liked Laurie. She was strong and solid but more mellow than her intense mom. Should she tell Laurie's mom about that creepy boyfriend? No, she might resent it, kill the messenger.

"Why aren't you in Boston?" Jessica asked, interrupting Mini's ruminations.

"Boston?" Mini stopped short. "We had no novice team, so we canceled," Mini said with a curious glance at Jessica. Something's up, she thought.

"You mean Laurie never went?" Jessica asked in disbelief. She knew that Laurie was the star of the novice team.

Mini shook her head. "No one on the team . . ."

"Oh!" Jessica stammered. "I—I'm mixed up, I guess." She tried to look Mini in the eye.

"Say hello to Doug, will you?" she said, and quickly walked away before Mini could respond.

FEAR WAS STILL in Laurie's stomach at the thought of Kevin's vicious outburst. How could she be so *stupid*? Her mother couldn't be right. She couldn't! But as she clutched her pillow, she couldn't help thinking of Kevin's scary look, his bizarre mood shifts. She remembered how his fists had clenched and unclenched. And finally the heartbreakingly anguished look on his face when she told him to leave. Had she provoked him? Yes, no doubt. Still, his reaction . . . Was Kevin having some kind of breakdown? Was *she* responsible in some way? Making demands on him? Or should she break it off? Her world was turning upside down. The doorbell rang. She put the pillow over her head. Maybe she could just pull the covers up and stay in bed forever. But she dragged herself out of bed and raised the window blind. A delivery boy with a huge bouquet of flowers stood outside. She turned on the light, buzzed him in, and opened the door. The perfume of freesia and lilies and forget-me-nots suffused the room. The flowers were magnificent. Attached was a poem and a note in Kevin's handwriting: "Please don't let the rumor be true/that we are through. I love you."

The poem was typed.

Autumn Song
Once more the crimson rumor
Fills the forest and the town;
And the green fires of summer
Are burning—burning down.
Oh, the green fires of summer
Are burning down once more
And my heart is in ashes
On the forest floor.

She felt a rush of hope lifting her from her despair of a moment ago. She was at least partially to blame for being such a big mouth. Maybe they could still work it out. . . .

"LIES, LIES, LIES," Jessica was saying as she banged shut the door to her apartment, went to the phone, punched Laurie's number, and listened to the rings, furious at her daughter. Eight, nine, ten. She let the phone ring on and on, finally slammed the phone down, and thumbed through her address book to find Tom's new office number. But she held the receiver in the air. She couldn't do it. What she didn't need now was a lecture about how Laurie was trying to escape from her mother's clutches, that finally the only way Laurie knew to get free of her mother was to lie. He would somehow find excuses for Laurie, and then she would feel she was the heavy. Still, in spite of all that, Tom did trust her and he was right to. She rarely went on a crusade half-cocked. But about Laurie . . .

What she needed now was ammunition; then she would call Tom. Kevin was corrupting her daughter—Laurie, to her knowledge, had never lied before. She made another call, but it wasn't to Tom. One she should have made a long time ago. "Putney information, please," she said. We'll see about that aunt in Vermont. "Tina Glade," she said to the operator. "I have no address."

"There is no listing for that name," came the reply.

"Try Bettina," Jessica said.

"There is no Glade listed in Putney."

No Glade in Putney. She had another idea. "Give me the number for the Putney School," she said, calling Putney information again. The story she would give the school first thing Monday morning was forming rapidly in her mind. She felt much better. Taking action always made her feel better. Now she could call Tom and Laurie. But she wouldn't disclose a thing. Not until she had proof positive that Kevin Glade was a fraud.

JESSICA ATE A spoonful of sweet potato topped with marshmallow before covering the dish with tinfoil. "It's just the way my mother always made it. No wonder people get heart attacks after Thanksgiving." She watched Tom rinse the last dirty dish and stack it in the dishwasher.

"I can understand Rozsi going to sleep early," Tom said, adding soap to the machine. "But Laurie?"

"Her eyes were all puffy. My mom thinks she's skin and bones."

"Rozsi thinks anyone under two hundred pounds looks like a concentration camp victim."

"I'm glad Kevin wasn't here," Jessica said suddenly. "Maybe they had a fight."

"Look here, Calamity Jane. Your daughter has a cold, and Kevin's visiting his aunt in Putney." He turned on the dishwasher.

Jessica attacked the baking pan with the scouring pad.

"You're just upset because she didn't win a trophy in Boston."

Jessica gritted her teeth.

"Maybe Laurie's blue because she wants her mom to like her boyfriend—"

"Wait a minute," Jessica said. "Stop the dishwasher."

She moved quietly down the hallway and listened at Laurie's door. Was Laurie crying? She hurried back to Tom.

"I think she's crying . . ."

"If you jump to conclusions, you'll never find out what the problem is," he told her. "You'll hurt your relationship with her, and she'll never confide in you again. At least she called and said she wanted some time at home."

"You think it's me!"

"She hardly talked all evening. Jess, slow down and let me try to find out what's going on with Laurie."

Jessica nodded, kept her silence. She was right not to have brought up Laurie's lie. It would push Laurie further away—and right into Kevin's arms. Silence for now. Tomorrow Tom would leave for Brazil, and she would be free to discover the truth about Kevin Glade.

CHUCK HILDEBRAND HAD been a skier and a swinger in his day, but now he was grounded by arthritis and cataracts. His wife, Lilly, made the phone calls and did all the driving up to Vermont from their New York apartment these days. She had been the mousy one when she was young, but she was emerging with her new responsibilities.

"Let's sell the chalet," she said. "I'm sick of hounding renters for money." This was the time to push the idea. Their tenant, Tina Sedgewick, who had always paid her rent just when they had given up hope every month, was now two months in arrears. But Chuck had always resisted, somehow clinging to the idea that he might ski again, nostalgic because their kids had learned to ski at the little Putney resort close to the Brattleboro vacation home. She knew he loved the covered bridge they crossed to get to the ski lodge, that he could still picture their sons dressed in woolen hats with pom-poms, that he remembered how the children slid down the hill by the chalet in their snow boat. It was hard to give up memories, but she wanted the money so they could go south in the winter. Riverdale, on the outskirts of Manhattan, was a place where you definitely needed a car, so in the winter they never ended up walking anywhere. She was aching for activity and felt guilty about playing tennis and running around town without him. If it wasn't for the indoor pool in their building, the Century, he would never stretch his muscles.

"I checked the lease," Lilly said. "Tina gave her mother as a reference. It's a New Jersey address. I'll give her a call."

Chuck nodded. "Good idea."

"Then we'll put the house up for sale," she announced.

"*If* this doesn't work out," he said.

"Chuck, you're dreaming. Tina doesn't answer the phone or answer your letters."

"Call the mother," he said, motioning to the telephone with his head.

Lilly got a response on the first ring. "Is this Mrs. Sedgewick?" she asked.

"Ye-es," was the suspicious response. Lilly knew this call was a waste.

"Tina Sedgewick's mother?"

"Oh," she answered. "Is she in trouble again?" Before Lilly could reply, Mrs. Sedgewick finished her thought. "If she is, I don't want to hear about it. I've bailed her out of trouble for years, and I'm not paying any more of her bills."

"She owes two months' rent," Lilly said quickly. "If she doesn't pay, we'll have to evict her. I just thought you would want to—"

"I don't want anything more to do with her."

"Do you want my name and phone number in case you change your mind?"

"I'm through with her," the woman said with finality.

Chuck could figure out the situation by listening to Lilly's responses. She summed it up for him: "She's a hippie bum, and her mother wants nothing to do with her."

Now they would have to go up to Vermont, evict her, clean up the mess that Tina was bound to leave, and put the place on the market. This wasn't what Chuck Hildebrand had had in mind for his golden years.

"Well, let's get cracking," he said. "We'd better get up there and see Tina before winter sets in. You know how Vermont laws are. Once it's winter, you can't evict anyone even if they haven't paid a nickel."

"We'll take a room at the Putney Inn and make a holiday out of it," Lilly said, trying to sound cheerful, then began pulling down their overnight bags from the closet.

JESSICA HAD CALLED Triple A; the drive to Putney would take five hours, so she canceled all her appointments for two days straight and booked a room at the Putney Inn, then allowed herself to sit back and relax for a moment.

Very early that morning, as soon as she arrived at her office, Jessica had pushed aside all of her messages and called the Putney School.

While waiting for Ms. Osgood, the records secretary, she looked out her window at the beautiful buildings of Rockefeller Center. She could see the skating rink from her office, and today there was the gigantic Christmas tree that had just arrived from New Hampshire. She remembered the joke her secretary had told her two years ago, right after Jessica had started at the foundation. "Rockefeller bought his children blocks for Christmas this year," she had said. "Yes, Fiftieth Street, Fifty-first Street . . ."

"I'm doing research on teenagers," she said when she was connected to Ms. Osgood. "A young man named Kevin Glade was recommended very highly, and I would like to get in touch with him. He graduated last year. I'm director of social work at the Foundation for International Child Development in New York, you can check with my—"

"No problem. Give me your number and I'll call you right back," Ms. Osgood said.

Jessica shook her head. At least outside New York people were still civilized. She sorted through her mail, waiting for the phone to ring. When it did, she picked up before her secretary could.

"I've checked our records for the past three years," Ms. Osgood reported. "I'm sorry, Ms. Lewisohn. There is no record of a Kevin Glade."

Chapter Seven

"WHO'S BILL OWENS?" Tina asked.

Fear clutched his gut. Suddenly the young woman whom he'd counted as his friend, who had taken him in when he needed a place to crash, whom he'd called Aunt Tina even though she was in her twenties, looked like a young Jessica Lewisohn in hippie clothing. And he had looked forward to spending the weekend with Tina, no questions, no hassles. Tina was often in a Mary Jane high, but she was also a trusting love child, someone you didn't have to be wary of. She was guileless. As a matter of fact, he hadn't even needed his key to get in because the door was unlocked, as usual.

"I'm telling you, Tina baby, lock your door," he had warned her when he walked in on her just by turning the knob. She was on the floor in front of the television set smoking a joint, and hadn't even heard him over the noise of the TV she was watching. "You leave your jewelry and your rent money lying around, and someone could walk in on you—"

"It's the ones I know that I hide my money from," she said, laughing. "You've really gotten to be a city slicker, worrying about locking doors. This is Brattleboro, honey, not the big, bad city."

She was right. In Vermont people took you at your word. The young men all looked like Olympic athletes, and the women were simple and clean-living. Even potheads like Tina were harmless and wholesome compared to New York druggies.

Tina worked as a waitress and a salesgirl. She sold drug accessories like mirrors and pipes to the locals, sometimes venturing to nearby towns with her wares. A regular traveling saleswoman, she joked. The company she worked for was actually called High Time. Tina was lovable and always good-humored, but often she was so spaced out she didn't know what day of the week it was. Luckily for her, rent was cheap in Vermont, and she had been living in this pretty chalet for almost two years. She had made a special effort to keep up with the rent because the house, built on the foundations of a church, had a garden, overgrown now, a pond, and "real good vibes." Tina believed in numerology—she favored the number three—and she was into astrology and crystals. Kevin liked all of this otherwordly stuff too. It was a good place to escape to.

Tina was rummaging about now in her closet, opening shoeboxes until she found what she was looking for. He had followed her into her bedroom. His heart hadn't stopped pounding since he'd heard Tina speak his real name. He was just about to leave for Ithaca, having stayed for three days, and had given her a supply of drugs for her hospitality. He had refused her a large cache, for the sake of her health.

"Don't you . . . ?" she had asked, amazed that he didn't partake.

"This is strictly business with me," he told her. "I buy in the city, sell up here, and it takes me through the semester."

"You don't look too prosperous," she remarked.

"I do it only to cover my expenses. I can't afford to fuck up and get booted out of school. I plan to go to business school, make some serious bread. Let's just say this is my endowment for the arts." He chuckled at his wit; Tina had joined in, not too sure what the hell she was laughing about.

Finally she pulled out an old photograph of a man. The edges were worn off and it was creased. It was a photo of his father, the one he had kept in his wallet. He couldn't believe he had left it there. He turned it over. "Bill Owens" was penciled on the back in his father's handwriting.

"I found it after you left, in a book," she said.

"Not mine," he said. The man looked like him. Should he have said it was a relative? "Maybe someone who stayed here," he tried, knowing she had lots of roving friends who could have spent the night. He hung onto the picture, hoping he wasn't calling attention to it. But he had no choice. He tried to look into her face, but she just led him out of the room, shrugging her shoulders. He decided to loosen up on her dope allowance. Maybe she was better off high after this.

"Gee, thanks, Kev," Tina said gratefully after he doled out another hit. She sensed he was in a giving mood. "How 'bout some more?"

Kevin hesitated, looking into her eyes, then gave her what she wanted. "It's your funeral," he said.

THEY DROVE INTO the parking lot of the Putney Inn, the familiarity and the gentle pace of country living already overtaking them. They had never made a reservation in the twenty years they had come to dine here, and they knew they would have a good table. The food would also be good, if uninspired, and the waitresses would be friendly, sparkly clean, and cheerful. The easel in the entranceway between the restaurant and the bar said that the Green Mountain Boys were billed for the week's entertainment.

"Read me the menu," Chuck said after he pulled out his oak chair and sat down at the big round table. "I've forgotten my reading glasses." The waitress lit the kerosene wick under the hurricane lamp.

"You know the menu by heart," Lilly said. "It's lots of cholesterol and overcooked vegetables."

At the next table Chuck noticed a woman sitting alone, which was unusual up here. He knew she couldn't help overhearing him. "It's fresh game. Has no hormones or poisons," he insisted. The woman smiled at the remark. He smiled back.

"What would you recommend?" Jessica asked. She was studying the menu.

"I bet you're a New Yorker," he said.

"Yup," she said. "Manhattan."

"Riverdale," he said. They all laughed.

"I could tell by the way you're dressed," Lilly said. Sporty but classy, she thought. The woman wasn't wearing the sweater with reindeers or the short strand of pearls or the comfortable shoes that so many well-to-do New England women seemed to favor. Of course, walking on the muddy roads, she had learned, wasn't conducive to patent or suede.

"If you don't like rabbit or venison or quail, I think their roast duck is always good," Chuck said. "Wouldn't you say so, Lilly?"

Lilly closed the menu. "I always order duck," she said.

"And the kids always ordered hamburgers," Chuck added.

Jessica took a sip of her wine. "You winter here?" she asked.

"No, we have a house in Brattleboro a few miles from here. Trying to collect rent from a hippie-dippie renter." Lilly gave him a nudge. "Just mixing a little pleasure with business," he continued.

The waitress arrived at Jessica's table. "Thanks for the tip," Jessica said, skipping the fish and ordering the duck.

"Remember bringing the kids here and ordering from the children's menu?" Chuck turned to Lilly, reminiscing.

"Now they'll take us to dinner and order the senior menu," said Lilly.

"Are you trying to cheer me up?" Chuck said. The waitress moved to their table. "I'll have a draft beer and the rabbit. I need to fortify myself for when I deal with Tina the space cadet," he added.

"I'll have the duck," Lilly told the waitress.

JESSICA LOOKED AT the thick biography of Simone de Beauvoir on her night table next to the phone. She gave herself a pat on the back for driving to Vermont. Never mind that Tom would think she was bonkers. She was always on target when she followed her instincts. Now she was too revved up to finish the book about her former mentor. She picked up the phone to check on Laurie. What would she say to her daughter? She was glad she hadn't reached her last weekend, when she was so angry. She knew she would have exploded and driven Laurie further away. Now she would wait and see, play it smart.

"Over your cold?" she asked Laurie innocently. "Your voice sounds funny," she said.

"Yes, Mom. Yes." Laurie's voice was husky from crying.

"Are you sure there's nothing on your mind?" she asked. "I don't much like the way you sound." I could die repeating myself, she thought but compelled to go on. "I don't want to sound like a broken record, honey, but after eighteen years of being a mommy I just can't stop cold turkey."

"I understand, Mom. You're right to ask. . . ."

There's something wrong, Jessica thought.

"But you can stop now that you know I'm okay," Laurie added quickly, changing her mind about admitting her mother into her pain.

Oh, thought Jessica, the kiss-off. "Kevin's still away at his aunt's?"

"Just arrived, I think."

Was that a sigh in her voice?

"It was kind of nice being alone for a while. I mean, everybody needs some private time, right?"

So it *was* Kevin! Why did you lie about Boston? was on the tip of her tongue.

"Where are you?" Laurie asked.

"I'm, I—I'm on a short business trip," she said. "Be home tomorrow if all goes well. I'm meeting with some people here in . . ." She almost said Vermont. "Boston. Your trip inspired me." She couldn't resist.

"Well, have a good meeting. Gotta go, Mom. Talk to you soon."

"See ya, kiddo," Jessica said, feeling clever. She took up her coat and bag. It was time to snoop around Putney.

She drove into the town, which was five blocks long, and if nothing else promised at least a fattening dessert in a coffee shop. She parked in front of the country store, the windows of which told her she was in a different world. Hunting caps and matching plaid shirts were laid out alongside thick work gloves, Coleman stoves, and red lanterns. Here hunting was a sport. In New York it was a trade. She picked up a *New York Times* from the outside rack, then added a *Brattleboro Reformer* and a *Penny Saver.* Inside, she wandered past jars of candy and shelves of canned goods, past ice skates and clothing stacked high on shelves. She picked up a bottle of raspberry-apple juice from the cooler, chose two slices of locally baked carrot cake, and paid for them at the counter. She strolled out into the clear, cool night and dropped her package onto the front seat of her Volvo, breathing in the fresh air. Surprisingly, it was colder in Hartewoods, and the air in Vermont was less redolent, if crisper.

She looked up at the bright stars and walked up the empty street to the food co-op. But a stab of nerves caught her up. Was she wasting her time? What exactly was she looking for? She peeked in the window. The store was dark, but she could make out the organic produce, bins of grain and jars of loose tea. Sawdust covered the floor, and wine stood on the shelves. She could almost smell the inside of the store just by looking in. She crossed the dirt road and passed the white colonial church, the crafts market, and the hardware store, all deserted. Unless she wanted to drink at a local hangout, a converted barn on Main, she would be forced to head for her room and watch a B movie or finish reading about Simone babying Sartre.

There was a light on in the library and she went in, finding herself in a modern room with a bland atmosphere. The tables were empty; two other browsers were wandering among the stacks. The casual, unhurried air was so different from the charged bustle, the depths of silence, in the St. Agnes library on Eighty-third Street, or the main library on Fifth Avenue, where scholars perusing their tomes sat sandwiched between the deranged and the homeless.

She roamed about, enjoying the displays. The children's room was downstairs, but of course it was closed. The poetry section featured several volumes by well-known writers, and above the display hung prize-winning poems by local talent. She approached the bookcase. Yeats, Eliot, Cummings, Rupert Brook, Aiken, Dickinson, Tennyson—and Hopkins. Gerard Manley Hopkins! She stared at the wall, and then the prize-winning poems from the poetry contest of the Putney Public High School.

Astonished, she read the first-prize winner, "Vert Mont." Word for word, the poem was the same as the one she had read before. But the name of the poet was *not* Kevin Glade! It was Betsy Wilcox.

She fairly ran out the door, causing a small stir. Crazy New Yorker. When she reached the country store, puffing and sweating, she leafed through the pages of the directory attached to the wall under the pay phone. Only one Wilcox in Putney. She dialed, searching her brain for what to tell the parents of this child. She had to talk to them, to find out about Kevin, and to tell them he had stolen their daughter's poem.

JESSICA DROVE UNTIL she saw the barn by the driveway on Falls River Road and then made a left as instructed, following the curve down into a ravine. The falls pounded in her ears before she could see them. Suddenly a wall of granite cut the early morning sunlight, and she passed a grand waterfall and a narrow, rushing river. My God, she thought, did the average Vermonter live with such beauty and take it for granted? But of course there were also trailers along the roads, and acres of discarded auto parts marring the landscape, and she saw poverty almost as bad as anything she had seen in New York.

A small, unimposing house faced the magnificent natural phenomenon. A small woman with dark, curly hair and intelligent gray eyes stepped out of the door when Jessica turned off the motor. Inside, the house was cozy and small and low-ceilinged, and she wondered if Nicole Wilcox's husband was small too. The house did have the appearance of a casual dollhouse, with furniture that Jessica imagined had been gathered at random. She had learned from their phone conversation that Nicole was a nurse at the psychiatric hospital and that her husband was a film teacher. Nicole's shift was the four o'clock one today, so she had invited Jessica to come in the morning.

Nicole had a faint French accent, Jessica noted. Vermont was filled with French Canadians. The soft voice she had first heard on the phone fit in with the relaxed air of the house. Sometimes Jessica envied the laid-back life but knew she couldn't let go enough to live that way herself. She had to accept the fact that if a chair was out of place, if a color didn't match, she was moved to action. But such intensity took its toll. Even now, when this calm woman who had cheerfully assented to talk about Kevin—he had dated her daughter—and seemed eager to tell all she knew without a trace of reserve, even now Jessica was jumpy, anticipating trouble as she listened to Nicole.

"The poor boy was an orphan. Naturally we felt sorry for him," Nicole began. "He stayed with us quite a lot. He worked in the crafts co-op."

Everything's a co-op in Vermont, Jessica thought.

"He worked himself up to manager within a few months," Nicole continued. "A very responsible young man. Very independent. I tried to invite him for meals as often as possible, a boy of eighteen out on his own. He had an aunt in Brattleboro that he never talked about, but other than that he had no family. His parents were killed in a car crash when he was young—"

"Did you say eighteen? He must be nearly twenty," Jessica said.

"Maybe he was embarrassed because he was a couple of years behind. Teenagers tend to do that."

"I suppose," said Jessica.

"Kevin was a perfect gentleman with Betsy," Nicole went on. "She was a junior last year, and I set the rules for dating. He never brought her home later than ten on weeknights and midnight on weekends.

My husband, Paul, said he'd never met a nicer boy. We were very proud of him when he was accepted at Cornell last spring. He's a smart boy, he deserved the scholarship."

"What about the poem?" Jessica asked. "Don't you resent the fact that he plagiarized it and gave it to my daughter?"

"Kevin studied night and day for over a year for his SAT exam, and he doesn't have a family to back him up. He's a talented artist, but maybe he didn't have the time to give her something he painted. He took a shortcut. It's not really so terrible. As for giving the poem to another girl, your daughter, Betsy missed him a lot at first, but now she's editor of the school newspaper and busy with her life. I think you would hear praise from her about Kevin too."

Jessica looked skeptical.

"I wouldn't worry, Mrs. Lewisohn. Kevin's a good boy. If he borrowed Betsy's poem, I honestly don't think she'd mind. Maybe she'd be a bit jealous, but I know they parted friends."

"He told us he graduated from the Putney School, not the local high school."

Nicole looked at Jessica. She had noticed the expensive car as Jessica pulled in the driveway. "Maybe he's changed . . . I guess he puts on some airs now. When he was in Putney he was truthful as far as I can tell."

Jessica looked at the clock on the wall and got up from the table. "Maybe you're right. I hope so."

Nicole smiled, but her eyes told Jessica that she was thinking, oh, these New Yorkers. They do like to exaggerate.

AS LILLY DROVE them up the hill to the chalet, Chuck examined the grounds, looking for signs of deterioration or destruction. His initial reaction was one of relief. At least there was nothing obviously wrong. The wooden gate to the garden was hanging off its hinge, but that was normal wear. The weeping willow had grown another six inches in the past two years, and he recalled that it had been no taller than he was when they bought the house. Twenty-two years ago on Memorial Day weekend they had fallen in love overnight with the little chalet with a cathedral ceiling and picture windows overlooking the pines and maples and nineteenth-century farmhouses. He remembered the time his neighbor had tapped Chuck's maples and sugared in the barn next door, supplying him and Lilly with quarts of syrup. What a kick it was pouring syrup from your own trees over the kids' flapjacks.

Lilly pulled into the driveway, and he was happy to see that no smoke was coming from the chimney. The girl was using oil instead of the wood stove that fouled the air and was ruinous to the house.

The kitchen light was on, which meant she was home and they would have to confront her. He looked up at the bedroom window and saw the blue-and-white clover-leaf-pattern curtain she had sewn for the window. At least she hadn't skipped out.

They stood at the door, waiting for her to answer the bell. The last renter had kicked in the door, having lost his key. The marks were still visible, and the door frame didn't fit quite right.

"We shouldn't have rented to her," Lilly argued. "She didn't even look like a responsible person. And she was late with the security."

Lilly was right. She was better at business than he was. "You always know the answer from hindsight," he said. "We didn't have much choice at the time, did we?" He turned the knob.

The door was unlocked, and he pushed it open before Lilly could object. He stepped in, taking a deep breath, preparing for the worst.

He looked around quickly. Everything appeared to be normal. He actually felt like an intruder, nosing around while his tenant was away. But he was satisfied the house was intact.

"There are dishes in the sink," Lilly observed.

"Anyone home?" Chuck called out.

"Gone shopping," Lilly said.

"Or never came home."

Lilly started up the stairs to the master bedroom. Chuck paused at the bottom, looking through the window at the weedy garden, which was on a level below the house. The steps and the wall were hand-layered in flat stones, Vermont style. Chuck had always loved the early American stone fences demarcating the land between farms. He remembered sitting by the fire, looking out at his small plot of land, contentedly staring at the snow on the pines, the powder piling delicately on the branches. He climbed up the steps after Lilly, the weight of years heavy upon him today. Reaching the top of the staircase, he looked down, just as he would do on Christmas morning when the kids were little. The lighted tree in the living room always looked like a picture postcard, snow scenes in every direction. They had those perfect moments in this house, maybe because they had come only on holidays and spent the hard work days in the city.

Lilly was just ahead of him. "Hurry up," she said. "I don't want to do this myself." She led the way into the bedroom through the open door.

"Jesus, she's still in bed in the middle of the day," Lilly whispered. But her heart beat faster as she approached. She could tell something was wrong by the stillness of the body as they noisily entered the room. She moved closer to the bed. And then she gagged. Blood was clotted around Tina's neck. The skin was gray. And the eyes were wide, staring into death.

Chapter Eight

MILDRED SEDGEWICK LOOKED down into the satin-lined coffin at her dead daughter, who, dressed in her pretty flowered dress, looked younger than her twenty-seven years. The person in the casket, though, was not her daughter at all but the outline of a memory of another human being.

Mildred's husband, Jack, who was standing beside her, interrupted her thoughts. "I knew she would come to a bad end," he said.

Jack's words should have sparked Mildred's irritation, but she realized he was probably covering his grief with his talk. Mildred had tried to harden her own heart against her daughter, to blame her for bringing misfortune and finally her own death on herself. Mildred had also tried to prepare herself for this kind of tragedy, but of course it hadn't helped any. She looked at Tina's head, which was turned to the side to hide the horrible neck wound, and she saw instead the image of her daughter as a schoolgirl. Tina's finger was still encircled by a simple gold wedding band.

"Tina went along with anything," Mildred said. "I don't think she really wanted to get married, but she liked the white wedding dress and the party. Pete just talked her into it."

"Pity he couldn't talk her into being a regular wife," Jack said.

Mildred started to cry. "I wish he had. I wish *we* had."

Jack touched her on the shoulder. "There was nothing you could do. You couldn't change her."

Mildred gazed at her daughter for the last time. Suddenly she realized that one finger of Tina's right hand was bare. The opal ring she and Jack had given Tina for her eighteenth birthday was gone.

KATHLEEN PORED OVER the descriptions of nursing courses in the McClintock Junior College catalogue. She would attend McClintock in the spring. Brendan was asleep, her father was out, and the house was silent. She felt in charge of her life. Hard work was paying off for her, and she had a real sense of satisfaction. One day, after she became a nurse, when she was self-sufficient, she might even find a young man to marry, someone who would love Brendan. But a twinge of guilt marred her good mood. She worried about whether she had made the right decision about the skull.

The house had been chilly that evening when she and Brendan came back home from the quarry. She had decided to continue her routine, to put their frightening discovery out of mind, at least until she could think more clearly. Fortunately, she had prepared a stew for dinner before she left, and as soon as she arrived back she put it on the stove to simmer. It would be done in time for her pop's return. She wanted nothing to seem out of the ordinary, nothing to alert her father that there was anything wrong.

After giving Brendan a few carrot sticks, she rewarded him with a treat. He had been so patient and well behaved just when she needed it, when she had been desperate for quiet. While he munched on the cookies she had baked the night before, she ran him a warm bath. She also turned up the thermostat, knowing her father would object. But on that dark day, after what she had been through, she felt she needed some special comfort.

After bathing Brendan, rinsing his shiny, soapy skin, and drying and hugging him, Kathleen stopped shivering. At the quarry she had told Brendan it was a human skull he had found. She had told him because she had screamed; he had known she was scared and she decided it was better to tell him why. Besides, she was determined never to lie to him. For Brendan's sake she had forced herself to calm down, and in no time the incident had flown from his young mind.

While she made the salad, she took peeks at him from the kitchen, playing happily in his pajamas, busily pushing his dump truck across the carpet in the living room. Meanwhile she worked on pretending it was an ordinary evening. Preparing the salad dressing, she sampled her mixture of olive oil and balsamic vinegar with a shaky finger before swirling a teaspoonful of French mustard into it. She was teaching herself to be a gourmet cook. A touch more vinegar . . .

She was beginning to feel almost normal as she rinsed the leaves of the Boston lettuce, then sipped the soothing Earl Grey tea, flavored with milk, that she had prepared for herself. And warming her fingers around the mug, feeling cozy and warm in her kitchen, she began to believe there was no reason ever to tell anyone about her grisly find.

Why should she call the police, open herself to questions? Maybe the skull Brendan had found was an animal's, not human at all. Maybe it was her overwrought imagination that had led her to connect Billy to the skull in the quarry. His girlfriend April was probably safe and sound.

But where *was* April? She had been missing for more than a year. Kathleen stared at the telephone and wondered, Should I call the police, let them decide? But she smelled the aroma of beef bourguignon wafting from the pot, and when she heard the sound of the stew bubbling, she made no move. If she told the police her story, she would also expose herself and her son to the scorn of their neighbors. Everyone, including her father, would know she had been raped. And one day, if her worst fear proved true, Brendan might learn that his father was a murderer.

THE BRIDGE OVER the river, connecting the Bronx to Manhattan, rose slowly, blocking traffic and stalling Jessica on her way to visit Rozsi. It amazed her that the lone, tall sailboat sliding under the bridge could halt dozens of cars, and that so many people were forced to sit and wait five full minutes for the bridge to close. It was another interesting if quirky aspect of the city.

Jessica hated driving through her mom's bombed-out neighborhood but enjoyed visiting her mom's apartment, cluttered with knickknacks and silver and century-old mementos Rozsi had brought to the U.S. from Europe. Laurie always said that the apartment reminded her of an antique shop. For Jessica, it brought back memories of her childhood, especially the carved-wood scenes of Hungarian peasants, the petit-point flowers displayed in oval frames, the tapestries and prayer rugs decorating the walls, and her mother's favorite chair, which Jessica's father, Morris, had upholstered in rich silk brocade. The rooms, filled with history, were like vaults hidden in the depths of some pyramid. The streets outside Rozsi's apartment resembled the teeming bazaars Jessica had seen in third world countries. Bronx avenues, with their ethnic shops, had flavor and bustle and life, but in every side street danger and death lurked, waiting for nightfall.

Rozsi, like every other law-abiding resident, was ever vigilant but philosophical about her situation. But unlike Rozsi, who could afford to leave, many of her neighbors had nowhere else to go. They had no choice but to resign themselves to the terrors. They watched out for one another when they braved the streets, and lived their nights barricaded in their apartments. Rozsi had a locked steel gate on the bedroom window that led to the fire escape. And the police lock she had had installed in her front door contained a steel rod that was bolted into the floor.

Still waiting for the bridge to close, Jessica rolled down her car window. It was a beautiful fall day. She decided to check out Rozsi's latest sculpted creations and then whisk her off to MOMA, the Museum of Modern Art, to see the Matisse exhibit. Clicking off the radio, which was broadcasting static instead of news, she idly thumbed through the copy of the *Brattleboro Reformer* that she had bought before leaving Vermont. She didn't see the bridge closing or hear the honking of the horns behind her; she was jolted by the headline "Landlord Finds Tenant Murdered" printed on the inside front page of the paper above photos of Tina Sedgewick and Chuck Hildebrand. But she couldn't continue reading. Shouts of angry drivers and insistent blasts of car horns finally intruded on her consciousness. She could barely concentrate on the road as she made her way off the bridge and to her mother's place.

DID I DO the right thing? Kevin asked himself. He toyed with the opal ring that Tina, already high, had offered him in gratitude for the drugs and money he had given her. He had accepted the ring only reluctantly. She had, after all, taken him in when he had had no place to go, when he was lonely and, literally, out in the cold. He had been living in Brattleboro in the Flying Crown Hotel, a seedy rooming house down the road from her when the ramshackle building burned down. Tina had already been a drug client, and since she needed drugs and cash and he needed a place to live, she had said he could move in with her. It was strictly a platonic arrangement, at his insistence. He could keep his emotions and his needs compartmentalized when he had to, and it wasn't hard with Tina. She wasn't his type. She was too old and her boozy, laid-back, druggie life was convenient, but it wasn't his style. Her wavy brown hair, her disheveled clothes, and her small, slight figure didn't turn him on. Besides, the parade of guys in and out of her bedroom had convinced him that she might even be a health risk.

Then he met Betsy Wilcox and told her he was living with an aunt. How could Betsy or her family understand his arrangement with Tina? He had hated giving Betsy up, but things had gotten dicey between them, and Cornell had saved the day. He tried not to think about it.

His thoughts turned back to the ring. He lay on his bed in his dorm room, holding the opal up to the light. Yes, he had done the right thing. He hadn't wanted to hurt her feelings. A knock on the door interrupted his thoughts. It was Laurel. He had been afraid she would go back on her word and not show up. But the flowers and his charm when he phoned her had done the trick.

Suddenly, he remembered the ring. But before he could put it safely away, Laurel walked in and saw him trying to hide it.

"Is it for another girl?" she asked, tugging at his hands playfully.

"Oh, no!"

"Well?"

Suddenly he held the ring out to her. "It's a present for you. To make up for . . ." His voice dropped. "My anger earlier," he said. "I was going to give it to you at dinner."

Laurel saw that the ring size was small but slipped it on her pinky. It was a no-obligation present, one she could enjoy without having to make any deeper commitments. She noted that the small opal was mounted in a delicately wrought antique gold setting.

"It was my aunt's," Kevin said.

JESSICA UNLOCKED THE front door to Rozsi's apartment building and waited nervously in the deserted lobby for the elevator. She always sweated it out until the elevator brought her to the sixth floor, where her mom lived. This time when the creaky elevator arrived, it took her up and opened on the third floor. To her relief, Jamie Hernandez, a young buddy of Rozsi's, got on.

"I watch your mom from my window or from the stoop when she goes out shopping," Jamie had once assured Jessica. "And I feed Matchka sometimes," he had said, laughing. "You know *matchka* means cat in Hungarian?" Jessica had nodded and laughed along with him. "I don't have my own mother, so I love Rowzshi. I told her if she ever needs me, give me a call." Jessica had been touched by his offer and had begun to understand why her mother refused to leave the old neighborhood.

But as Jessica stood at her mom's door, she was preoccupied with the details of the gruesome murder she had hurriedly read about while double-parked out front. And for once she didn't worry about her Volvo being robbed or its battery being stolen; she worried about whether to tell her mother about the murder in Brattleboro. Rozsi eyed her through the peephole in the door and let her in.

"Is something wrong?" she asked, seeing the anxiety in Jessica's face.

Jessica showed her the news story. "Kevin was just there in Vermont—visiting her! And he lied about the school he attended. I checked up on him." She sat beside Rozsi on the plastic cover that protected the sectional couch in the living room. "I drove up to Vermont because I just knew there was something fishy about him," Jessica said. "And now this young woman is dead. Bad things happen around Kevin."

"This is his aunt?" Rozsi asked, referring to the news photo of young Tina.

"I don't like it, Anyuka. It's too much of a coincidence. A Tina in Brattleboro."

"Call Laurika," Rozsi said, pulling the phone from the table next to her and placing it between them.

"I can't, Mom. I've called her so often. She resents me."

Rozsi removed the receiver and held it away from her ear. "Dial me Laurika's number," she commanded. "I've lost my reading glasses." Jessica punched in the number, and Rozsi gave up after ten rings.

There was nothing they could do but keep trying until Laurie answered. Jessica remembered her car, jumped up, and looked out of the window. To her relief, it was safe, a parking ticket fluttering in the windshield wiper.

After Jessica found her glasses, Rozsi pressed redial until at last she reached Laurie. Jessica listened in.

"Hello, my darrling. Is everything okay?" Rozsi asked.

"Hi," Laurie responded cheerfully. "I'm terrific. Why?"

"How is Kevin, your boyfriend?"

"He's okay too. He just gave me a present."

"How is his aunt?"

"Kevin's present is from his aunt."

"His aunt is healthy?"

"Why shouldn't she be? Why are you asking about his aunt?"

"Didn't he just come back from Vermont?"

"Yes, and he brought back a present for me. It's beautiful, *Nagymama.*"

Rozsi loved to hear the Hungarian word for grandmother from her only grandchild.

"What is the present he brought back, my darrling?"

"A ring, *Nagymama.* An opal ring."

"AM I NUTS?" Jessica asked. "Kevin's aunt is alive and well, and Laurie has a present from her? Am I totally crazy?"

"Crazy like a fox," Rozsi said.

Jessica noted the Bronx phone book on the table and quickly found the Riverdale listing for Charles Hildebrand. She tried the number, ignoring the sound in the street of a car door slamming. She could tell that Hildebrand was thrilled to get her call. He confessed that he hadn't had such attention since the *Riverdale Press* had printed his letter to the editor.

"She was young," he told Jessica when she questioned him. "In her late twenties, poor thing. We found her," he said, his voice heavy with melodrama. "It was horrible. The police think it was a robbery. Her purse was stolen. And her mother just called to ask me to keep my eyes open for a piece of jewelry when I go back to clean out the place."

"What kind of jewelry?" Jessica asked.

"A ring," he said. "An antique opal ring."

Icicles probed Jessica's spine. She cut short the conversation and phoned Brattleboro information and got the number of the local police. But she also knew that before she made the call to the police, she would have to explain it all to her mother. And if her mom became too upset, her blood pressure would shoot up.

"Give it to me straight," Rozsi said, seeing the expression in Jessica's eyes. "I can take it."

"Tina's opal ring is missing," Jessica said. "I think Kevin killed Tina Sedgewick."

SHERIFF SNOW TOOK the call at his desk.

"I have information about the Tina Sedgewick murder," Jessica announced.

Sheriff Snow turned around and rolled his eyes at the deputy manning the traffic desk behind him. "Yeah?" he said, turning back and speaking into the phone.

"A young man, Kevin Glade, was visiting Tina at the time of her murder."

"You think he killed her?"

"I—I don't know for sure. But I thought you should have this information."

"What makes you think he killed her?"

"A ring. An opal ring. Tina's mother told the landlord that her daughter's ring was missing. And Kevin Glade has the ring."

"The murder has been solved, ma'am. We caught the sleaze asleep in a ditch last night and he confessed. We have the purse, the money, and the knife he used."

"But the ring! What about the ring?"

"Is that the world's only opal ring? Even if it is Tina's ring, her mother told us that she hasn't seen her daughter in ten months. So she couldn't be sure if she sold the ring, lost it, or gave it away before she was killed. By the way, who is this Kevin Glade?"

"He's my daughter's boyfriend."

"You have some kind of grudge against him?"

"Thanks for your help," Jessica said, and hung up.

"All roads lead to Kevin," Jessica told Rozsi. "And each time I follow one, I slam into a brick wall."

* * *

SHERIFF SNOW HUNG up and turned to the trooper.

"Another full-mooner?" the trooper asked.

"No, this one didn't confess to the murder. This one turned in her daughter's boyfriend."

"Usually it's an ex-husband."

"Lucky we have this one wrapped up," the sheriff said, slapping his hand on the desk.

JESSICA PACED HER mother's living room.

"Call Tom," Rozsi suggested.

"Oh, sure. Tell him I accused Kevin of murder and the police blew me off?"

Rozsi looked weary, and Jessica could tell that she was trying to control the urge to issue advice.

"I'll do better than that," Jessica continued. "I'll confront Kevin with everything I learned about him in Vermont. And I'll get the truth out of him about this nonexistent mysterious aunt of his."

Jessica reached for her pocketbook and pulled out her car keys. It was time to take action, and to get her mother out of the middle of this. Rozsi didn't need this kind of aggravation.

"I'll call you as soon as I speak to Laurel," Jessica said. "If she and Kevin can't come to the city, I'll drive up to Cornell this weekend."

Jessica's adrenaline was pumping. The elevator couldn't get her down fast enough. When she hit the sidewalk, she couldn't believe her eyes. Her Volvo was gone, ticket and all.

JESSICA WAS APPROACHING Ithaca when she saw a bumper sticker bearing the words "I send my money and my daughter to Cornell," and she had to laugh. The Cornell campus was one of the most beautiful in the country, she thought as she spied Lake Cayuga. And she realized that Laurel probably took it for granted. Jessica, on the other hand, was still a product of her past. It was inspiring for her just to be setting foot in any one of Cornell's sixteen libraries, which varied from sleek and modern to the ones she loved best, which were church-like in architecture and atmosphere. There was *something* to be said for being poor, Jessica thought, remembering her childhood.

Jessica knew she was fortunate now. She had rented the BMW she was driving and, at her pleasure, would replace her stolen Volvo. She was glad she and Tom could afford to send their daughter away to Cornell. If only Kevin Glade were out of the picture.

She pulled into the Hilton Hotel parking lot. She had just enough time before her date with Kevin and Laurel to shower, dress, and plan her strategy. And then, damn it, she would unravel for Laurel Kevin's skein of lies.

THE RESTAURANT JESSICA picked was one of the places parents of Cornell students took their kids on special weekends like graduation and homecoming. It was located in an old railroad depot, and a Victorian railroad car attached to the restaurant served as its bar and lounge. Jessica had avoided choosing a student hangout for the sake of privacy; she wanted no beer-hall hubbub, no interruptions when she confronted Kevin. She wanted to focus on his reactions. She arrived early, chose a secluded table, and refrained from ordering her usual gimlet.

She greeted Laurie with a big hug and a kiss and forced herself to shake Kevin's hand. Laurel looked healthy, and Jessica had to admit the two of them did make a handsome couple. The impression brought a moment of panic, thinking about her mission. Laurel looked so happy. She had just gotten a good grade on a bio quiz, she said, and Kevin seemed proud of her, positively beaming.

"She rocked on that test," Kevin crowed after they all sat down. "And it was no lame exam either," he said, gazing lovingly at Laurel.

He's a phony, Jessica reminded herself. Get on with it. She looked Kevin in the eye.

"I have bad news, Kevin. I hate to be the one to tell you."

Kevin looked confused. But then his eyes sharpened.

"Tina Sedgewick is dead."

Kevin looked stunned.

"I just saw her," he said.

"She was murdered," Jessica said.

Kevin's face paled.

There was no faking that, Jessica thought. She saw his lips tremble slightly.

"Tina? She was my friend," he said, more to himself than to Jessica.

"My God!" Laurel said.

"Someone cut her throat," Jessica said.

Laurel looked at him in horror.

"Why did you call her your *aunt*?" Jessica asked.

"She was older." He faltered. "I had no family. . . . I wanted you to think I had someone who cared about me, that I had a place to go, like most people. Especially at Thanksgiving."

Jessica bit her lip.

Kevin put his head in his hands. "Now I have no one. She was real good to me. I warned her this would happen."

Jessica, in spite of herself, thought she was seeing genuine grief. "I'm sorry," she said, and meant it. "They caught the killer," she said, and saw Kevin's shoulders drop.

"Thank God," he said.

"He was a drug addict, they said. He killed her for her money."

"I *told* her to lock her door. Oh, man, I gave her the rent money because her landlord was about to evict her . . . and she insisted on giving me the opal ring." He turned to Laurel. "I shouldn't have given it to you. I'd planned to give it back to her. I was scared I was losing you. It was dumb of me."

Laurel slipped the ring off her finger. "Now I understand," she said. "I wondered why you acted so funny that day." She laid the opal ring on the tablecloth.

"I'm sorry," Jessica said. More than he knew. She *had* been unfair to him, she told herself.

Kevin looked at them through his tears.

He had Jessica now. He had lost Tina, but he had the dragon mother in the palm of his hand. He thought back to the day Tina had taken him in. "I'm your family now," she had told him.

He reached his hand out to Jessica.

"You're my family now," he said.

Chapter Nine

WHEN LLOYD MARTIN, head of the county homicide unit, called Sandy Ungar to alert her that a serial killer was loose in Indiana, she couldn't help wondering if this new case was somehow linked to the disappearance of April Meadows. Over the past year and a half, the killer had murdered three women. And last night, the most recent victim, a twenty-three-year-old waitress, had been found, garrotted with a rope, a gun barrel stuck in her vagina. She had been placed in an obscene pose so that the cops would see the "still life" as soon as they entered the woman's apartment.

But April Meadows had simply vanished, and the M.O. of the serial killer was to flaunt his victims, not to make them disappear. He had decapitated one woman in her apartment and set her head on a bookcase facing the entrance to the living room. Also, April was a "low-risk" victim, if she was a victim at all. The other women were high-risk types. The first had been a go-go dancer in a topless bar; the second had been a hooker. The waitress may have been what was termed "a victim of opportunity," a stranger in the wrong place at the wrong time.

Sandy noted that the murders had been committed at least a hundred miles away, and that all three known victims had been in their twenties. April, of course, had been only fourteen. Sandy momentarily pictured herself as a schoolgirl of fourteen. God, she thought, I was just beginning to live.

DRINKING HER BREAKFAST coffee, Kathleen spotted the newspaper article reporting the murder of a waitress in the very town where Kathleen's own grandmother had died. Kathleen pushed her chair back, stood up, and reread the last sentence of the piece. "The police are investigating the possibility that the murder might be related to two other homicides in the area."

She reached for the telephone. She could no longer in good conscience hide her discovery. Not another second. She dialed the police, and interrupting the trooper as he tried to identify himself, she let her words explode.

"I found a skull, a human skull—in the quarry off Euclid." Instantly she clicked off before the trooper had time to ask the question she dreaded. What's your name, lady?

SANDY UNGAR CAME awake fast and was quickly out of bed when the phone rang. Early morning calls were never good news. It was the boss's son, trooper Dan McKenzie. Brian was in the next town investigating a bank scam, so Dan had called Sandy, second-in-command, to tell her about a woman reporting a skull found in a nearby quarry. If it wasn't a crank call, Sandy thought, it might be the work of the serial killer. *Or* the skull might be April's. . . .

After alerting the medical examiner and the county crimes team that she might need technical assistance, she drove to the barracks, where, thick braid swaying, she rushed into her office, where Dan and rookie cop Johnny Greenmeyer waited for her.

"You may not know this," she said, looking at the rookie, "but several years ago a homicide, the child of a big cheese around here, was bungled, and badly. Lloyd Martin tells *his* team that if any one of them is careless and if there is even a suspicion of anyone disturbing the crime scene, he will personally see to it that semen samples and pubic hair samples as well as prints will be required of every man."

"What about the women?" Greenmeyer asked, being careful to smile when he said it.

Sandy had to laugh. "Needless to say, Lloyd's crime scenes are pristine."

THE INVESTIGATIVE TEAM swarmed over the quarry. It was eerie the way they crept and crawled and gingerly stepped over every inch, photographing, nudging sticks and stones aside, hunting for evidence, depositing even discarded soda cans into collection bags. When they spoke it was in low tones, the sort of respectful murmurs heard at a funeral. They were looking for the rest of the skeleton.

The brownish-colored bones they finally collected had been dragged into bushes by animals. It would be up to Dr. Silver, the medical examiner, to determine the race, sex, and age of the skeleton from the shapes and lengths and development of the bones. If there were enough teeth left, the forensic odontologist would be able to try matching the teeth with the dental x rays of missing persons.

Let it not be April, Sandy said to herself. Then Dan, snagging his sleeve on the rim of the culvert, eased some bones from the opening. They were the bones of a foot enmeshed in decaying fabric. Bits of pink polish were still stuck to a toenail.

A half hour later, the M.E. approached Sandy to tell her that the remains were definitely those of a female. He guessed she had been fifteen years old. He would, of course, need to confirm his opinion in the lab.

Sandy felt now, in spite of her hopes to the contrary, that these were April's remains, and she was depressed. Further, in spite of all the new technology, no fingerprints, footprints, or other evidence that would lead to the killer had apparently survived.

Dr. Silver, as they walked to their vehicles, told her, "The animals and the elements did the killer's work for him. He was a shrewd one, not burying the body or sticking it in a plastic bag."

Sandy got in on the passenger side of the police car, glad that Dan was driving, too discouraged to speak. She watched as Dan brushed dirt off the sleeve of his uniform and fingered the tear in the cloth.

Suddenly Silver knocked on the window and pulled the skull from the evidence bag. "I thought you should know. I'm taking the skull back to the lab myself. I don't trust anybody, things get lost, and I'm sure this is important."

"What's the story?" Sandy said.

"I've determined how she was killed. Blunt trauma. Look for a hammer."

"Who was the caller?" Sandy asked Dan as they pulled out onto the main road. "She didn't just happen on the quarry—it's deserted and creepy. What was she *doing* there?"

"I hardly spoke to her," Dan said. "She hung up before I could ask her name."

"Obviously she's trying to hide something. What exactly did she say?"

"She talked real fast, like she would change her mind if she stopped for a breath. Told me she'd found a skull in the quarry and hung up pronto."

"That's more than odd. Usually a hunter stumbles across a body in the woods, and no one has anything to hide."

Dan turned east. "It was very early in the morning."

"Right. Good point. Any background sounds?"

"Nothing."

"Did she sound young, old? What was her speech like? Foreign accent? Mannerism? From around here?"

"She sounded like a local high school girl. There was nothing unusual about her, except she was in such a hurry to hang up."

"What was a young girl doing in an abandoned quarry? You live nearby. Is it used by high school kids?"

"Nope. There are a lot nicer places to make out," he said, somewhat embarrassed.

"How can we find her?" Sandy asked as he pulled into the lot behind the barracks.

Dan was pleased she was asking him for advice. But he didn't get the chance to come up with a suggestion. As soon as he turned off the motor, Sandy jumped out of the car and rushed indoors.

"I'd really like to get my hands on her," she said over her shoulder.

ON THE WALL was a sign that read: "Let conversation cease. Let laughter flee. This is the place where death delights to help the living."

Dr. Silver looked up. "A colleague in New York sent me that when I took this job," he said, watching her read the words. "Pretty strong stuff, but to the point."

Sandy nodded, and Silver went back to his work, examining the skeleton they had found in the quarry. As he worked, he seemed to forget she was there.

Finally he spoke again. "Sorry to disappoint you," he said, "but it's just what we were afraid of—we've got no tire tracks, prints, nothing but bare bones to go on, literally. The body was deposited there about eighteen months ago. Rain washed everything else away."

"But the toenail, the nail polish . . ."

"I've seen nails last fifteen years," he said. He picked up the thigh bone. "Fits the stats of an adolescent, as I predicted. See those lacy threadlike cracks? They were etched by freezing temperatures over the winter. And those gnaw marks are the work of rodents, who generally don't begin until the bones are at least a year old."

"Any news on the x ray?"

"Dr. Hess just got back from Chile." He picked up the phone and dialed. "She helped identify victims found in a mass grave—for the families. I told her it was a rush on the x rays. We won't wait for the written report," Silver said as he listened to the rings, waiting for someone to pick up.

"Hello, Estelle? This is Sol. I know you just got back but . . . They match! Sorry to hear that. I know, I know. Fifteen years old. You're a pal, Essie. I'll buy you a drink."

Sandy didn't have to ask what the odontologist's findings were. April hadn't run away; it was just as her parents had said. April had been murdered. Probably in her own house. The killer had used a hammer to smash her phone, and then he had bashed her head in.

God, she thought, the parents . . . She had called to tell them they had discovered the skeleton. Now she would have to go out there and tell them it was their daughter.

"Tell me about the hammer," Sandy said.

Silver picked up the skull. "See the depression in the bone? Round, like the ball of a hammer. The sternum, the breastbone, was also smashed, indicating a similar blow. But the top part of the sternum was hit with the claw. Can you see those flat, squarish depressions?"

Sandy nodded. "How much blood? The house was clean the night she disappeared."

"If he hit the jugular, lots. It would take at least a half hour to clean it up—if he was cool and didn't panic."

"And if he knew he had enough time to do it," Sandy thought out loud.

"When did the parents come home?"

"About five hours after April arrived home from school."

Neither spoke, both searching for possible answers.

"Lloyd Martin thinks it's the serial killer," Sandy said.

"I worked on the last victim, the waitress. Of course, we don't know what was done to this girl before she was murdered. Or after. The difference is the other women were strangled, from behind. This child was not killed by a stranger sneaking up on her. It's no premed. It looks like out-of-control, face-to-face rage."

"And the serial didn't hide the bodies," she added.

"Maybe she was his first," he said, though he clearly didn't buy Lloyd's theory either.

Sandy winced. "What's so important about finding the hammer?" she asked. "There would be no blood on it by now."

"The claw had a piece missing, a distinct groove. The mark it made in the bone reflects it." Silver shrugged. "That's all we've got."

Sandy shook her head, miserable and frustrated.

"Listen to this," he said as Sandy started toward the door, then stopped and leaned against the doorframe. She suspected a joke was coming. Silver always told jokes—gallows humor—to keep his spirits up, especially when the victims he autopsied were young.

Sandy waited.

"A guy goes to the doctor. The doc tells him, 'I've got good news and bad. The good news is you have only twenty-four hours to live.' The patient asks, 'What's the bad news?' The doc says, 'I should have told you yesterday.' "

MARJORIE MEADOWS HAD dusted her daughter's room every day, keeping it ready for her return—until she found the splintered pieces of April's telephone in the kitchen. After that, as each day passed, the hope that had always been mixed with her dread receded. And every time the phone rang, she steeled herself. She secretly hoped, in loyalty to April, but her whole body was tensed, her emotions knotted like a fist against the terrible truth she knew she would hear one day.

Then Sandy had called about the skeletal remains found in the quarry, and today she had come by to tell her that the M.E. had positively identified the body as April's. Marjorie sank into a chair and sobbed. Now as she stood beside her husband in their living room facing Sandy, she asked the question her husband couldn't bear to ask.

"How was my daughter killed?"

Sandy could barely get the words out. "Do you . . . own a hammer? He used a hammer."

LLOYD MARTIN, HEAD of the county homicide unit, sat on Sandy's desk, trying to appear casual. He knew that behind his back he was called "Pretty Boy Lloyd." Although he was well liked, he also had the reputation of being a square, partly because he always wore a suit and tie but also because his hair was combed back in the old style, his black wing tips were highly polished, and, albeit with a smile, he liked to follow procedure to the letter.

"Check out any parolees in the area with a sexual assault or assault record," he suggested. They were both aware that rape could be plea-bargained down to assault.

"I have a suspect," Sandy said.

"Oh!"

"But he's not your serial killer. He's local talent. The boyfriend of the victim. He left town after he graduated."

"What makes you think *he's* not the serial?"

"The M.O., the timing—he was in high school when the first victim, the prostitute, was killed. Two hundred miles away. How could a kid travel all those miles unnoticed? This one knew we were keeping tabs on him because April had just disappeared. Plus, he was a good student, had excellent attendance." Sandy paused for a breath. "I checked," she said. "He didn't impress me as the type to mutilate bodies and then show them off."

"You met him?"

"Yeah. When April Meadows was first reported missing by her parents."

"Look, Ungar," Lloyd said, "Bundy didn't look like a vicious killer either. Serial killers are often charming and intelligent. They're well organized and methodical, and masters of deception."

"Bundy murdered at least twenty-three women," Sandy said, "but he never laid a hand on his girlfriend. Serial killers don't usually whack out their girlfriends, as I understand it."

"Does this boyfriend have a name?"

"Billy Owens."

"What makes you think he did her?"

Sandy fiddled with the paper clips on her desk. She looked up and saw Brian McKenzie standing in the doorway waiting for her to answer.

"Nothing concrete . . ." she admitted.

And just as her meeting with Lloyd ended, Sandy caught her next case—a floater pulled from a nearby lake. She had to leave the two men to discuss the bank scam that Brian was tracking; a couple would deposit five hundred dollars in a bank, go to separate ATMs and, at the exact same time, remove the five hundred, thereby doubling their money. Sandy didn't wait to hear the details.

She headed for the lake, not looking forward to viewing a bloated body; she hoped it wasn't a child. She had no proof whatever that Billy was involved in April's or anyone else's murder. It was true that lots of kids left town after graduation. Even April's parents believed in Billy. She parked at the lake beside a police van and headed through the trees to where the action was. Maybe these people were right about Billy, she thought wearily. Maybe he was innocent.

HE WAS TANNED and wholesome-looking, just like the young men in the ads for the Colorado resorts he had worked at: Telluride, Aspen, now Vail. He fit in nicely at Vail. Most of the ski instructors were bright and athletic and wanted to escape from some unpleasant reality.

He looked out over the slopes from the window of his condo. It was warm enough that sunny morning to have his croissant and coffee on the small wooden deck, which faced east. He took up his mug and newspaper, stuffed the croissant between his teeth, and pushed the screen door open with his right foot. He sat at the small round table and, while he sipped from the steaming mug, opened his hometown Indiana newspaper.

He hadn't been home since his parents had died. For a long time, with no relatives in town, he hadn't felt any desire to return. He had only two connections to his old life. The newspaper, which he had never stopped reading, and the house, which he had never sold. One day he would return and take care of it. He was almost ready. Lately he had been getting tired of the transient life. He had bought the condo only because he had been left a lot of money; both of his parents had been physicians, and he had been expected to follow in their footsteps. But the ski slopes were fast and made him feel free, and the social life and the outdoors had helped him forget his loss. Now, little by little, the vacuous life that had been so appealing was beginning to pall.

As he wiped a drop of coffee from one of the inside pages of the paper with his sleeve, an article caught his attention, an article that he read with shock and horror. The remains of a young girl had been found in the quarry near the high school.

No, he couldn't go back, he realized with building anxiety. When he thought of his hometown, all he could remember was the plane crash. He pulled his car keys from the pocket of his jeans, rushed down the spiral staircase, and jumped into his Porsche. He needed the wind in his face now, the speed, the cold blast that the slopes provided when he skied downhill.

He backed out of the driveway, floored the pedal, and shot off. The dust thrown up from the road as he accelerated to eighty covered the six letters on his vanity license plate. The letters spelled his name: K. Glade.

Chapter Ten

"COOK THE ONIONS until they are glassy," Rozsi directed as she dropped a handful of chopped onions into hot oil, then stirred with a long wooden spoon.

"I see you've taken the skin off the chicken parts," Jessica remarked. "Chicken paprikash the modern way. I'm impressed."

Rozsi added the chicken to the pan, along with generous doses of sweet-and-hot paprika and black pepper.

Jessica sat on a stool across from Rozsi at the cooking island, sipping her Tokay wine. Rozsi's glass, Jessica noted, was almost empty. Dr. Helpern, who was almost as old as Rozsi, allowed her two small glasses a day. "I can't give up everything," she had told him. And he had agreed.

"So the Kevin scare was a false alarm," Rozsi said, turning the chicken parts as they browned.

"He has no one, Anyuka. No family, it turns out."

"I understand about the aunt, the ring. What about the story of that fancy school—what was the name?"

"The Putney School. That's part of the picture. It seems his crime was trying to keep up with the Joneses. And I guess we're the Joneses."

"Was he ashamed when you cornered him?"

"Once I realized *why* he'd been lying, I let it drop. I wasn't exactly eager to let him, and especially Laurie, know that I've been checking up on him."

Rozsi finished off her wine. "So that's *it*? Everything is hunky-dory now?"

Jessica filled Rozsi's glass with wine. "I had to lie and say I saw a small article about Tina in a New York newspaper. I didn't want to complicate matters."

"You're the boss," Rozsi said.

"Drink your wine, Mom," Jessica said.

"Are you trying to make me drunk?" Rozsi joked. But she knew that when Jessica used the English word for mother, she was irritated.

"Laurie has a good heart," Jessica said. "She picks up wounded birds and stray cats, like your *matchka.* That's what I think we have here—she's taking care of a wounded person."

"I remember when she was a tiny little girl and we were in the zoo, she stepped on a bee. How she cried when you told her it was a living thing and she shouldn't kill it." Rozsi turned the chicken with her spoon and began cutting a shiny green pepper into slices. "She's *too* good," she said.

Jessica sighed, annoyed.

"You too," Rozsi said. "I don't know how you put up with those crazy people you used to take care of."

"No more," Jessica said.

Rozsi cut four plum tomatoes into quarters. She was trying to decide whether to irritate her daughter even more with an observation about Kevin.

Jessica broke the silence. "Okay, out with it."

"Next you add water and the raw rice, and throw in the green pepper and the tomatoes."

"Uh-huh."

"Then you cover the pot."

"Uh-huh."

Rozsi took the plunge. "No matter how poor we were when you were a little girl, no matter how high and mighty your friends were, did you ever lie? Try to tell people you were somebody you weren't?"

Jessica took a large gulp of her wine.

"Don't forget to check under the lid and add more water," Rozsi advised.

THE BASEMENT OF the Meadows house was uninviting, Sandy thought as she reached the bottom of the steep staircase. The windowless rock walls made the deep space beneath the house unusually dark and damp. Gary Meadows located the toolbox and opened it for her.

There was no hammer inside.

"I'm not a fix-it type," he said. "I rarely use these tools, but I checked the toolbox first because that's where I usually kept it. When I saw it was gone, I searched everywhere just to be sure. I've even called my neighbors—they borrow things occasionally. I checked both cars. And now I know it was in the box where it was supposed to be."

The metal box was stored out of the way in a dark corner. The killer had to search for the hammer. Or else he knew where to find it, she thought . . . Gary Meadows shut the box and kicked it back into the corner. Sandy gladly followed him up the stairs into the light.

Marjorie Meadows was waiting for them in April's bedroom. She pointed at the bent nail, still on the wall.

"April or someone else must have used the hammer to pull out the nail," she said, trying to keep her voice steady. They all knew that Billy's poem had hung on that nail.

"You're sure the hammer was in the toolbox before . . ." Sandy asked.

"I'm sure," Gary said. "We had the downstairs rooms painted a month or so before April disappeared, and Marjorie reminded me this morning that she had been after me for weeks to rehang the pictures. I'm sure I returned it to the toolbox after we hung the pictures. I haven't touched it since."

"Do you remember any grooves or imperfections in the hammer?" Sandy asked.

"It had a nick in the claw. It was my dad's old hammer, and it had years of hard use before it came to me."

Neither of them had noticed that Marjorie was crying until she covered her face and sat down on April's bed. Gary sat next to her. The house was quiet. They could hear the sound of a plane overhead.

Sandy wished there were softer words for harsh news.

"The hammer wasn't found in the quarry," Sandy said. "It's still missing, and from what you've just told me, I think it's your hammer we're searching for."

"April was killed in the kitchen," Marjorie said, wiping her eyes. She stood up, and they followed her downstairs. "Who killed her? A stranger? The serial killer? Someone who followed her home?" They stood in the kitchen, looking around as if they were seeing it for the first time.

"Someone she knew," Sandy said quietly. "Someone who could be sure he had enough time . . ." She couldn't say the words, "to mop up the blood."

"Billy! You're trying to say it was Billy Owens."

THEY ALL MET for lunch in the diner closest to the barracks to discuss cases. Lloyd sat next to Sandy in a booth across from Brian McKenzie and his son Dan.

Sandy had finished off her scrambled eggs and was working on the hash browns, still in the breakfast mode, having missed breakfast this morning. McKenzie was talking about another bank scam. This time a phony Nigerian official had suckered an Indianapolis bank into lending millions to his government at 30 percent interest. Interpol had documented losses of at least two hundred million dollars to corporations and banks worldwide.

"You'd be surprised at how naive so-called sophisticated bankers are," McKenzie said.

"Greed triumphs over good sense every time," Lloyd said.

Sandy watched as Dan, in a new uniform, listened intently to the talk, but she couldn't help thinking back to her visit with the Meadows family. They had let it slip that soon after the funeral many of their friends and neighbors had stopped calling. Sandy had seen it before. Almost unconsciously, people treated tragedy like a contagious disease. At first, thinking April had run away, they had probably blamed Marjorie. And when they learned that April had been murdered, they blamed her parents for not being watchful enough. Some, Sandy was certain, secretly blamed April. Finding blame, Sandy knew, allowed people to believe that if they were vigilant, if they did the right thing, nothing could happen to them.

She sipped her coffee, not listening closely until Lloyd spoke. "That Billy Owens came up smelling like a rose," he reported. "We interviewed his family and a few girls he dated before he met April."

"Of course, the girls aren't going to tell you anything nasty or kinky about him. Billy hasn't been accused of a crime. You think they're going to expose themselves?"

"Why not?"

"Because in this town, a girl sleeping around is a slut. A guy doing the same thing is a stud."

"Maybe," Lloyd said.

"Girls who are dumped on are too ashamed to admit it," Sandy said.

"And if a girl complains, she's bitchy," Dan put in.

"Hey, my son's a regular women's libber," said McKenzie.

"So what's the story on the hammer?" Lloyd asked Sandy.

"April was killed with her own hammer, probably in the kitchen. The killer was someone who knew he had enough time—at least half an hour—to clean up a lot of blood. It was someone who knew when the neighbors came home and when her parents were expected. We need a break here."

"Why don't you talk to someone at the paper? Arrange for them to publish your name and phone number in the next story about April," Dan suggested. "The follow-up should hit the streets tomorrow. Use Cassandra instead of Sandy and ask for info about the murder, strictly confidential. A woman with a secret might confide in another woman."

Sandy looked at him with new eyes. "That's an excellent suggestion, Dan," she said. "And I like your new jacket."

"The city is paying for this one. I tore the other in the line of duty."

"How's that?" Sandy asked, suddenly remembering Dan's torn left sleeve.

"At the crime scene. I tore it on the culvert. On a piece of metal at the opening trying to get that girl's remains out."

Sandy could barely get the rest of her coffee down. *I know who murdered April,* she thought. But she said nothing, because she still had no proof. But she knew that fresh gash she'd seen under Billy's left thumb the day after April's murder and that sharp metal on the culvert that had torn Dan's jacket was no coincidence.

KATHLEEN LIFTED A restless Brendan from the shopping cart to stop him from yanking cans off the shelves as she wheeled him down the aisle. Shopping before the dinner hour was always risky. She knew that a full-blown tantrum would result in another tuna-fish casserole for dinner if she wasn't able to pick up the ingredients for the pasta dish she was planning. She tossed a package of ground chicken into the cart beside a can of stewed tomatoes, keeping an eye on Brendan, who was letting off steam running along the refrigerated meat cases. Kathleen held her breath as he weaved in and out between shoppers. She started after him just as a tall, familiar woman coming around the corner collided with him.

"Oh, I'm so sorry," the woman said, bending down to Brendan. It was clearly Brendan's fault; he'd run headlong into the woman. "I'm sorry," Kathleen began, "I shouldn't have let him—"

"Please don't worry," the woman said. She smiled at Brendan. "He's a cute little boy. I remember how it was. Mine is all grown up now. . . ."

"Good night, now," Kathleen said nervously as they parted ways.

She put Brendan back in the cart and headed to the checkout, and spotted the woman as she turned down a nearby aisle. It was a shock as recognition finally came to her. I know who that woman is, Brendan, she thought. She's your grandmother.

SANDY STAYED LATE in her office the next evening. If Ms. Mystery, as she and Dan had named their anonymous caller, decided to respond to her request, she would be ready. Her name and number had appeared in the paper that morning, and the television spot could come on any minute. She'd already received calls, but none had been the one she was waiting for. Sandy was horrified by the number of molested teenaged girls who had phoned in to implicate their brothers or uncles in April's murder. So many young women out there who had been suffering in silence. No less depressing was the unidentified vagrant who had been pulled from the lake the other day. He hadn't even been reported missing.

All day long, each time the phone rang, Sandy had tensed. Another call from a molested teen? A crazy confessing to April's murder? When the phone stayed silent for ten minutes, she had dispatched Dan home to his fiancée. Now she thought about going home too, but she picked up the newspaper again, reread the story of the search for April's killer, and finally tore out the article. Her request was printed in bold letters beneath the story. She slipped the clipping into her desk drawer and dropped the rest of the paper into the waste basket.

It was a quiet night. The barracks wasn't busy. No, she wouldn't give up yet. She eyed the clock, hoping for a slow news night—the less news there was, the greater chance April's case had of being a top story. She leaned her elbows on the empty desk, waiting. The silence around her seemed to grow louder. She thought about how Dan had inadvertently led her to believe she knew April's killer. And now she was sitting on the info, hoping that Ms. Mystery could verify her admittedly small piece of evidence that it was Billy Owens who had stuffed April's body into the culvert eighteen months ago.

KATHLEEN WAS FOLDING laundry while she watched the evening news, leaving the socks for last. For once she paired them and they actually came out even. She didn't mind folding the clothing, and she loved the clean smell of the towels and the sheets. She stacked the clothes and linens neatly at the end of the couch, glad of the chance to complete a chore at the same time the evening news improved her mind. She was also grateful to be over the flu and back to her old schedule. And three pounds thinner to boot! She would start exercising as soon as she felt stronger. Tonight's meal had been a bowl of soup and a few chunks of a French baguette.

Brendan was beginning to have a bit of a social life. They'd joined a new play group, and Kathleen was pleased that he had already been invited on a play date. Since he was eating dinner at his new buddy's house tonight, Kathleen could relax. She was hoping to become more friendly with Allison Oliver, his friend's mother. She checked her watch. She would put her coat on at the commercial after the news ended and have Brendan in tow by seven-fifteen.

She stretched out on the couch, putting her feet up on the piles of laundry. She was glad her father was out bowling. He needed a break; he'd covered for her for the last three days. She watched the news wind down—and suddenly April Meadows's face appeared on the screen. It was her junior high graduation photo. And Kathleen couldn't believe what the anchorwoman was saying.

"This is April Meadows, who never lived to graduate from Centennial Middle School. Her remains were discovered in a quarry near Euclid Road two days ago, a year and a half after her parents reported her missing. There are no clues or suspects, and the police ask that anyone having information related to this unsolved murder contact the police. Please call the number on the screen. It is the private number of Inspector Cassandra Ungar. Your identity and all information you provide will be kept strictly confidential."

The news was a blur. The commercials came on, a sitcom flashed on the screen, and still she made no move. The police were asking *her* to call, she thought. She knew it. Yet they had made no mention of her anonymous report of the skull. Holy mother of God! It was April's skull. She nearly gagged as she thought of Brendan holding it in his hand.

Perspiration dotted her neck and her forehead, and she began to feel ill again. She had picked up the phone to dial before she realized she hadn't gotten the number. Her face felt flushed. She had to pick up Brendan. If she was late, Allison would resent it. Sweat dripped down her back as she dialed information for the police.

SANDY HAD JUST about given up when the local news ended. Ms. Mystery still hadn't called. But at six-fifteen a trooper received a request for Inspector Cassandra Ungar's number, the one that had flashed on the news, and the caller had insisted on speaking only to Sandy. She was put through immediately.

"I'm the one who reported the skull. April's skull . . ."

"Did you know April?" Sandy asked, trying to stay calm.

"I can't talk now—"

"All I need is your name," Sandy said quickly, afraid that Ms. Mystery would hang up on her. "*Strictly between you and me.* No one else will know. We can talk later. I need nothing else now. If you have something important to tell me, I need your name."

"I can't give it to you. I can't. Why do you need my name?"

"There are so many weirdos calling, we can't take anonymous information seriously. If you can't talk now, I'll come to see you myself."

"No."

Sandy heard the woman's panic. "Out of uniform. Just the two of us. As if I were a friend visiting."

"I don't think—"

"I *promise* you. Your name stays with me. *Strictly confidential.*"

"How can I be sure?"

"You have my word." Sandy then took a chance that she hoped wouldn't scare off the caller. "Look, this is about a young girl brutally murdered. I think you have an obligation."

A moment's silence. Two. Then: "Kathleen Sullivan. Sixteen Grove Street. After eight. You have to leave by nine." And the line went dead.

Sandy was elated. She had, finally, Ms. Mystery's name.

She hurried home, took a shower, and changed into a tailored but feminine outfit. Then she paced around, planning her strategy, unable to eat even to kill time, until it was finally the hour to leave.

ONCE AT THE Sullivan house, Sandy got out and stood in the driveway for a few moments before climbing the steps to the front porch. It was an old house on a well-lighted, tree-lined street. Yellow leaves were strewn on all the sidewalks. The steps were now underfoot, and the porch.

She looked around, then checked her watch before ringing the bell. She had been told to come after eight, and she didn't want to make any mistakes, risk spooking Kathleen Sullivan. The porch light was on, a good sign. She noted the plastic tricycle that was leaning against the wall and next to it a milk carton filled with toys. Sandy understood now why she'd been asked to come late. She knocked only once, not too loudly, so as not to wake the sleeping child inside.

Kathleen opened the door, and Sandy wasn't surprised at how young Kathleen was, or how pretty. What surprised her was how tall she was, and how blond and blue-eyed. How much she resembled April. Sandy knew this was going to be one hell of a night.

As Kathleen invited her in and sat down on the couch, motioning for Sandy to sit beside her, Sandy made note of several details as she crossed the room. On an old upright piano were displayed framed photos of a little boy about three years old. A man, who appeared to be the boy's grandfather, smiled out of many of the shots. Another picture, this one in a silver frame, held a photo of a couple. The man was the same one as in the other pictures, only younger. Sandy surmised this was a photo of Kathleen's parents. None of Kathleen, or of a husband.

Kathleen was tongue-tied, Sandy soon realized. Sandy herself would have to find the path that led into the secret Kathleen was keeping. Start out slowly, she told herself.

"I guess you saw me on TV," Sandy said. "Or was it in the paper?"

"I haven't seen the paper for days. I've been sick. It's my first day without fever," Kathleen said.

"So you found out about April for the first time tonight on the TV report."

She nodded. "It was a shock. I didn't know her, but I'd seen her in school."

Sandy wanted to take notes but was afraid it would scare Kathleen off.

"Did you find the skull?" Sandy ventured.

"Brendan. My little boy Brendan found it."

"God," Sandy said. "That must have been awful for you." Then, trying to sound casual, nonaccusatory: "What were you doing in the quarry?"

"I had to face something. And no one, not even my father"—Kathleen looked at the clock on the bureau. "He's coming home at nine. I never told him. It was something I couldn't tell anyone. That's why I hung up the first time I called."

"But now that you know April was murdered, you want to tell me something because . . ."

"Because I feel I must. In case, just in case—if you know what happened to me it might lead you to the murderer."

"You can tell me," Sandy said. "I know what it's like to keep secrets. And I'll never tell a single soul."

"SUCKS TO BE you, baby," Kevin said aloud into the silence of his dorm room. He had just written the words down in his Lexicon of Hot Words for Over-the-Hill Dudes. But the phrase made him think of Tina, and he put his pen down on his desk. Christ, he was lucky they had caught the guy who wasted her. He had been right on the money about Tina. With enough drugs she would never have remembered the snapshot of his father or the name on the back. But he hadn't counted on her dying. He missed old Tina.

He opened his desk drawer and pulled out the photo of his father.

Why did he keep a picture of his father when it was his mother's voice he had such a longing to hear? He had barely thought of his mother in a year and a half. As a matter of fact, he had taken some satisfaction in knowing that she was sad without him, that she was probably worrying because she hadn't heard from him once, except for the time he had called and hung up. And she hadn't even gotten a single postcard from him. He knew his father didn't miss him, and when he looked at his father's photo he felt nothing. But now, after all these months, he had the urge to hear just a word spoken by his mother.

It was late afternoon. A time when his mother might be home from work, when his father would be out. He picked up the phone and dialed his old number. The phone rang, and he hung up quickly before she could answer. It would be a mistake, a foolish mistake he couldn't afford.

Chapter Eleven

"I WAS ONLY sixteen at the time," Kathleen began. "So innocent. Dumb. I was so sheltered, my parents never talked about sex."

"It's the fastest way to get a daughter pregnant," Sandy said. When she saw the surprise in Kathleen's eyes, she knew she had hit pay dirt. But Kathleen said nothing. "If sex is a dirty secret," Sandy ventured, "kids find out by themselves—the hard way."

"That's why I'm going to be a nurse," Kathleen said. "No more secrets."

"Except for this one," Sandy said.

Kathleen lowered her eyes.

"I know what you're going through," Sandy said. "I was married when I was twenty. To a guy my parents disapproved of. We met in college. By the time I graduated he was into drugs, but I didn't know it until I got pregnant and he got busted. So I had an abortion no one knows about and got divorced. I haven't told anyone I work with because—"

"You're ashamed?"

"I guess I want to protect my image," Sandy said. "I don't want anyone to know what a chump I was, what a mess I made of my life."

"I was raped at the quarry!" Kathleen blurted out.

"My God," Sandy said. "Was it . . . someone you knew?"

"A boy in my class, a *nice* boy, or so I thought. A real popular boy. A handsome boy. I was so naive. . . . I went to a deserted quarry with him. I really never thought that kind of thing could happen to me. . . ."

"What was his name?" Sandy asked, holding her breath.

"Swear you won't tell," Kathleen said. "Swear it."

"Why are you protecting this scumbag?"

"He's Brendan's *father.*"

"I swear," she said. "Tell me."

"It was Billy Owens. April's boyfriend."

LAURIE SMELLED THE sweet scent of the strawberry candles as Kevin kissed her, interrupted by the jarring sound of the phone.

Kevin jumped up.

"The phone again!" He began to blow out the candles he had placed all over the room, and in his anger he knocked over the vase that held the tulips he had brought her. He banged his fist against his forehead.

"Kevin, please. It's *okay."* Ignoring the phone, she turned on the light, righted the vase, and mopped the water with a towel. She was beginning to dread their nine o'clock dates. Not dates. They were becoming more like rituals, and she felt obligated to be at home so they could have sex as planned. At first it had been novel, then sort of a joke. Now it was getting to be a real pain. Tonight she was missing a lecture by Stephen Jay Gould. Last week it had been a jazz concert. She watched Kevin as he grabbed up his clothes and began getting dressed. Maybe if he left she could still catch some of the lecture. Sold out, she remembered. In spite of herself, she felt guilty for wanting him to leave. Why did he have that effect on her? And why *was* he leaving? They were so unnecessary, his tantrums. Over nothing, really. God, more and more she felt she was walking on eggshells around him.

"I'm so clumsy," he said. "I'm sorry. It was dumb of me. . . ."

Laurel rearranged the flowers in the vase. "It's okay," she said and sat back down in the middle of the bed, her knees drawn up.

"Why can't your friends leave us *alone*?" He felt like throwing the telephone across the room, but suddenly his mind replayed the sound of April's telephone splintering when he smashed it with the hammer.

"My friends don't call anymore," she said.

He was dressed now, buckling his belt, humming that tune he always hummed when he was tense, *Kokomo, Indiana.* He leaned over her.

"Let's go to Hartewoods. It's the perfect setup. Your parents think you're on a debate trip, winning tournaments for the greater glory of the school, and we're off at their summer house for a good time."

He tried to kiss her, but she pushed him away and pulled the cover up. "We can't, Kevin. Do you realize how far behind I am? I've got two papers overdue, and I'm going to fail my French ex—"

"Oh, please, not again! All you do is complain. Get it together." He stared at her. "What's wrong with you? You have no sense of humor lately. Everything's so serious with you." He was standing at the door, his hand on the knob. "So get your work done," he said, and stormed out, slamming the door behind him.

Maybe it was her fault, at least partly, she thought. But she couldn't work, couldn't think. Couldn't breathe around Kevin. So why did *she* feel guilty?

She left the unmade bed and looked into the mirror. Her hair was scraggly, her complexion splotchy. She thought of the missed lecture. The topic complemented the bio course she was taking, the paper she should be writing. And she would have enjoyed it.

She missed those carefree times when she giggled with Doug and Mini, but no way could she cope with the team now. Her mom would be so disappointed if she quit. And if she had a clue that her brilliant daughter was worried about *failing* a course . . . All this lying was getting her down. She pulled the phone onto the bed, sat down, and reached for her address book. She'd call her dad in Brazil. Maybe she could tell *him* the truth.

THE ANSWERING MACHINE at the other end of the line whirred. Gary Meadows had ninety seconds to describe how April was murdered. If he could convince the producers of the TV show *Wanted for Murder* to dramatize his daughter's slaying, one day soon millions of people across America would be looking for Billy Owens.

From the pitch and modulation of her voice, from her diction and confident sound, Gary estimated that Lisa, the show's associate producer, his best hope, he figured, to nail Billy Owens, was a lady in her mid-thirties, who took notes on a legal pad. A no-nonsense lady in a business suit, judging from her clipped speech. A blond Californian with a tan. He had called an eight hundred number in L.A. to reach her.

Quickly, as succinctly as he could, Gary recounted on tape for Lisa the horrors of April's murder. He knew his wife, Marjorie, would have been upset had she heard this calculating delivery, his depiction of the discovery of their daughter's remains. He glanced at his study door. At any moment Marjorie could open it and overhear his pitch. As the tape spun toward its ninety-second deadline, toward Lisa's verdict, stage fright quickened his pulse.

Finished, Gary wiped the sweat from his forehead. Marjorie had been spared this ordeal. The truth was, she had never been able to believe that Billy was guilty, even though he had disappeared so conveniently. It would be cruel to put this on her now. He would wait it out alone. He only wished he knew a way to speed up the painful, pitiless ticking of the clock.

KEVIN WASN'T A bit surprised to hear her voice, Jessica thought. He acted as if it were altogether normal to get a call from his girlfriend's mother. She knew she was being hysterical, but she wouldn't be able to sleep until she had reached her daughter.

"Laurie's not picking up," he explained. "She's pulling an all-nighter to get a paper done."

Jessica relaxed some. Laurie at home working. Good. "I wish she would use the answering machine I bought her," Jessica said. But she suspected Laurie felt freer not having to return her mother's many calls.

"I wish she would too," he said.

"I guess I'm just being a nervous mother tonight because—"

"I understand, Mrs. Lewisohn. But don't worry, please. I'll take care of Laurie."

Jessica was sorry she'd called him. She had the feeling that she'd played right into his hands. She just didn't *like* Kevin Glade and she never would. No matter what his past life had been, he was too smooth, too practiced. . . .

"Laurel won't be too happy that I called . . ." she said.

"No sweat. You thought you could catch up with her here. Perfectly natural."

Jessica mumbled thanks and hung up, praying that Laurie would get rid of this guy. And soon.

* * *

WHEN LAURIE FINALLY got through, the phone connection to Brazil was so poor it was difficult to hear her father's voice, somehow making her even more aware of the distance between them.

"I don't know, Dad. I feel . . . overwhelmed lately. I can't get anything done."

"Maybe you should quit debate. Maybe it's too much, going away every weekend."

Laurel burst into tears too long held back. "I think I will."

"Are you okay, hon?"

Laurel took a deep breath. "Yeah, but I could just really use a hug right now."

"Things okay between you and Kevin?"

"Yes . . ." she said reflexively. She just wasn't ready to say no. She still hadn't sorted it out, their relationship.

"Okay. But if something, anything, is wrong I want you to tell me. I know it's hard to reach me. I'll try and call you again soon."

"Thanks, Dad. I feel better already."

And she did. It was good just hearing her father's voice. And at least she didn't have to lie anymore about debate. I'll quit the team tomorrow, start pulling myself together.

"LAUREL'S QUITTING DEBATE? It's Kevin! It's *his* influence." The phone crackled around Jessica's voice. "Why, Tom? She's a champion debater."

"I suggested she quit."

"You?"

"Cornell is a lot more demanding than high school, Jess. She's only a freshman. She needs time to adjust."

"Why didn't she tell me?"

"Come on, Jess. Let me help out when I can. You know you two have a touchy relationship right now."

"That's not fair, Tom. Because I try to protect my only daughter from a boy who lies—about the Putney School, the poem, the 'aunt' who turned up murdered—"

"As I see it, he pretty well explained all that."

"I don't care. He's bad news, Tom." Suddenly the line cleared up.

"Jess, we're talking about someone who attends Cornell University, not Alcatraz."

"But he's taking up all her time, and she's changed since she met him."

"Our daughter needs a social life; she's entitled to one."

"Of course she does. I would love a boyfriend for Laurie, a real one, made of flesh and blood."

Tom sighed.

"My mom doesn't like him either."

"Oh, the Hungarian CIA is back on the case?"

"Not funny," Jessica said, half smiling in spite of herself. But nothing Tom said could convince her Kevin wasn't poison, causing trouble between herself and Laurel, and now even between herself and Tom.

Sandy was still awake at three a.m. She closed her eyes but could not stop thinking about Kathleen. Why did I even mention my life? For the first time in years she was thinking about her ex. She had no idea where he was, and she didn't want to know. She was a totally different person from the one who'd married Jeff. Now she was nobody's easy mark. She took care of herself, didn't need her parents, and could handle one of the world's toughest jobs.

Actually she knew why she had confided in Kathleen; it was to befriend her, gain her trust. But opening up like that left her feeling vulnerable. Maybe that's the real reason I can't sleep, she thought.

Billy Owens. Billy Owens. The name drilled itself over and over into her brain. She turned onto her stomach and put the pillow over her head, trying to stop the thoughts from coming.

"Billy killed April," she had said to Kathleen, trying to get her to accuse Billy. Not exactly by-the-book questioning, but she was running out of options. "I can only go after him if you press charges."

"He raped me. But that doesn't make him a murderer."

"Rape is aggression. It's not about sex."

"But the serial killer . . . maybe he did it," Kathleen said, hoping it was true but knowing deep down that Billy was guilty.

"The serial killer didn't kill April, Kathleen. Billy was too far away to kill those other women. And now I have evidence to prove he bludgeoned April with her own hammer. But I need your help."

Kathleen was silent.

"When he hid April's body—pushed her into the culvert—he cut his hand on a piece of metal on the opening. I saw the cut—"

"You *saw* it?"

"After the murder I went to his house. I don't blame you for trusting him, believing in him. Everyone did."

But at that point Kathleen had refused to listen to another word, had practically pushed her out the door.

So she was back to square one. She had nothing on Billy. That cut she'd seen on his hand wouldn't even tempt a D.A.

Sandy turned onto her back and looked again at the luminous blue square on her clock. Three-fifteen. She had to get up in three hours. I must be slipping, she thought. She had seen the tear in the left sleeve of Dan's uniform that day at the quarry, but she hadn't connected it at the time to the cut under Billy's thumb. If Dan hadn't reminded her, if he hadn't worn his new jacket at the diner yesterday . . . Or was it the day before? She was getting sleepy, and the last coherent thought she had before falling off was, Why had Kathleen called the cops if she really thought Billy was innocent of April's murder?

Chapter Twelve

LISA FRANKINO, TWENTY-THREE, was short with light brown, wavy hair and extremely fair skin. She hadn't sunbathed for nearly a year; last January she had had a suspicious mole removed from her face. A former UCLA journalism major, she had decided to break into TV after seeing a Jane Pauley interview, and now she was working her way up. She was dressed in coral, raw silk culottes and a matching jacket and pale, multicolored sandals. Her only jewelry was a pair of slender gold hoop earrings. She dressed to impress, but in good taste.

One thing Gary Meadows had been right about; she had taken notes. They were penned in her clear, even handwriting on a sheet of underlined white paper. She had numbered her observations as she jotted them down. "1. Bad guy wanted for *questioning,* not murder. 2. B.G. had *not* fled. 3. Mother of victim may *not* appear on TV." Number four was highlighted in red. "Possible legal problem. Evidence circumstantial."

The case had possibilities, Lisa thought. But she had already approved so many other clear-cut manhunts that she was seriously backlogged. She affixed a coded label to the tape and dropped it, along with her notes, into a folder. Then she opened a metal cabinet and filed the folder under M. The drawer was labeled L.P.—low priority.

WHEN DAN GOT the call from Vince Pazzolini, a private eye in L.A. who wanted info on Billy Owens, Dan immediately put him through to Sandy.

"Inspector Ungar here. What do you need on Billy Owens?"

"So, he's got a long sheet?" Vince asked.

"What makes you think that?" Sandy asked.

"I'm put through to a detective in a hurry. . . ."

"No sheet. Not even a traffic violation." She was giving none of her evidence to this guy until she heard more. Maybe not then.

Vince said, "Here's the deal. My client is a movie star. She's been getting obsessive letters from this fan for a number of years. Billy Owens. The postmarks on the letters were from your town, so I decided to check him out."

"What's the most recent postmark?" Sandy asked.

"Eighteen months ago. The *point* is, when he got sick of writing, he began calling. Then two weeks ago he suddenly stopped the calls. It's probably nothing to worry about, but I'm checking all possible kooks. My client is jittery. The soap actress who was shot in L.A. is giving all the female stars in Hollywood nightmares."

"He's a suspect in some serial killings," Sandy said evenly.

"Christ! I thought this was gonna be a routine call."

"Myself, I don't believe he's a serial. But some around here do. Who's your client?"

"Lorna Barrett."

Sandy whistled.

"Off the record," Vince said, "does my client need to worry?"

"Serials don't usually write letters or call their victims. But I think Owens murdered his girlfriend. And I know he raped a girl."

"Holy shit!"

"Off the record. Strictly off."

"I didn't expect this."

"Officially speaking, he's only wanted for questioning."

"I hear you."

"I'm telling you this for your own good, and mine. I would very much like to find this kid. I can use all the help I can get."

"How old is he?"

"Nineteen and a half."

"Well, send me your bulletins," Vince said. "And a photo." He gave Sandy his address.

"Keep in touch," she said, and hung up.

But she knew that Lorna Barrett wouldn't get another letter from Billy. No way. He had gotten too smart.

* * *

AT THE LAST minute Patricia Van Etten Owens ran into her bedroom to check to see if the letter was still where she had left it. She knew it was, but she checked anyway. . . . This Detective Ungar was coming to see her. She pulled her top dresser drawer way out and felt the underside. It was still taped there. There was no need to read it; she had memorized it, read and reread it for some deeper meaning. Maybe somewhere in that letter was the solution, or at least a clue, to the mystery of their lives, the truth about whether or not her own son had killed April. That was why she had never destroyed the letter. She was still trying to find its hidden message, as if it were the Rosetta stone she had learned about in college.

She shut the drawer and rushed into the living room to collect herself, took a deep breath, and tried to reassure herself that she had nothing to worry about. But just in case, she had carefully timed the meeting so that her husband, Bill, wouldn't arrive home from work while the officer was still in the house.

Bill, of course, didn't know about the letter. She had found it only recently, when a man doing repairs had pulled the washing machine away from the wall. The letter, along with a stray sock and T-shirt, had fallen behind the washer. It had been wadded up in a ball. If Billy had been home as usual, she would have thrown it out. But now anything he had left behind was precious to her. She had smoothed it over and over again, so much that most of the wrinkles had been pressed out.

She dreaded the meeting with Sandy. Just tell the truth, she reminded herself. She had lied about only one thing to the police. She had arrived home the night April disappeared shortly *after* Billy had. She had felt the heat still coming from the dryer in the laundry room and assumed Billy had dried his wet jacket; it had been raining hard and his wet tracks in the hall had still been visible when she arrived. And withholding the letter wasn't really a lie, since the letter belonged to Billy. She stood up suddenly to get the letter, to burn it, but the ringing doorbell stopped her.

Sandy was in full uniform. Although she was invited to sit down, she stood over Billy's mother and opened her black leather notebook. She was trying to intimidate, and she was succeeding.

At first Billy's mother had looked sad. Now she just looked defeated. She was hiding something, Sandy felt. But if she took her apart the way she wanted to, the woman might get a lawyer. Sandy wished she could tap the phone. And through all of this she also felt sorry for the mother. Which made going after her harder.

"Have you heard from Billy?"

"No, I haven't." She lowered her eyes.

Was she lying? Ashamed?

"In all this time? Isn't that odd?"

"He's young. Kids don't like to report in to their mothers."

"Did he have a good relationship with you and his father?"

"Yes," she answered quickly. "But he's closer to me."

"Did he ever exhibit violent behavior as a child?"

"Why are you asking me this?"

"Mrs. Owens, your son is wanted for questioning and he's disappeared. April, we now know, was murdered, and we need some answers from Billy. April was only fourteen. . . ." Had she gone too far?

"Billy was a good boy. He never did anything wrong, he *loved* April. . . ."

"Has he contacted your husband?"

"Bill sells insurance now, he's on the road a lot." And saying it, she looked over at the wall where their wedding picture hung.

Suddenly a picture of Kathleen's little boy popped into Sandy's head, along with the realization that this couple had a grandson they knew nothing about.

"Do you remember the cut on Billy's hand, Mrs. Owens? The culvert where April's body was hidden had a sharp edge—"

"Are you accusing my Billy?"

"I just want to know where he is," Sandy said, clapping her notebook shut.

"So do I. Believe me," Mrs. Owens said, wiping her eyes with a tissue and blowing her nose.

A terrible feeling of guilt came over Patricia Owens then. But it wasn't because she was keeping something from the police. What she was hiding she was hiding from herself and from Billy.

* * *

THE LETTER SHOOK as if a gust of wind had caught hold of it. But it was her fingers that had lost control; she could barely hold the paper.

She blamed herself for all this—for marrying Bill. How could she have married him? She had asked herself the question so many times over the years and come up with the same answer. She had fallen for a smooth talker, a wheeler-dealer. Her parents had never said a word, though they thought she had married beneath her. Even when she quit school, and even though they paid the Owens's family bills until they themselves died, they never said anything.

It hadn't taken long for Patricia to see the signs that she had made a terrible mistake, but back then she had thought she could change him, that love could change anything, everything. It was the missionary spirit in her—she'd inherited it from her family. But what had she gotten? A ruined life and a son who did anything to gain approval. He was always the best child, so well behaved. But it was too much, unnatural. At first he had fooled her with his show of goodness. Then, when it was already too late, she had tried to reach him, but nothing had worked. She never had a clue to what he was really feeling. Billy just became more endearing, cajoling, winning—and, like his father, slyer. And finally, when Billy tried to turn the charm on her one time too many, her heart had gone cold and she accepted she had failed.

So why was she protecting him now? A mother's job was to protect her child, wasn't it? And she strongly felt she had failed her son, again and again, failed to get through to him, to understand him, to influence him. She had, to be truthful, given up on him. She read the letter now for the last time before she burned it. Its precise, perfect handwriting made her shudder. It was dated the day April Meadows disappeared.

April—my life, my best friend,

I never thought you would betray me. I thought you cared about me. But now I sense you have become someone else. Is it possible that you—who I thought was my own—my very own forever—would desert me?

Patricia stopped reading. For the first time she realized the letter could have been written to *her.* He resented *her* for what he considered deserting him. . . .

> I may come across proud, assured, but I *need* you. You're my dream come true. Don't ruin my dream, April. Please don't.

The letter continued with a heart that Billy had drawn. Inside the heart he had printed "Billy." An arrow pierced the heart, and drops of blood spilled from the wound.

As she burned the letter, her tears were not for Billy, as Detective Ungar had imagined. Her strongest sense of remorse was for April. Her feelings of pain for her own son were mixed, blotched and blemished by a dark memory over a decade old. She had never stopped wondering. Could she have saved Billy from his father? He felt she had deserted him. But had she also betrayed him? Yes. It was her fault that Billy had become calculating, soulless. He had been only five years old then. . . .

FROM HER KITCHEN Jessica could hear the elevator gate open and close, and recognized the sound of Ricky's footsteps in the hallway. Of the four tenants on the floor, only Ricky had a fast, almost staccato walk. Jessica had already gotten into her long flannel nightgown and robe, but she opened the door.

Ricky, still wearing her khaki parka, was putting her key in the lock. She turned around as Jessica's door opened.

"Hi, Jess, come on in. I have something to show you." The wind whistled through the vents, and Jessica pulled her robe more tightly around her. "Be right there," she said, and ran back into the kitchen, grabbed her keys and the pot of broccoli soup she had been heating, and walked out, locking the door behind her.

Ricky had left her door unlocked for her, so Jessica bolted the door and looked around, deciding Ricky must be in the bedroom.

The apartment was cluttered and artsy. Huge paintings done in acrylic adorned the walls. One, a naked woman, hung over the couch and practically hit you in the face as you walked in.

"Some broccoli soup?" she called out to Ricky, who was changing into pajamas.

"Oh, yes!" Ricky answered. "Bless you."

Jessica knew that Ricky's eating habits were tailored to her late-night schedule, that Chinese take-out and pizza were her staples.

They sat around the round oak table in the dining area and spooned their soup without talking until they were almost finished.

"So you got a letter from the man of your dreams and you're madly in love," Jessica ventured.

Ricky finished her soup. "This was homemade heaven," she said, sighing. "You know I don't believe in love anymore. It's an illusion."

"Oh, Ricky, you've been in the theater too long."

"People lose their grip on reality when they quote fall in love end quote. I've done it, Jess."

"Well, you may be on target, kiddo. Freud called love a mild psychosis."

Ricky stood up, got her briefcase, took out a pack of letters and tossed them on the table. "Read 'em and weep," she said.

Jessica took up the packet and thought of the ad she had dreamed up for Ricky, who had sent it to the personals column of the *New York Review of Books:* "Young, creative woman looking for someone to light up my life."

"Are they really all pathetic? I can't believe my brilliant copy didn't attract a possible." Jessica stuck the letters into the deep pocket of her robe.

"Jess, I just want to meet someone who isn't married or borderline schizophrenic."

"Or both. My aunt Ilona once advised me to marry a woman."

"Women are more sensitive."

"Except when they're teenagers and twist their fathers around their little fingers . . ."

"Something's on your mind, Jess. Let's hear it. And does it call for a drink or just tea?"

"Coffee, please."

Ricky moved toward the kitchen.

"Tom said that I don't have a good relationship with Laurel."

"Just because you fight?" Ricky called out. She measured coffee into the basket, poured water into the coffeemaker, and turned it on. She sensed that Jessica was just barely managing to hold back tears. She returned to the living room. "You love each other?"

"Yes!"

"Laurie respects you?"

"Yes . . ."

"Confides in you?"

"Not anymore."

"All teenaged girls fight with their moms, Jess. You've told Margo that whenever her girls go off the deep end. Remember Marianne's kid and the Hell's Angel? The closer the relationship, the harder the daughter has to fight to break away. Right?"

"My very words coming home to roost."

"I think I'm being objective. I've seen you and Laurie over the years, and I would be very happy to do as good a job if I were lucky enough to have a daughter."

Jess had tears in her eyes as she hugged Ricky.

THE ANSWERING MACHINE in Jessica's study blinked, indicating a single message. She turned on the light and pressed Play.

"This is Nora Berry. Remember me? It's been, what? Six years? I've got something important to tell you. I'm on duty at the institute until midnight. Call me."

Jessica reflexively pulled a curl down on her forehead to cover her scar; Nora had been there the night she was assaulted. She picked up the phone before she realized that Nora hadn't left the number, and stood there for a moment, remembering the night.

Ed Polley had been high on drugs. Officially, he was a mentally ill substance abuser—like many homeless people who had been thrown out on the streets. Ed was a paranoid schizophrenic, a violent one. Someone she had found difficult to sympathize with because the crime that had landed him in the observation unit was murder: he had shot a Good Samaritan and then smashed his head in with a stone—his way of saying thank you to the young man who had stopped to help him with a disabled car.

Now the number came back to her. Nora picked up. "I heard

about your job as director at the foundation. I was so happy for you," Nora said.

"And I heard you're a supervisor. Congratulations."

"Thanks, Jess. I'm really happy to have gotten here—finally. Listen, I only have a minute, so I won't beat around the bush. I thought you should know. Ed Polley's out. *Cured,*" she added sarcastically.

"What? When?"

"Early this morning. Discharged from Ward's Island Hospital. He's probably forgotten all about you, but I wouldn't have been able to sleep without calling."

Nothing more needed to be said. They had been through the mill together, watching dangerous men go through the revolving door of the psychiatric health-care system.

"Thanks for warning me, Nora," Jessica said, trying to keep her voice steady.

She hung up the phone and rushed to the front door to double-lock it. She locked the terrace door and all the windows near it even though it was virtually impossible for anyone to climb to the twenty-fourth floor. And even though she knew Ed Polley didn't have her address, and her phone had remained unlisted since her days at the psych institute, she called the doorman and reminded him that *no one,* under any circumstances, was to be let up unless she gave the order.

It was too late to call Tom. Too late to call anyone. She thought of buying a small handgun, of bringing the shotgun from Hartewoods. What was she thinking? She paced the apartment until she calmed down. It had been years since Ed Polley had even seen her. Surely he had made many more enemies in those years, was frying his brain this very moment by smoking crack. She was the last thing on this madman's mind, she told herself. And two glasses of sherry along with two old movies helped her some to believe it.

Finally she fell into bed and slept a fitful sleep, dreaming too many dreams. In her last one she smelled the aroma of broccoli soup. She had just ladled a spoonful into Laurel's bowl. She was in Laurel's dorm room, and her dream had provided a kitchen. Suddenly a fire engine screamed . . .

Jessica opened her eyes. The phone was ringing. She reached over to her night table and grabbed the receiver.

"Hello," she whispered. But the caller abruptly hung up. Exhausted and confused, she stared at the clock. Six a.m. When she put down the phone she had a terrifying, unavoidable thought. Ed Polley!

Chapter Thirteen

PATRICIA VAN ETTEN Owens wore her hair straight and short, was soft-spoken, and still had a musical laugh when she allowed herself an unguarded moment. Her wholesome Midwestern shine was not entirely dulled by the dark circles under her eyes and the spidery lines beginning to form at her mouth. But she knew that the years of living with Bill had changed her.

She sat now on the worn-out couch, waiting for Lord knew what, assessing her life now that she had the security of knowing that Bill was dead. Not for the first time she noted the irony of living in a house furnished with cheap catalogue pieces that were almost exact imitations of the authentic early American antiques she had grown up with. What was she waiting for?

She opened the small metal box that lay in her lap and stared at the lumps of gray ash and the bits of bone. Her husband's remains. She shuddered. He wasn't really dead; he was living on in their son.

"I deal in death," Bill had announced on the day he retired from the steel plant and began selling life insurance. But he was struck down by illness too soon for him to enjoy his new career, or for her to enjoy his stint on the road. And when he lay in his bed helpless, paralyzed, and unable to speak, she knew that, had *she* been ill, he would never have cared for her. One day he read her eyes and showed his fear. He knew she had a score to settle with him.

ALEX, THE RUSSIAN doorman who had known Laurie for years, shifted uncomfortably in his heavy uniform. He rang Jessica to announce Laurel and Kevin. "New rules," he explained, glancing at Kevin. "You know your mother."

Kevin tried to look cool, but he was burning inside. He got the message. To Jessica he was still a stranger.

Upstairs in the kitchen, Jessica had prepared a spread of cheese, hummus, pita, and fruit, along with an assortment of nuts and chocolates. "You really needn't have come," she told them. "I'm convinced now it wasn't Ed Polley calling me. I haven't had a call since that morning. It must have just been a wrong number hang-up." She watched with satisfaction as they sampled the goodies. "Of course, I'm glad you called, happy to see you . . ."

"It's okay, Mom," Laurie said. "We're going dancing after dinner." Kevin looked at her, surprised. Laurel had brought him along on impulse. He had looked so forlorn when she told him where she was going.

"But you should be careful, Mom."

"You're preaching to the choir, Laurie. This place is a fortress. So where are you going dancing?"

"A happening club." She looked at Kevin, who smiled weakly.

KEVIN WALKED ALONG the stone wall on Riverside Drive, imagining Jessica sneaking a look out the window. In the apartment he had felt her looking him over. When he excused himself to take a walk, to allow mother and daughter some private time, he said, Jessica had obviously been pleased. And worst of all, Laurie had seemed relieved. Well, never mind, he had another motive for cutting out.

The stone wall reminded him of the nursery rhyme he had always hated. "Humpty Dumpty sat on the wall, Humpty Dumpty had a great fall," running through his head as he searched for a pay phone. It was a sunny afternoon. Families strolled by, and down in the park along the river he could see couples jogging together, children biking under the watchful eyes of their parents, and lovers holding hands as they walked.

Abruptly he turned off the Drive and on to Ninetieth Street. "All the king's horses and all the king's men," he thought as he dropped the first quarter into the phone slot. Fear stirred as he heard the coins clang inside the box. What if his father was home? He looked at his watch. Too early. He had always treaded lightly around his father, terrified he would do something wrong. One misstep and he would fall like Humpty-Dumpty. And all the king's men wouldn't be able to put him together again.

"Hello."

It was his mother's voice, and there was urgency to it. She knew it was him. He didn't answer.

"Billy, is that *you*?"

Still no answer.

"Your father is dead, Billy. I wish you could come home now."

Silence.

"But I know you *can't* come home," she said.

He heard the tears in her voice and the music was gone. He hung up.

He leaned against the phone, unmoved by the news of his father. What was there to cry over?

But he got gooseflesh at the thought of being caught, of his own death. His mother *knew.*

A flash of anger. Now he would never have the chance to tell his father how much he hated him.

AFTER BILLY'S CALL, Patricia sat in her armchair, completely still. She stared into the dining room, remembering again the scene that had changed all of their lives. Would Billy ever forgive her? Should he?

She heard Billy's laughter, the laughter of a mischievous five-year-old boy. And she heard the sound of him running, high-spirited and agile, to elude his father's grasp. But then the heavier footsteps, pounding after Billy, had halted abruptly.

She had run to the doorway. Too late. Bill had grabbed his son by the arm, jerked him over to the gun cabinet, yanked out a revolver, and held the gun to Billy's head.

She had known at that moment that if she uttered a sound, made a move, he would punish her for protecting Billy, and both of them would be dead. Bill was crazy enough to pull the trigger.

"Next time I'll blow your head off," he had said as he dropped the gun to his side and let go of Billy.

Her screams, her tears had compressed into a knot inside her—until Bill left the house. Then she had held Billy close and rocked him.

But there had been no tears to kiss away. He was inert in her arms, a wooden soldier, his eyes green marbles.

She cried now for the baby she had borne, not for the man he had become.

"SO YOU'RE WORRIED about me, my Laurika." Jessica hugged Laurel and gave her a juicy kiss on her cheek. "Rozsi sends you a big kiss."

"Did you tell her about that loony getting out?"

"Absolutely not. And I told Daddy not to come home, I'm fine."

"Well, then, I guess we'll be going back tonight."

"All right, but no drinking tonight."

"Mother . . ."

"Did you bring the new poem?"

"Yes, but not for your approval. I'm only showing it to you to let you see his better side. I know you think he's a barbarian."

Jessica said nothing as Laurie pulled a folded sheet of paper from her purse and thrust it at her.

" 'Autumn Song.' Nice title," Jessica said. She read on quickly. "Very expert."

Laurie waited.

" 'My heart is in ashes on the forest floor.' He sounds depressed."

"I *knew* it was a mistake bringing it," Laurie said, reaching for the poem. How could she explain that it had been an apology for his off-the-wall anger?

"Can I keep it?" Jessica asked, not letting go, "I'd like to read it more carefully. Do it justice. It wasn't a mistake," she said, trying to sound sincere, wondering where he had ripped this one off. She'd show it to Marianne, the poetry police.

KEVIN FOUND LAURIE in her room dressing for the evening, but not before he checked out Jessica's bedroom through the open door. It was the most casual room in the house, with a brass bed frame and eclectic, comfortable furniture. Large windows with an unobstructed view of the river and the sky gave the feeling of being suspended over the earth. A large TV was set on a bookcase against the wall across from the bed. A lamp, a clock, and a pile of books were stacked next to the antique telephone on one of the night tables.

Kevin stored the information and watched Laurie as she squeezed into a black dress, low-cut and short, not her usual style. She looked stunning.

"You need to show some skin if you want to get into a club," Laurie said, and tossed her leather jacket at him. "Take this," she said. "We need to look hip, or else we get stuck at the Wetlands."

He checked out the jacket in the mirror. "What's wrong with the Wetlands?"

"Too whitebread." She put on a short fur jacket she had found long ago in a thrift shop. "So where do you want to go?"

Kevin looked baffled, and Laurie suddenly realized he knew nothing about the club scene. "It's the pierced-nose, combat-boot brigade in Pluto's. But I feel like glitz tonight. How about the Palladium?" She doubted he would appreciate the transvestite scene at Versailles.

She led him into her mother's bedroom, rummaged around in a jewelry box until she found long rhinestone earrings. "Funky, huh? They're Rozsi's."

Kevin snatched up a sheet of paper lying on the dressing table. "What's this doing here?" he asked, shoving the paper in her face. It was his poem.

Laurie nearly dropped the earring she was trying to clip on. "My God, Kevin. You scared me!"

"I—I . . . Why did you give it to her?"

"To show you off!"

"I wrote it for *you.*"

She looked into the mirror. The rhinestones sparkled as she fixed them to her ears. "I was trying to impress her, for you."

"Well, it's personal. What if she hates it?" Or finds out he didn't write it.

She turned to face him. "Kevin, it's great. Really."

He replaced the poem, controlling his anger. Jessica was like an octopus, her tentacles reaching for Laurie, pulling her away. As he followed Laurie back to her room, an idea crept out of his brain like a parasite that had burrowed there and was now slowly emerging.

* * *

IT WAS PITCH BLACK in her bedroom. Two a.m. Jessica's outstretched arm lay on Tom's empty pillow. Suddenly her head twitched at a jarring sound. She struggled to open her eyes and reached blindly for the phone.

"Hello? Hello, Tom?"

Her stomach clenched. Someone breathing in the deathly silence. Ed Polley for sure.

AS KEVIN CAME back from the telephone near the men's room, he noted dancers performing in cages hung high above the dance floor. The action was fierce at the Palladium. The crowds surged. People cruised the crowd, looking for drugs, for trouble. They wouldn't get it from him. Not from Billy Owens. He was a good little boy.

JESSICA HAD INVITED Marianne and Ricky to her health club to exercise, swim, and sauna, and, she hoped, to cheer her up. She badly wanted to believe that maybe, just maybe, as the telephone company rep had suggested, the calls were still being made by a whacko who had dialed her number at random. After all, New York was nutcase city. The calls, and there had been only two of them, could also have been from a malicious teenager. The one at six a.m. could even have been a wrong number. If she changed her phone number now, Tom, still away from home, would be unable to reach her. And she would have to call dozens of friends and business associates. Once again, because she wanted to believe it, she was willing to believe it wasn't Ed Polley. Almost.

Marianne interrupted her thoughts. "So, where's Kevin's latest masterpiece?"

Jessica clapped her hand to her head. "I totally forgot it!" She got up and ran to the locker room, forgetting to bring her towel. Feeling like a fool standing there in the nude, she twisted the dial on her combination lock, found the poem in her bag, and hurried back to the warmth of the sauna.

As Marianne read the poem aloud, it seemed depressingly obvious to everyone that the poem was far too mature, far too subtle to have been written by Kevin. " 'Crimson rumor, green fires of summer,' " Marianne said. "If he wrote those words, Laurie's got herself a major poet."

"Can you find out who wrote it?" Jessica asked as they headed toward the showers.

"I'll research it. Call me in about a week."

"Sounds like a Victorian to me," Ricky said.

WHEN THEY SAID good-bye outside the empty street, it was dusk. Marianne took off in a cab, and Ricky and Jessica started walking home together. Impulsively, Jessica grabbed Ricky's arm. "You know something? This is the first time since I was a little girl that I've dreaded the night, the first time ever I've been afraid of sleeping in my apartment alone. I'm always looking over my shoulder—"

"Jess, if it is Polley calling, and you've been told that's very unlikely, you're playing into his hands by letting him get you off balance. If you can't think straight, you can't protect yourself."

"I know, I know. I've got to get myself together."

"That's my Jessie. This is New York, hon. You have to be tough."

"I think I just bit into a worm in the big apple," Jessica said as they crossed Ninety-sixth Street.

"DON'T GO. *Don't,*" Kevin was saying. She stood in the doorway a moment, trying to smile and make light of it.

"Later," she said, backing out of the door as she closed it, then hurried across the campus, hardly noticing the clock tower and the Gothic buildings. The grand architecture of the quad, steeped in tradition, usually lifted her spirits. But she was so immersed in her thoughts that later she couldn't even remember how she had gotten to the party. Noise greeted her from the stairway. The entire dorm was jumping.

At brunch, when she had told Mini and Doug that she was quitting debate, they'd surprised her by accepting her decision without a fight, but they wouldn't take no for an answer when they invited her to their party.

"Everybody's showing up, and you've got to be there tonight. No one's seen you for centuries," Doug had said.

"There's a hot guy been staring at you in psych lecture. Have you noticed? He's coming too," Mini had said.

She had arrived early, but it was already wall-to-wall. She got a beer from the keg and, spotting Mini and Doug at the other end of the room, realized it would require major elbowing to reach them. They waved at her, and then Mini, smiling broadly, pointed at a young man who was standing with his back toward her. Laurel recognized him. He had sat next to her in the lecture hall a couple of times, and she had been well aware of his presence. Alan. She remembered his name just as he turned to her.

"I was hoping you would be here," he said.

Laurie felt herself blushing. Was she so out of touch she was flustered when a cute guy just spoke to her?

"Hi, Alan." She held out her hand, and he took it. His palm was warm. Holding his hand for a moment, she had an emotion she didn't want to feel. And she felt a sensation of easiness, of lightness, from his smile, from the comfortable way he led her into conversation. Though it seemed like minutes, it was hours before she thought of anyone but him.

They meandered into the crisp night, staring at the stars that were shining over the valley like a protective dome of diamonds. The mood and his company had pushed aside her early guilt over leaving Kevin, and, deep in conversation, they stopped to sit on a bench. But it was way past midnight, and the longer they talked and the later it got, the more the old guilt intruded.

"It's late," she said nervously. Alan stood up.

"No," she protested. "I'll walk home myself." She saw his surprise, but he only said, "I enjoyed the evening, anyway." He looked into her eyes. She could have kissed him. Easily.

She walked away feeling *good.* The air seemed thinner, clearer.

When she arrived at her dorm, she flung open the door, half expecting Kevin to be waiting. He was gone. She dug through her closet for the journal her mother had given her the day she left for Cornell. She dated the first page and wrote, "I'm so confused, now that I've met Alan. . . ."

* * *

ALAN HAD ALREADY finished his breakfast when he spotted Mini and Doug. Sound was subdued in the cavernous Student Union dining hall thanks to the marvelous hundred-foot ceiling. No noisy chatter or clatter of trays. Just the place to start the day, he thought. He picked up his coffee, walked over to Doug and Mini's table, and sat down.

"Nice party," he said.

"I saw you leave with Laurel," Mini said.

"Do you approve?"

"Dynamite debater," Doug said.

"What's her story?" Alan asked. "She's cute, friendly. In lecture she asks awesome questions. I like a woman with brains. Is she neurotic, or what? I think she likes me, but the minute I get close, she acts sort of weird. Can you help me?"

"She's a very private person," Doug said. Mini nodded her head.

After Alan finished his coffee and left for an early class, Mini poked Doug. "Why didn't you tell him?"

"That Kevin threatened us?" He buttered his croissant and added raspberry jam. "It's not my business to do Kevin's dirty work."

UNDER HER DOOR that morning Laurel found a card made of green construction paper with a square piece of rice paper glued inside. On it was a stunningly accurate rendering of delicately colored nasturtiums in a plain jar. Below the drawing, two tiny red hearts stood side by side, one with the letter L, the other with a K imbedded in it.

That evening, Kevin arrived at exactly nine to apologize for his behavior the night before.

"I know it sounds seriously screwed up, Laurie, but . . . well, I was afraid you wouldn't come back . . . like my parents," he said, kissing her lightly on the lips.

His pain, his vulnerability, touched her. She couldn't help it. "Don't you worry," she said, caressing his hair. "I won't leave you." She kissed him back. "The card, it's beautiful, Kevin."

That night Kevin made love to her, ever so sweetly. And as he slept, his head on her pillow, she marveled at how tender and helpless he looked.

* * *

"I THOUGHT YOU *were dead!" he said, and raised the hammer high. Down it swung, again and again. Her head cracked wide open, and he looked inside the wound. Blood had splattered on the wall. He would have to clean it up. He bent down to see if she was still breathing.*

Was that the door? It creaked open. His whole body shook. . . . Laurel was gently shaking his shoulder. His eyes came open. He was all sweaty, not sure for a moment where he was. It was always the same. In every dream a woman appeared in the doorway, but his fear woke him before he could identify her. Today Laurel had stopped him.

"Just a nightmare," she whispered. "God, you're as white as a ghost!"

"There's always a woman . . . she's standing in the doorway. But I never see her face."

Chapter Fourteen

KATHLEEN WENT INTO the community center meeting hall long after everyone else was seated, not wanting to risk meeting up with Sandy Ungar and be pressured again to prosecute Billy. She found a seat in the back row and tried to concentrate.

Sandy was concluding her first topic, "How to Avoid Being a Victim of Crime." Kathleen had never seen her in uniform. She looked so strong, so official. And she spoke with an authority that went with the look.

"It *can* happen to you. So don't look vulnerable. Be a tough target . . ."

Kathleen thought about what an easy target she had been.

Sandy continued, "And remember: If you find yourself in a tough spot, yell 'Fire,' not 'Help' or 'Rape.' "

The next subject, "How to Protect Your Child from a Kidnapper or Molester," was the one that had gotten her to come here, but she couldn't stop thinking about what Sandy had asked her to do. A victim once, she refused to be a victim again, this time of the court system. They would probably never find Billy anyway, and her sacrifice would be wasted.

At the end of Sandy's talk, when members of the audience crowded around her, Kathleen slipped out, got into her car and pulled out of the lot in a rush. She had just turned right, hoping to meet up with Dartmouth Street, where the twenty-four-hour supermarket was, when she saw the sign for Edgewood Road.

Last week, when she had looked up Allison Oliver's number, her eye had caught "Owens" and she hadn't been able to resist. "William Owens, 200 Edgewood Road." Impulsively, she made a left onto Edgewood.

Slowly, she drove past each house, struggling in the dark to read house numbers until she reached 200. The house looked smaller and more rundown than any she had ever envisioned for spiffy, fast-talking Billy Owens. A light came on in the living room, and she slowed almost to a standstill. A woman's figure hovered in the window. Billy's mother. Kathleen stepped on the gas.

"You will never know you have a grandson," Kathleen said to the woman outlined in the lamplight.

KEVIN WAS THE perfect roommate, neat as a pin, never had rowdy parties and paid all the bills. Last week, when he had paid the phone bill, he had put a check mark in the box next to the statement that read: "I would like an immediate all-call restrict placed on my telephone number." Now he could call from the comfort of his room at any time of the day or night, and no one—even someone who owned the device that automatically recorded incoming numbers—would be the wiser. He had his reasons for keeping his number secret, and he had wondered, as he signed his name to the form with a flourish, if Ed Polley had been smart enough to restrict *his* number.

GARY MEADOWS WAS grateful that his wife was off to work every day well before the mail arrived. Although she would never open his mail, her schedule saved him the effort of lying about the letter he was waiting for. At last it arrived. He stood at the mailbox, tore open the envelope, and read the letter.

> Dear Mr. Meadows,
>
> Thank you for turning to *Wanted for Murder* in your time of loss. We would very much like to help you by airing the tragic story of your daughter. But at this time our legal department advises us that we would have a much stronger program when new evidence emerges incriminating Billy Owens.
>
> Please inform us immediately of any new developments in the investigation.
>
> Sincerely,
> Lisa Frankino

Back in the house, he carefully tore the letter into pieces and flushed them down the toilet. Tears of disappointment blurred his eyes.

LAURIE FELL ONTO her bed, aimed her exam booklet at the bureau, threw, and missed. The French test, with its F circled in red, landed on the floor. She had never failed a test in her life, and it felt horrible. She had failed it because she had been with Kevin instead of studying. In the past she had always managed to juggle a social life and good grades. That was pre–Kevin.

And another bio paper was overdue, and even if she managed to finish by tomorrow, the best she could do would be a C. She was too exhausted to pull an all-nighter anyway.

The phone rang. Oh, great, she thought dramatically, the inquisition.

It was Jessica. The conversation began amiably, but before long the strain of keeping the F a secret and dodging her mother's questions began to give her a searing headache.

"It's just that I'm worried about you, Laurie. You always loved concerts and lectures. And I haven't heard you talk about a single play or concert you've seen on campus. Not even parties."

Out of spite, Laurel held back about meeting Alan. She didn't wait for her mom's next remark. "Listen, Mom, I know you don't want to see it, but Kevin . . . well, is very different. He's talented, Mom, and he's special. Beneath the button-downs, the Docks, the Shetland sweaters everyone wears, well, there's a lot more." As she listened to herself, she wondered if she was talking to herself as much as to her mother. Was she protesting too much about Kevin? Trying too hard to justify him?

Her mother didn't respond.

"I've had it easy," Laurel went on. "I just won't abandon someone who's had a hard life, run away from the first problems I face."

"What problems?" her mother asked, trying not to sound as alarmed as she felt.

"Mother, *please,* I just don't want to talk anymore," and she hung up.

Now what? Kevin would arrive at nine as usual, with his candles and romantic music on tape, with wine and flowers—the whole so familiar routine. She got up off the bed, grabbed her bio books, and sat down at the computer. She opened a new document and stared at the screen, the enormity of writing a paper in one night descending on her. She didn't even have a topic. She thumbed through the index of the basic text, hoping for an original idea, but her mind kept wandering. Her room was a sty, and Kevin would be irritated. She needed to wash her hair, change her clothes, and . . . Over and over she read the first line of the chapter describing Darwin's voyage on the *Beagle.* Finally, she closed the book, turned off the computer, picked up the test booklet, and dropped it into the circular file.

TOM LOOKED INTO the patchy glass of the hand mirror in what barely passed for a hotel room and realized he had lost quite a bit of weight during this trip. Jess would be shocked if she could see how gaunt his face was. He wouldn't tell her about the murder of a young Swedish environmentalist who had happened on a poacher in the jungle. She had enough to worry about.

He picked up the phone to call Jessica, vowing to gain some weight by the time he returned home for the holidays. But now Laurel's voice rang in his ears. He had just called her after trying Jessica without success. *"Daddy, can't you make her stop?"* He hated being in the middle of these conflicts between mother and daughter. He tried to relax so he could start his conversation with Jessica on an upbeat note. But the memory of Laurel's upset was very much with him.

"I'm *failing,* Dad," she had blurted out. "I don't know what to do. I failed French, I owe two papers in bio, and I have one due in English. . . . God, don't tell Mom. Please."

Jessica's voice broke into his thoughts.

"Hi, love."

"Oh, Tom. It's you at last," Jessica said, her voice flowing over the continents.

How much should I tell her? he wondered.

KEVIN APPROACHED LAUREL'S yellow VW Bug, looking for the "Indians discovered Columbus" bumper sticker. The words were not only meant to be an eye-opener, they helped him identify her car. It turned out there were two yellow VW Bugs at Cornell—one owned by a crunchy granola, and Laurel's. One time Kevin had hidden in the wooded parking lot of the Campus Hill Apartments until two a.m., certain she was at a party there, only to discover, after the owner of the Bug finally came out, that Laurel was fast asleep in her room. Then she had added the bumper sticker her father had sent her, but having no idea of being spied on.

The door was unlocked and he opened it casually, hoping anyone who saw him would think it was his car. He found a notebook and fingered it lovingly.

He rummaged through her tote bag. Class notes were scattered inside along with a half-eaten corn muffin. Laurel had been acting very odd lately. He needed to find out why. He had to know everything about her, anticipate her every move. He was losing her and if she left, he would be totally alone. He flipped open the glove compartment—and suddenly the voice that hung at the edge of his dreams, the question he heard when he saw the woman in the doorway, came into his consciousness. *"She loves me, doesn't she?"*

Whose voice was it?

LAUREL HAD HOVERED around the classroom door, not even entering the lecture hall until she was sure all the seats near Alan were taken.

Now, after the class, she hurried out, but a hand caught her by the arm.

"Are you avoiding me?" Alan asked. "I'm not exactly dangerous, you know."

Laurel smiled. "I'm not so sure."

"I'll take that as a compliment. How about I treat you to a cappuccino?"

When she hesitated he held up his hand. "No strings."

Laurel saw in his open smile an uncomplicated invitation, and she followed him to a popular spot in College Town. When they were seated at a small table near the window in the crowded café she actually, for a change, began to enjoy the fall day, the hubbub of students' voices, the clatter of dishes, and the background music of 10,000 Maniacs. She *relaxed.* And when Alan leaned toward her, describing in detail the Gould lecture she had missed, she began to feel like her old self again.

He even suggested a topic for her paper. "You know, with all this discussion of creationism, you could explore Darwin's religious beliefs. It turns out he was quite religious, but he came to believe that God didn't interfere in the world of nature."

Laurel's eyes came to life. "What a good idea." She leaned her elbows on the table. "I could throw in a few other scientists. Examine their religious beliefs and how it affected their scientific investigations."

"Gould told an anecdote you might be able to use," Alan said. "When the British biologist Haldane was asked by a theologian what his study of nature revealed about the deity, Haldane said, 'God has an inordinate fondness for beetles.' "

Alan laughed but stopped short when he saw Laurel's face turn pale. "You're supposed to laugh, Laurel." He leaned away from the table. "What's the matter?"

The matter had nothing to do with Haldane. She had seen Kevin's face in the window.

"It's nothing, someone I know . . . in the window." She couldn't explain further.

"Let's go," he said, seeing that she was too distracted to finish her coffee. "I'll walk you to the quad." Her expression told him she was grateful that he had asked no more questions.

They walked in silence until they reached the quad. "I've got Darwin's letters," he said. "I'll drop by and give you the book tonight."

"No."

"No? Why not?"

Laurie pictured Kevin sitting on her bed, waiting for her to come home to confront her about Alan. Then at nine he would reappear. . . .

"Not tonight. I . . . have to go out."

"Okay," he said, trying to be cool but actually feeling upset.

And she could see it in his eyes and hear it in his voice, but her anxiety was too great to worry about his feelings for the moment. And, somehow, she felt she was protecting them both from a fate worse than a broken date.

* * *

"HELLO?" JESSICA SLAMMED down the phone.

"You're shaking like a leaf. What's the matter?" Rozsi asked.

"Some crackpot calls and hangs up."

"New York, New York, it's a wonderful town. No reason to jump out of your skin. It happens."

"The phone company says these kooks call from pay phones or don't allow their home numbers to show. So there's no point in getting one of those new ID boxes that show the caller's number."

"It wouldn't hurt."

"Look at this," Jessica said, to change the subject. "Laurie sent me a note and Kevin's latest artwork."

"Why his artwork?"

"God knows." Jessica took a moment and thought it over. "I complimented her on his poem," she admitted.

Rozsi laughed over Jessica's white lie.

"She doesn't send me A papers anymore. I never hear a word about her classes."

Rozsi scrutinized the nasturtiums Kevin had drawn.

"They're so damn perfect," Jessica said.

"He should be a CPA. Take up numbers munching."

"Number *crunching.*"

Rozsi shrugged. "Have it your way." She tapped the drawing of the flowers with her finger. "They have no life, these pretty flowers."

"Bloodless," Jessica said.

Rozsi took off her glasses and looked up at Jessica. "Maybe that's why Laurika sent this. Maybe she senses there is something wrong with Kevin. Maybe she's asking for our help."

Chapter Fifteen

"I PROMISE YOU, Tom," Jessica said. "I'll change my number. Don't even think of coming home now. We're counting on a long Christmas vacation." Jessica gripped the phone and realized her voice was growing louder as if to compensate for the distance between them. "Still, I hope you're not going to take the example of the guy at Harvard who went to the Amazon to study curare and stayed fourteen years."

"He didn't have you to come home to."

"Ah, Tom, dear. You do say the right thing."

"I hope I said the right thing to Laurel. I just spoke to her."

"So, how is she?"

"Laurel? Okay, I guess."

"Well, I think she's in trouble, Tom. I'm worried about her school work and—"

"Freshman year is the hardest, Jess, Don't you remember? I almost dropped out my first year."

"I'd bet my life on it, she's fighting with Kevin. He's behind the problems. I know it's her freshman year, that there are adjustments to be coped with, but Laurie is no airhead, she's a good student. I tell you, Tom, something is very wrong. I just feel it, I know it. . . . Mr. Wonderful sent her such a cri de coeur poem. 'My heart is in ashes on the forest floor.' He probably stole that one too. Perfect for getting her to feel guilty if she dumps him."

"I hear you, Jess, but let's give it a rest. Even if he is part of the problem, we'll be sure to do more harm than good if we alienate her."

"You're right," Jessica said into a long silence. But didn't altogether believe it.

"Didn't Rozsi cut you some slack when you were young? You made the right decisions. You married *me,* didn't you? We've got to let Laurie grow up, Jess."

She let that one go by. He did have a point.

* * *

THERE WAS NO blood on the sheet when Laurel woke up. Another circle on the calendar! Oh, my God, what if I'm pregnant? Her stomach was so tight that for the third straight day she skipped breakfast. Was it morning sickness? So soon? She'd have to get one of those home pregnancy tests.

A scary thought occurred to her, and she rushed to her bureau drawer, found a round plastic container, clicked it open, removed her diaphragm, and held it to the light. Intact, no flaws. And she never took chances, never.

But what would she do if she *was* pregnant? Nothing made you a hundred percent safe. She *couldn't* be tied to Kevin for life. She didn't want a baby, and she didn't want an abortion . . . well, she would *have* to have one.

She took a deep breath, feeling awful, but her anxiety wouldn't let her cry. She found her journal and entered the date: "Fourth day of no period. What to do? What to *do*? If I tell Kevin, he might want the baby. Do I have the right to decide by myself?"

She put her pen down and put her head in her hands. Too much, she said to herself, rocking back and forth. Too much . . .

"I CAN'T STAY. I didn't leave food for Matchka," Rozsi said.

"That cat! You treat it like a baby," Jessica said. But she knew Rozsi was using the cat as an excuse. Rozsi treasured her independence.

Jessica dangled Kevin's drawing of nasturtiums between two fingers.

"He's a cold fish," Rozsi said, repeating earlier impressions.

"I'll drop this in the mail to Laurel along with a check," Jessica said.

Rozsi smiled at the obvious device.

"She needs to be cheered up," Jessica went on. "I wish I could tell her how I feel about his drawing." She slipped Kevin's card and a check into a priority mail envelope. She'd send it down the mail chute on her way to drive Rozsi home.

"I'll write to her," Rozsi said. "She listens to me."

Jessica ignored the dig and handed her a piece of note paper and a pen.

"Darling Angel," Rozsi wrote, "I hope you are healthy and happy and having a good time. And also maybe learning something. We recieved your short note and the card that your boyfriend made for you. Is this artist friend Kevin making my *draga* Laurika happy? You deserve the best, my darling. Write to your *nagymama* and spill your heart out to me. Love and million kisses, Rozsi."

Jessica read the letter, admiring the rounded, curlicued elegance of Rozsi's European penmanship. She placed the letter in the envelope, deliberately ignoring a misspelled word. "Perfect," she told Rozsi as she helped her into her overcoat.

A TEAR FROM Laurel's eye plopped onto Rozsi's letter. Rozsi's love, radiating from the letter, had made her cry, and the melodrama of the tear splashing on the page made her laugh, made her feel better. She could allow herself to hope that she wasn't pregnant after all, that maybe her period was just a week late. The home pregnancy test *had* been negative. But when she had visited the infirmary to double-check, afraid her own test was inaccurate, the nurse had convinced her to return for a blood test on the tenth day. Now she decided that if the test proved positive, she would tell Rozsi, swear her to secrecy. She was wise, she would help her. . . .

Laurie took her journal from the bureau: "Seventh day and still no period. The truth is, I'm scared. Mom hates Kevin. So I can't tell her. I want to tell my *nagymama*—but she's eighty. Is it fair to worry an old lady with my problems?" She paused a long time before she wrote the last lines. "I want to tell you all about Kevin, my little *nagymama.* About how unhappy I am. But I think I love him and I'm so confused. . . . I know I can trust you, so I'll wait three more days, and if I am pregnant with your great-grandchild, I'll ask you what to do. About everything!"

AS ALWAYS, KEVIN looked around before opening the car door. He had decided to intelligence-gather between classes. Early in the afternoon she had called to cancel out on tonight, saying she had to work in the library—her excuse now for coming home later and later for their nine o'clock dates. And she'd been jittery all week, not interested in sex.

He found her appointment book and thumbed through it. When he reached the pages for the current month, he peered out the window. No other cars in the lot behind the dorm, not a soul to be seen. He scanned the entries, searching for the unusual—library books due, psych paper, exam, exam. Then he found it; a notation in red with exclamation points—"gyn. 9 a.m.!!" An appointment three days from today.

Suddenly the musty interior of the old car nauseated him. She was pregnant! Was that why she'd been so cold to him? He replaced the book and casually headed for the front of the building to watch the dorm entrance and her window. He could make out movement behind the slats in her blind, so he crossed over to the playing field and stood by a tree, certain he was hidden by the branches of a huge bush. In any case, she wouldn't head his way. She would turn left to the lot and drive her Bug to a class at the other end of the campus. He took a sketch pad out of his book bag and began to draw her from memory. But the vision of her pregnant, of her belly bulging out, kept getting in the way. He almost gagged at the thought of fucking her while a fetus was growing inside her. Her visit to the doctor might be routine, he tried to tell himself. Well, he would soon find out. Then decide what to do.

The sun was showing through the blinds when Laurel checked her watch. She saw it was past eleven. She shut the journal, tucking Rozsi's letter inside and quickly placed it, along with Kevin's card, beneath her undies in her bureau drawer. If she rushed, she might catch Alan at the bagel place in College Town, his favorite hangout.

KEVIN TIGHTENED THE slats of the blind. He had let himself in with his key, but he had no legitimate excuse for being there. Well, he could say he had misplaced his wallet or his keys. He listened for footsteps or voices outside the door. Sometimes Laurel forgot stuff and had to come back. The top drawer of her dresser was open slightly. He opened it wide and looked in, noting at once a familiar object peeking out from under Laurel's bras. His card to Laurel. He had wondered why it was no longer stuck in the frame of the mirror. Then her diary! He had struck gold! A letter was folded between the last two entries, but he couldn't take the time to see who it was from. First he had to read Laurel's secret thoughts.

Fear and anger took over as he began to read. *Alan?* Who was Alan? And what about the gyn appointment in the book. *Was* she pregnant? Was it even his baby? Just who the fuck was Alan? A deadly calm took over as he read, "Mom hates Kevin." He thought he had neutralized that bitch. He forced himself to go on reading, relieved somewhat that the one test had been negative, and even more relieved when he read she thought she still loved him. But things were falling apart. He had to find a way to make things right again. He would marry her, then later . . . But read the letter.

When he had finished, he folded Rozsi's letter and placed it neatly back into the book. Laurel was planning to ask the old hag for advice. She was more important to Laurel than he had thought. He had work to do. He would have to take care of the old Hungarian.

KEVIN CROSSED THE quad to get to his next class. Often there was no way to avoid Mini and Doug, the joined-at-the-hip Bobbsey Twins, who had a class nearby. Although all were well aware of the others' presence, they usually pretended not to see one another. Sometimes Mini and Doug even veered off at an angle, or blended in with other students to forestall a meeting. Today Kevin spotted them first, walking toward him, and zeroed in on them.

They had been talking animatedly, and before they knew it he was there, right in front of them.

"Hi, folks!" he said.

Doug looked at Mini for only an instant. He took hold of her arm and pulled her away, trying to move around Kevin. "Sorry we don't have time to chat," Doug said.

"Well, I have an announcement about Laurel I think you'll be interested in."

They hesitated.

"We're getting married. That's right, we're tying the knot," he said and strode past them, leaving them speechless.

"I'm in *major* shock," Mini finally said.

"How do you think Laurie feels?"
"Tying the *knot*?"
"More like tying the noose," Doug said.

LAUREL HURRIED TOWARD Ollie's bagel shop, experiencing her first hunger pangs in days. She spotted Alan, seated alone at a large table, munching away on a bagel with lox and cream cheese. The friendly, sunny restaurant had plants and windows everywhere. It was just the cheerful kind of place Alan would choose.

She watched him for a moment. His legs were crossed, and he was glancing at a newspaper opened up before him. He looked so relaxed in his sweatshirt, jeans, and an old pair of Keds. Why was she running to Alan? And why hadn't she told Alan that she had a boyfriend?

She sat down across from Alan as he looked up, broad smile on his face, and it struck her that those brown eyes of his weren't searching her face for assurance, for direction, for anything. Alan was just glad to see her. That simple. What a relief!

She would be as open and direct as Alan was. She would tell him about Kevin.

MCKENZIE, WHO WAS parked on Sandy's desk, picked up her phone and held it out to her. "It's Lloyd Martin again," he said. There was a smirk on his face as he hopped off the desk and left her alone in the office.

Sandy held the phone a moment before speaking. So it was true. Lloyd was coming on to her. She had sensed he was interested, that he made excuses to call her. But she had never been attracted to him. He wasn't bad-looking, but he was so—so conventional. She tried mentally to redesign him. First he would have to cut his long, slicked-back hair . . . or maybe let it grow. She almost laughed out loud at the image of a ponytail over the back collar of his neat, proper suit. He had a nice bod. In a pair of jeans and a T-shirt. Those wing-tipped shoes had to *go.* Maybe if he grew a beard. But a blond beard? She put the phone to her ear. "What's up, Lloyd?"

"Sandy? Hi. I have news. Important news. You can close the case on April Meadows. The serial killed her. We nailed him a few days ago—just finished questioning him—and he confessed to everything, with all the details. We've got a signature and a videotape, and he's willing to be polygraphed."

Sandy was stunned. She looked up at the photo of April still tacked to the bulletin board.

"Are you sure? Who is this guy?"

"Some creep who was seen picking up the waitress in a bar the night she was murdered."

Sandy put out her hand and touched the photo. "I can't believe it."

"I knew you would say that. If you're not convinced, why don't you come up here this evening? Talk about it over a brew."

"I don't think so, Lloyd. I've got work piled up—"

"One less case now," Lloyd said.

Sandy hung up, still staring at April's picture. She couldn't pull the photo down. Not yet.

SANDY FELT THAT for the past hour Lloyd had been eyeing her across the table with more than professional interest. And it made her self-conscious. She had changed her mind and at the last minute accepted his invitation. Why, she wasn't entirely sure, but after she'd hung up on him and looked at that picture of April Meadows, she just didn't want to be alone. She finished her beer and squirmed in the booth's leather seat while Lloyd paid the check.

She would give it one last try to persuade him that the serial had duped him.

"The psycho who killed April was meticulous," Sandy said. "Do you really think a serial freak who leaves body parts around would scrub up April's blood . . . ?"

"I *think,* Sandy, that you're obsessed with this Billy Owens. Why can't you just accept it? The case is closed."

Sandy pulled her car keys from her purse. "I don't know why the moron confessed. But you admitted he couldn't even remember where he got the hammer. And his story about April letting him into her house to make a phone call is pure horseshit." She stood up. "Thanks for the beer."

"What's the rush?"

"I'm *not* closing out the case, Lloyd."

Chapter Sixteen

ALAN AND LAURIE stopped on the bridge at Casadilla to look into the gorge. "You mean you can't even be *seen* with a guy?" Alan asked.

"I don't want to hurt him, Alan. Kevin's been hurt enough."

"But . . ."

"Is this the bridge despondent students hurl themselves from when they flunk out?" she asked.

"That's a myth," Alan said, looking at Laurie with some concern.

She laughed. "Don't worry. I'm not jumping off a bridge just because I'm overdue on a couple of papers."

"Do you know the story of the two lovers kissing on the Fall Creek suspension bridge—and the bridge tips over?"

"Kevin and me?"

"Well, from what you've told me about Kevin . . ."

Laurie kept her eyes on the falls and gripped the sides of the stone wall.

Alan glanced at her. "Is it my imagination, or were you looking over your shoulder as we were talking?"

She turned to him, embarrassed. "Alan, it could be all this is more my hang-up than his. I mean, I do tend to exaggerate, to dramatize."

"But I still can't come by with the Darwin book?"

She laughed. "Come by at nine."

LAURIE STOPPED IN front of Rockefeller Hall and watched Alan as he strolled toward Baker lab. She had been so critical of Kevin, but she did have her reasons—Kevin's nine o'clock sex, and his weird humming when he was upset, his jealousy, even his not being able to swim—a grown man who couldn't swim? Too afraid of the water. Why? And suddenly Kevin was there, in back of her.

"What are you doing *here*?"

"I just wanted to see you."

"I have class. And I *told* you I had work to do after, that I have exams, papers. Kevin, why don't you listen to me?"

"I do, I do. I just thought . . . You seemed so . . . different. I don't want you to be unhappy."

"I only have five minutes—"

"Marry me, Laurel."

Students were brushing by them, hurrying to their classes.

"What?" Laurel whispered.

"I mean it. Maybe you still don't know how much I love you—"

"Kevin, what's come over you?"

"Tonight? We'll talk about it tonight?"

"No. I *can't.*" Laurel shook her head in astonishment and started up the steps. "I'll—I'll see you tomorrow."

He grabbed her arm, trying to pull her back. "I'm not good enough for you?" he said under his breath.

Laurel looked around, embarrassed, hoping no one was watching as she pulled her arm from his grip. Then, without saying a word or looking back, she ran up the steps into the building.

"DID YOU SEE the look on Alan's face when we told him Laurel was becoming the Bride of Frankenstein?" Doug waited at the debate office door for Mini, his finger on the light switch. "Why didn't you clue him about Kevin's threat?" Mini said, and took up her backpack just as Doug turned off the lights.

"At first I didn't want to tell Laurel because she always defends him. He has such a hold over her." Doug locked the door and checked his watch. It was after eight-thirty. They'd worked straight through dinner. "And everyone knows we can't make nationals without her, so they would assume we were just sandbagging Laurie's romance to get her back."

Mini nodded.

"And something always stops me from telling Alan about Kevin."

"I know what you mean," Mini said, clattering down the short flight of stairs alongside Doug. "To be honest, I don't want to get in

Kevin's face. I have enough problems. I worked until dawn, only slept three hours."

They stepped out into the crisp night.

"I hear what you're saying," he said. "And now that she's supposedly marrying the creep, Alan is out of the triangle."

"The Bermuda Triangle," Mini said. "And we all know what happens to people who wind up there."

LAUREL STAMPED HER foot in anger. "I don't *believe* it! I wonder how many people he's told that crazy story to."

"You mean, it's not true?" Alan said.

"Of course not. We're just going together. I mean, I only met him four months ago."

"I don't mind saying I'm very glad to hear it," Alan said. He sat down on the bed. "But I think you should rethink going with the guy. He sounds like he's losing it."

Laurie tried to laugh it off. "I was afraid you'd stood me up. Now I'm surprised you came at all."

Alan kicked off his loafers and leaned back on an elbow. "I guess I don't discourage too easily."

Laurel smiled. She reached over and put a CD into the player.

"Oh, before I forget . . ." He reached over for the book he had brought and put it on her desk.

"You're sweet," Laurel said, and flipped through the pages as they listened to the Dave Brubeck Quartet and Johnny Desmond's sax floating the notes in an old jazz tune.

WHEN SANDY WALKED into the prosecutor's office, she was glad she had decided to put in an appearance. A live human being made a bigger impression than a voice on the telephone. Wendell Wilkerson, the D.A., was squeezing her in between phone calls and frenzied requests from his secretary.

Sandy had outlined the April Meadows case, including her theory about Billy Owens, in a detailed memo and had faxed it to him. Now she looked Wilkerson over as she spoke. He was a pretty off-putting older guy, skinny, with wire-rimmed glasses. But he was her only chance.

"Don't try to pin the Meadows's murder on Jukes," Sandy began, hurrying to get out her story. "The victim's mother just told me that April was a member of Latchkey Kids, an organization to help kids of working parents. She was trained *never* to let a stranger into the house, even to make an emergency call. And the serial's stories about gaining entry conflict, on top of which his M.O. and profile don't add up to his being her killer. What was he doing so far from home? And why would he bash April with a hammer—he strangled all his other victims from behind." She took a breath. "The killer of April Meadows took great precautions to hide the body and clean up the blood—"

The phone rang, and while Wilkerson talked, she checked the clipboard on her lap for more ammunition. When he hung up, she continued: "The killer went to great lengths to hide the weapon, the picture, the smashed phone, and to collect April's stuff—the glass trinket, the wallet. It's just not the serial's style. He's a butcher, a compulsive chopper, a sexual deviant. He's an addict like the Ripper. April's killer is careful, has more self-control."

She stopped talking when Wilkerson stood up from his desk, looking pointedly at his watch. "A meeting," he said.

The clipboard clattered to the floor as Sandy stood up.

"Thanks," he said, extending his hand. "At least something to think about."

AFTER FRENCH CLASS Laurel proceeded over to Kevin's dorm, a place she hardly visited even though his likable roommate, Stevie, was out a lot. True to form, Stevie was about to split. And when he saw her face he rushed to make an even faster exit.

Laurel wasn't prepared for what she saw. The wall over Kevin's desk was covered with pencil, pen-and-ink, and charcoal drawings of her face. All the old posters had been removed, and the room looked like a shrine. But she would say nothing. She had come on other business.

There were dark circles under Kevin's eyes, but for once Laurel had no feelings of pity or compassion for him. He had probably been up all night obsessing over why she had canceled their date. Well, this time she wasn't about to lay a guilt trip on herself. She had come to tell him off. She would deal with the embarrassing Memorial to Laurel later.

"*Why* did you do it?" she said as soon as Stevie had shut the door. "The whole campus thinks we're *engaged*."

"Who told you?"

"That's *not* the issue here."

"Marry me, Laurel. I love you, and you—"

"Don't be ridiculous!" She tried not to look at the drawings. Do you put lighted candles under them? she almost asked.

"It's your family, isn't it? *They* disapprove."

"It's not that . . ." I disapprove, she wanted to say, but upset as she was, she didn't want to go too far with it, open up his anger. "We're too young," she said finally, weakly. She was furious at herself for holding back, but she knew Kevin. "What *possessed* you, Kevin?"

"I guess I let my feelings for you carry me away. I wasn't trying to hurt you, Laurie. I just love you so much I wanted everyone to know how much. I mean, in case you needed me—" He stopped short, knew the instant the words were out of his mouth that he had made a mistake.

Laurel was instantly suspicious. Did he know her period was late? How? But, of course, there was only one way—*he had been reading her diary.*

"This sudden interest in marrying me, Kevin . . . where does it come from?"

"I . . . saw you going into the doctor's office. The gyn on campus. Everyone knows it. I guessed you were pregnant. Well, is it true?"

"You just *happened* to be there?"

"I knew your schedule for that day, and I wanted to surprise you. I had a present for you. I wanted—"

"You *followed* me!"

"No . . . it wasn't that way."

"You *did.* What gives you the right?" She paced angrily around the room.

"You looked so unhappy and—and"—the next gambit was sheer brilliance—"your mother called."

"What? She called *you*? I don't believe it."

"She was worried when she couldn't reach you."

Laurel sat down hard on the bed and put her fists to her temples. "I can't win! I *cannot win*!"

THE NEXT MORNING, Kevin kneaded the cramp in his neck, the aftermath of the too familiar nightmare. *He was on his hands and knees, washing the blood, terrified that time had run out, that he would be caught. And sure enough, the door had opened, revealing a shadowy figure in the doorway. "She loves me, doesn't she?" the voice had asked.*

His meeting with Laurel had been a disaster. She was cutting him off, wouldn't even discuss why she was seeing the doctor. "It's my body," she had told him. "And it's my life. We are *not* getting married, and you must stop saying it." And now his head ached with the realization that he had made a terrible tactical error. He had infuriated Laurel and probably made an enemy in Jessica. Laurel was slipping away from him. He had one more hope. He had to make a visit to this Rozsi.

SANDY HAD TO admit Lloyd's interest was flattering, but it was distracting her from her work. She turned back to her computer. Case number 73136 involved an armed robber who had shot a store clerk in broad daylight, panicked, left the money behind, driven straight home in his own car, his license being ID'd by three witnesses, and sat waiting in his room for the police to arrest him. Every case should be this easy.

"He's not my type," she told herself while she added the finishing touches to her concluding statement. "But then, who is my type? A junkie, a guy who likes to live on the edge? A risk taker who has no control over his violent behavior like my ex?" In the available field, Lloyd was looking good. Maybe even pretty good. She took a last look at the screen and pushed Print. Her thoughts hummed along with the sound of the printer. What am I talking myself into?

The phone rang. It was McKenzie. "Hang on to your report. We just checked out our witless wonder. He's wanted in Michigan for whacking his wife."

* * *

"INSULTS ROLL OFF Wendell Wilkerson like water off a duck's back," his mother had once said. With a name like Wendell, which in grade school could become "Wendy," he'd had to develop a tough hide. Sometimes he thought he had chosen to become a prosecutor to settle up old scores, but he also felt he was even-handed and not vindictive in his practice. He rarely brought to a grand jury a case he didn't believe he could, or should, win.

He had just finished rereading Detective Sandy Ungar's memo. Appealing lady—woman, he corrected himself. He thought of his wife, Carrie, who had died two years ago. She had just decided to go back to school to start a new career. . . . Sandy looked a little like Carrie. And she had the same heartfelt dedication.

Forget it. He was too old for Sandy. And she probably wasn't attracted to him. He remembered how flustered she had been, not knowing that his taciturn manner, his stern appraisal of her, was simply habit. He had become even more silent after Carrie's death. And he probably appeared forbidding. Carrie had seen his softer side.

Wilkerson looked at his watch. Exactly nine o'clock. The legal aide, Joe Burns, who wasn't the type to be punctual, was walking past his secretary. Exactly on time. People understood not to mess with Wilkerson. He hated waiting.

Burns didn't waste time. He hoisted his briefcase up on the desk and removed paperwork on Gordon Jukes. "My client wasted the three bimbos, Wendell. But he didn't kill April Meadows."

"Who's going to believe that, Joseph?"

"It's a matter of justice. If *you* believe it, that's what counts."

"I've got him cold on all four homicides, Joe."

"He'll plead guilty to the other charges," Burns said. "No insanity defense. You get him put away for good. Insanity plea and he could walk."

Wilkerson looked unconvinced.

"He *didn't* kill the girl. The asshole confessed because he wanted to get a TV contract."

Wilkerson shook his head.

"It's the truth. I'm not bullshiting you. Not this time, anyway."

Wilkerson thought about Sandy's memo under Joe's paperwork. "I'll think about it," he said.

Either way, he couldn't lose on this case.

LAUREL UNDRESSED BEHIND a curtain in the examining room and dropped her clothes on a chair. She slipped into the light green gown the nurse had left and stepped up onto the examination table. Soon she would be splayed on the stirrups, feeling exposed and absurd. But most of all she would be embarrassed to face the doctor after the speech she had made in September on her first visit to decide on the right contraceptive.

"A diaphragm is ninety-nine percent effective," Dr. Colson had said. "And, unlike the pill, it has no side effects. If you're the responsible type, sticking to one partner, and you don't forget or become sloppy, or drink and—"

"I'm not going to forget!" Laurel had said indignantly. "I believe in a woman's right to choose, but I don't take the creation of a life lightly."

What a pompous ass she had been. After Dr. Colson had measured her for a diaphragm, she had never regretted the decision. She had even discussed it with her mother, who had approved.

The nurse came in, took her blood pressure, and sent her to the scale. After recording the results, she drew a blood sample. What would her mother say? Laurel wondered as the nurse left with the vial. Somehow this wasn't something to talk to her father about.

Dr. Colson, a tall, dark-eyed woman with sleek black hair, came in and peered at Laurel's chart. Laurel could see a long shirt and tights under her lab coat and white socks and sneakers on her feet.

"Are you in good health?" the doctor asked.

Laurel nodded.

"I see you've lost five pounds. On purpose?"

"Not really."

"Let's check you out." She stood at the head of the table as Laurel put her feet up in the stirrups. "Exactly ten days, huh? I guess you want to know pronto."

Laurie felt the doctor press once and quickly on her insides, and soon it was over.

"You look good," Dr. Colson said. "Everything's as it should be."

"That's it?"

"I warm the speculum and you don't feel a thing." The doctor removed her gloves.

"I don't understand," Laurie said, sitting up. "I was so careful. I never missed a night, and I checked my diaphragm." Her voice broke. "Am I the one percent? The unlucky one in a hundred who gets pregnant?"

"You may not be pregnant, if you were really careful. Your diaphragm's still new, and you haven't lost enough weight to warrant a change in diaphragm size."

"But . . ."

"I suspect the one percenters who get pregnant aren't all that careful."

"But it's been ten days."

"Hang on, Laurel. You'll know in a few hours."

Chapter Seventeen

"I'm no spring chicken anymore," Rozsi mumbled as she pulled her shopping cart up the three steps leading to her courtyard. She caught her breath at the top and peered into the cart. "Did I forget the parsnip for the soup?" she wondered. "No, there it is, in the shopping bag, next to the carrots and celery." The cold she was hoping to cure with chicken soup was sapping her energy, and she leaned more heavily than usual on her cart as she pushed it to the front door. She pulled her keys from her skirt pocket, fit a key into the lock, maneuvered her cart through the door. . . .

Too late, his shadow caught the corner of her eye. He shoved her into the lobby, ripping her pocketbook from her arm. She opened her mouth to scream, but the steel door clanged shut behind her. She was doubled over on her cart, the handle poking into her chest. It had only taken a push, and her small frame had catapulted through the door. She stood up straight, took three breaths, and felt the ache from the bruise on her arm where her pocketbook had been.

Rozsi listened to her heart as if it were someone else's. She was acutely aware of her surroundings, of the eerie quiet. The schoolchildren in the playground across the street had not yet been let free. The neighbors had done their errands. It was that lull in the day she had ignored—until today.

As she wheeled her cart to the elevator, the face of the thief flashed before her, and her hand shook as she reached out for the button. She listened for the sound of the elevator descending, terrified that before it did, the front door would open and this time the mugger would kill her. An irrational fear. The door was locked. But she waited for the elevator as if it meant life or death. Only three summers ago, just down the block, she had fought off a thirteen-year-old who had grabbed her around the neck from behind. She had somehow twisted free of him, smacked him hard with her pocketbook, yelled bloody murder, and brought all the neighbors to her rescue. Who would have saved her today?

The elevator bumped to the lobby and took her straight to the sixth floor. She unlocked her apartment door, closed it firmly behind her, and slid the steel rod of the police lock in place. With her coat still on, she dropped into her favorite chair to rest a moment. The groceries would have to wait. She watched in the mirror as the color returned to her cheeks and checked her angina patch. Then she patted her chest and smiled; she had outsmarted the crook. She removed her money, several bills folded in a handkerchief that after the lesson of the last mugging she always secured to her bra with a safety pin. The only thing this thief had gotten away with was an old pocketbook, a few tissues, a lipstick, and a comb! And the soft mound in her blouse had cushioned her fall onto the handle of the cart.

She reached for the telephone on the table beside her. All she had to do was press the button with Jessica's name on it. But she waited.

She so wanted to tell Jessica. But she wouldn't make the same mistake twice. Last mugging she had proudly told her daughter how brave she had been, and it had started Jessica on endless harangues. "Move out." "Move in with me." "Move to a senior residence."

"I'm not budging," Rozsi had informed her daughter. "Losing my freedom is a bigger danger than losing a lousy pocketbook."

But now she wanted to tell someone. She couldn't keep it all to herself. Still, she resisted the temptation. If Jessica found out her mother had been mugged again, she would declare an all-out war. The telephone waited next to her. She looked around her apartment, at a lifetime's accumulation of possessions. All that was left of her family, long gone, was within these walls: photographs in old albums, hand-embroidered linens stacked in the closet, letters yellowing in cracking cardboard boxes, and Old World paintings hanging on the walls. The bedroom set she had bought with her husband fifty years ago, the bed they slept on—with a new mattress, of course—were still in the bedroom. Even Jessica's baby hair and milk teeth had been saved in a hand-painted wooden box from Hungary. These were her memories, and she clung to them.

She looked at the phone. She could call her friend Esther, but Rozsi didn't need hysterics right now, she needed Jessica. She ran the tap in the kitchen, filled a glass, and drank. Back in her chair, she listened for a long time to the ticking of the grandfather clock.

Just as the clock chimed, the phone rang. "The world is full of surprises," she thought as she picked up the receiver. And she was glad to hear a familiar voice. Even Kevin's.

Rozsi could hear the tremor in her voice, and she struggled for control.

"Are you okay?" Kevin asked immediately. Rozsi doubted he cared.

"Yes. Yes. I'm healthy as an ox."

"You don't sound too good. Should I call Jessica?"

"Absolutely not!"

"Then tell me what's wrong."

Rozsi knew she had no choice. She had to tell him or he would turn her in. "I was mugged. But I'm *okay.* I'm not hurt—just shaken up. Don't tell Jessica."

"Why?"

"I haven't the strength to explain it now. Just do me this favor."

"Are you alone?"

"Yes, but my door is locked up tight."

"Call the police right now. I'll be there tonight."

"But—"

"I won't tell anyone—even Laurie."

The phone went dead. He had hung up before she could tell him not to come.

FINALLY, THE NURSE called Laurel into the office. As she waited for the doctor, she stared at the framed degrees on the wall, whistling the tune that Kevin hummed when he was nervous. She was a good whistler, but she stopped abruptly. The tune was the sizzle on the short fuse of Kevin's temper when he hummed it. It meant he was over the edge.

She tapped her heel nervously and whistled a different tune. "Nobody knows the trouble I've seen."

The doctor arrived and shut the door.

"Good news. At least I think it's good. You're not pregnant."

Laurie's whole body relaxed. Her shoulders dropped. "Wow! It *is* good news. Very good. But . . . what's going on with my body?"

"Since you're not a jock overexercising, I would say it's tension. Tension can cause you to miss a cycle. It's not that uncommon. Have you been under any special stress lately?"

"School. My boyfriend. My mother!"

The doctor smiled. "That will do it every time." She waited for Laurel to speak, but she seemed deep in thought. "Why don't you give me a call in a few days?" the doctor said. "Physically, you're A-okay."

AT THE SOUND of the phone, Jessica snatched it up and practically spat her "Hello!"

"What's up, Mom?" Laurel asked. "Is that loony still calling you?"

"Is it that obvious?" Jessica squirmed out of her coat and dropped her briefcase on the couch. "I'm just tired. I just got home, had a hard day at work, and then my cab got caught in a traffic jam on Park Avenue."

"Why didn't you walk?" Laurel knew her mother loved walking.

"I'm kind of exhausted today. That maniac called last night, and I couldn't get back to sleep. Then the garbage trucks arrived, grinding away. I had visions of shooting out the tires."

"Take it easy, Mom. Why don't you—"

"I know. Change my number. I will. Don't get excited. You just got me at a bad time. And you know how crazy I get when I'm awakened. Things seem much more dire in the middle of the night. I tend to panic."

Laurel laughed. "When I was a kid, if I had a cough at night, Daddy had to keep you from giving me mouth-to-mouth."

"Very funny. You sound cheery today, my dear."

Laurel was on a high. I'm not pregnant, I'm not pregnant, sang through her head.

She had floated home from the doctor in a happy daze after hearing the news. And when she'd found Kevin's note under her door, saying he had late studio hours that evening, she'd been doubly relieved. "I am cheery," she said.

"Well, *that's* good news."

"But I do have a bone to pick with you."

Jessica took the portable phone with her into the living room so she could make herself a drink.

"Did you call Kevin?"

"Only because I couldn't get hold of you." Jessica opened the bar and got out the scotch, recalling the conversation in which Kevin had tricked her. She poured the scotch. "It was awhile ago—"

"Mom, you're still treating me like a *child.*"

Jessica was silent. She added water to the glass, wondering what to say.

"Please don't do that again."

That skunk, that manipulator! Jessica thought. She took a big gulp of her drink. "I won't," she said. "Believe me, honey, I won't."

ROZSI IS THE queen bee, Kevin thought as he climbed the steps up to street level. According to the map, her building was seven blocks from the subway. Night was falling, and the sidewalks were bustling with men and women shopping for dinner on their way home from work. Hundreds of straphangers were streaming out of the subway. Kevin tried to read the store signs, written in Spanish, and wondered at the strange foods in the grocery windows. Exotic smells wafted into the streets and mingled in the brisk air. He heard no English spoken until he reached the schoolyard across from Rozsi's building. Suddenly a cacophony of sound assailed his ears. The rumbling of the underground subway nearby, the screeching of car horns, and children's intermittent voices worked in furious counterpoint to the banging of a basketball on concrete.

Kevin recalled one of his first dates with Laurel, when they'd talked about city noise. "Did you ever hear of John Cage, the composer?" Laurel had asked.

Kevin had learned fast not to pretend when he was ignorant. Even college kids couldn't know everything. He also sensed that Laurel enjoyed teaching him. "Nope," he had answered.

"He was a composer who thought unpleasant noise was music, like the honking of horns or garbage cans rattling."

"Yeah . . . like it may be awful but it might be art. Like that Karen Findley we saw last night."

"Right."

He knew he had scored points. And now he listened to the street sounds with new ears.

Rozsi rang him in through the intercom, and he used the time in the elevator to straighten his tie and brush his jacket. He pressed the buzzer and stood patiently outside her door, holding aloft the bouquet of daisies he'd bought in Grand Central Station.

The peephole opened, then the door, and as Rozsi cautiously greeted him, he thrust the flowers into her hands. The word about her that had eluded him leaped to mind.

Matriarch. That's what Rozsi was. And he had come to woo her.

The cat came rushing in as soon as he heard the whirring of the can opener, and Rozsi emptied half the can into Matchka's bowl.

"It was a push-in robbery," she told Kevin as she checked the pot. Good thing she'd made the chicken soup in time to feed him. "The policewoman, she told me. I described to her and her nice young male partner what the mugger looked like. Turns out he's been robbing all the old women in the neighborhood."

She sat down to join Kevin as he took another spoon of soup and shook his head sympathetically.

"I wasn't thinking after it happened." She ladled the last of the soup into his bowl and turned off the gas jet. "I'm glad you advised me to call the police. They came right up to my apartment."

He was glad he had missed them. When they were finished eating, he cleared the dishes and added them to those already in the dishwasher. The hot soup had flushed his face, and he opened the steamed-over window. "No, no," Rozsi warned. She pointed at Matchka. "The cat likes to stroll on the ledge." She tried to close the stuck window, and Kevin helped.

"I guess I'm getting old," Rozsi said.

"You had a bad scare today," he assured her.

"Let's forget that," she said. She made circular swoops on her Formica table with a soapy sponge and dropped it into the sink. "I have something to show you," and led him into the living room.

"You're an artist. Look at this!" Suddenly she turned off the lights and turned on another switch. On the coffee table next to a gift box was a ceramic sculpture. It was a hexagonal vase containing, surprisingly, a bunch of neon flowers in magenta, green, and blue.

"That's cool," Kevin said.

"It's called 'out on the edge,' " Rozsi said, turning the lights back on. "It's a surprise for Jessica."

"I've seen sculptures using lighting, but nothing like this before," he said.

"Jessica's friend Ricky is a lighting expert. She helped me."

"Wait till I tell Laurie."

"You mustn't!"

"I won't!" He raised his hand. "No one will ever know I've been here."

"It was very kind of you to come when an old lady was in trouble. Why *did* you come?" she said.

"I had some business in town, thought I'd drop by."

Rozsi knew he was lying. He was buttering her up. There's no fool like an old fool, she thought. But he's got the wrong old fool.

Kevin saw her back stiffen.

It was a no-go with this old witch, he thought as he excused himself. Walking into the bathroom, he noticed the dumb cat used a litter box under the sink and gave the box a kick.

He had a long drive back. Nothing accomplished so far. But then he looked at the black-and-white tiles on the floor and the frosted glass in the bathroom window . . . and the idea came to him. He was smiling as he lifted the window, just enough for a cat to fit through.

ROZSI STROKED MATCHKA, who was lying next to her on the bed, purring. But when Rozsi stretched under the covers, the cat jumped off. She reached for the TV remote but changed her mind and turned out the lamp. The dark seemed strangely comforting. She was exhausted. But as she lay there staring at the ceiling, her thoughts jumped from Kevin to the mugging to the police. . . .

She closed her eyes, feeling more tired than she could ever remember.

* * *

As the Greyhound bus sped away, Kevin was relieved to be on the road and away from the crafty old coot. He had tried to talk to her about his love for Laurel, his plans for marriage. But she had cut him dead. And the whole damn family was against him.

Usually Rozsi slept through the chiming of the grandfather clock, but this time her eyes snapped open. Something was wrong. She felt around her on the bed. Matchka was missing. He always snuggled against her at night, waiting until dawn for her to awaken and feed him breakfast.

Rozsi grabbed her robe and, barefoot, ran along the cold wood floors. She checked the chair in the living room where Matchka slept during the day. Not there. Was he sick? She looked in the kitchen. No Matchka. She checked the bathroom litter box. Not there.

Then she saw the open window, and panic took hold. No cat on the ledge. She raised the window higher, stuck her head out, and looked down. There was Matchka right under the street lamp, easy to see because he was all white, his fur so beautiful. He looked as if he were resting. Asleep. But Rozsi knew better. Matchka was dead.

She reached out for support, her palm finding the tiled wall. The fluttering dread became palpable, filling her chest. She took a step, but with each breath a vest was drawn more tightly across her chest.

She moved slowly, gingerly, and after interminable minutes she made it into the living room, where she lowered herself into her chair. Her glasses were right next to the phone. She found Jessica's name on her phone and with a trembling finger pressed the button. A new pain seized her.

The phone shook Jessica from a deep sleep. "Hello," she said, her voice stretching from a dream into reality.

She heard nothing. Then only a whisper.

"Who's there?" Another ghostly whisper.

She slammed down the phone when she saw her clock. It was two a.m. It was that damn psycho calling again. For an instant she pictured Ed Polley's face. She was groggy from the pill she had taken.

Rozsi pressed the button again, struggled to raise her voice, but the pain squeezed the breath from her.

Jessica finally answered after the fifth ring. More ghostly whispers.

"It's Anyuka, Jessica . . ."

But the words were too garbled to decipher. Jessica had to assume it was Polley.

ROZSI TRIED AGAIN. The line was busy. She hung up. I'm afraid, Jessica. I'm afraid . . . Her head felt light. And she slumped over, felt herself falling. She didn't know where she was. She tried to remember Jessica's face, Laurika's face.

It was her mother's face that appeared. Rozsi stretched out on the floor and soon felt a warm kiss brush her cheek. A kiss she had not felt in over seventy years. "Anyuka," she said, fitting herself into her mother's embrace, the soft arms cradling her.

It was Rozsi's last word on this earth.

Chapter Eighteen

As the rabbi read the prayer in Hebrew, Rozsi, in a simple pine coffin, was lowered into the grave. The awe of death and the sight of her father's tombstone beside the open ground numbed Jessica. She tried to imagine Anyuka's face, fearing it would fade away, wishing she had a brother or sister to remember with her. Anyuka's little ironic smile, the worry in her eyes, her look of unqualified love. . . . Who would look at her that way again—through a mother's eyes? Who would love her the way her mother had? Who would help her? For the first time in her life Jessica felt alone.

She felt a chill when she spotted Kevin standing close to Laurie, holding her hand tightly. He's got her in his clutches and you have to get her out, Anyuka would have said.

The rabbi chanted the familiar prayer in the language of her ancestors. And suddenly she could feel her mother's presence. There were so many questions about her mother's past Jessica had wanted to ask her. Why didn't you ever speak of your years in Europe during the war? How were you able to save yourself? She could never ask her now.

And then she thought she heard her mother's voice. "Don't cry, *eletem*," she crooned. Tears came from Jessica's eyes. *Eletem,* my life . . . her mother was consoling her even from the grave.

"I can't stop thinking about Anyuka dying alone," Jessica said when the last guest had left the apartment and long after Laurel and Kevin had said good-bye. The leftover traditional sweets served to the mourners after the burial were all put away, and Jessica sat next to Tom on the couch. She put her head on his shoulder, and felt his arm around her, holding her close. "And I keep seeing Matchka, and

Jamie picking him up in the alley. How he and the super unlocked Rozsi's door—"

"Stop it, Jess. We've been through this."

"And then the police sealing off the apartment. I still can't even get in."

"It's routine when someone dies at home. The cops told you that."

"I keep wondering if she suffered."

"The doctor said it happened very fast. That's probably why she fell off the chair."

"Why didn't she tell me she was mugged? But I know why. She was afraid I would nag her some more about moving."

"You were trying to protect her, Jess. And, face it, she was a very secretive woman." Tom stood up. "I need a glass of sherry. Want one?"

Jessica nodded. "I wonder what other secrets she kept from me?"

I HAVEN'T FORGOTTEN about you, Alan, Kevin thought as he ran his fingers across his alphabetized collection of CD's. He listened to them in order, and was now up to S. He pulled out a Bessie Smith CD and carefully dropped the disk into the player, knowing he would have complete privacy for another hour. Stevie was at his wine-selection class. Of course, Kevin never knew exactly when his roommate would return. He was erratic, whimsical, unlike Kevin. Kevin preferred routine.

Laurel's pregnancy scare had just about blown him out of the water. But when she had announced to him that she wasn't pregnant, he felt that at last he would have her all to himself. *If* certain people wouldn't get in his way . . . people like this Alan.

Kevin forced himself to listen to the music. Actually, it wasn't his favorite, but Laurel loved it. Weird and lugubrious, he thought, using a new word. Tom and Jessica had played it after the funeral.

He dusted his CD's while he thought about the old bitch Rozsi. Things had worked out better than he could have planned—the cat dying, the old lady croaking with a heart attack. The day after his visit she had been found dead on the living room floor! Had she planned to close the window and died before she could do it? Or had she been sick and, by accident, left the window open? Had she died of a heart attack after seeing her cat on the pavement? No one knew. And his secret visit went with her to the grave. Perfect.

But there was still a major obstacle to his marrying Laurel, to becoming part of her family, to hell with what Jessica thought about him. And the obstacle's name was Alan. All through the funeral the name had stuck in his head. He had to do something serious about Alan.

BETSY WILCOX ADJUSTED the strap of the book bag on her shoulder and walked down the dusty road toward home. It hadn't rained for a week, and the weather was unseasonably warm. It reminded her of the fall day when she had first met Kevin. And only now, after a year and a half, the thought of him was a bit less painful. Until lately she hadn't been able to think about him at all; when her mother questioned her about Kevin, she would put her off by telling her what she wanted to hear.

She'd been only fourteen and carefree on that sparkling morning. She had recently written a prize-winning poem, was on her way to the library to read it, and just as she opened the library door she caught Kevin's eye. He was lounging on the grounds of the church next door, watching her. The moment was vivid in her memory because she had a feeling then she'd never experienced before. Now, thinking back, maybe it was the exhilaration of winning the poetry contest that had spilled over. But it was also the way he looked at her. He made her feel she was the only girl in the universe, that she was frozen in a beam of light that came from his eyes.

He followed her and her parents into the library and listened raptly as she read her poem. And she floated home, flattered that he watched her every move, seemed to be listening in on her very thoughts. And she hadn't even met him or spoken to him yet. When they finally did go out, her friends gushed, "He's so hot," and she thought that maybe now everyone would stop thinking she was a bookworm. But after a while his flowers and cards, the notes she found on her desk at school, began to embarrass her.

On the other hand, Kevin was serious, intelligent, *and* handsome.

Some boys shied away from girls who were stars in school, but Kevin basked in her success. When she was elected class president, he escorted her around town, showing her off. Her mother seemed relieved that Betsy had taken her nose out of her books and shown some interest in the opposite sex.

Oddly enough, it was Anne Frank who helped her free herself from Kevin. When she read the words of the thirteen-year-old girl hidden in a room in Amsterdam, Betsy realized that although physically free, she was more a prisoner than Anne had been. Anne's spirit had soared free, over her walls. She carried the *Diary of Anne Frank* home with her from school the day she decided to break free of Kevin. And he did something that night she hadn't told even her best friend about.

As Kevin hurried toward Laurel, he listened to the birds chirping into the dusk, the roar of an airplane, and the rumble of cars rolling over the bridge. At last his life was almost under control. Laurel depended on him now, and the Dragon Lady, overcome by grief, was butting out of their business. No more scary phone calls for you, Jessica, he thought. Besides, calling her new unlisted number would give him away in a second.

He walked briskly, remembering to take long strides that were not entirely natural to him. He allowed himself the luxury these days of thinking about his namesake, his idol and mentor, the real Kevin Glade. Kevin had shocked friends and teachers by throwing all their expectations aside. No brilliant career, no more awards for him. And he recalled how wiped out he had felt when Kevin suddenly left town after his parents died in a plane crash.

At first Billy Owens had felt betrayed. Kevin had taught him how to act, to dress, to eat, how to charm the girls. The young Billy had even gone to Kevin's barber to copy his haircut, worn the same style of clothing, had successfully imitated his walk. Once, a couple of years before the real Kevin hit the road, an older classmate, mistaking Billy for Kevin, had actually called from across the street and run toward him before stopping in his tracks when he saw his mistake.

After Kevin blew their hick town, Billy missed him more than he let himself admit. If Kevin had been a girl, Billy would have loved her. Kevin Glade wouldn't recognize the new Billy, using his name. Hey, he wondered if Kevin knew which wines went with which foods. Fact was, Billy had surpassed the real Kevin Glade.

"I'M SO SORRY," Alan said. "I know how much you loved her."

He reached out and hugged Laurel as soon as he opened the door to let her in. She let herself cry into his shoulder, relieving some of her pain in a way she never could with Kevin.

Alan continued to hold her until she finally let him go. When they sat down on his bed, she reached into her book bag.

"I stayed up all night and wrote my Darwin paper," she said. "Thanks to you, pal. You really saved me."

Alan smiled and smoothed her hair lightly with his fingers. "Something's happened, Laurel. What?"

"Real misery made me realize how depressed I'd been before. Is that crazy?"

"Nope."

"Alan, I want my life back. I need my old friends now." She pulled a folder from her book bag. "Read this."

Alan took the folder.

"Hey, would you mind if Doug and Mini joined us for pizza later?"

Alan grinned. "Of course not." Making himself comfortable on the bed, he opened to the first page of her paper. "Give them a call."

Laurel glanced at her watch. "Oh, my God . . ."

Alan looked up, saw momentary panic in her eyes.

"I forgot about Kevin."

Alan was silent.

"Well, it can't be helped," she said quietly. "This is my *new* life."

KEVIN SEARCHED FRANTICALLY until he found Laurel's yellow Bug. And almost as soon as he hid himself behind a storage shed in the dark parking lot, out came Laurel with . . . Alan? He was a tall asshole, not even good-looking. Kevin watched as they got into a nondescript blue Toyota. Shucking his glasses, he squinted in the dim illumination coming from the windows to catch the license before the car took off.

At the front door he scanned the names on the intercom. Alan Levine! He slammed his fist against the metal plate.

This asshole needs to have an accident, Kevin thought.

"I'M SO *SAD*," Jessica told Laurel. It was their first phone call since the funeral.

"She wouldn't want you to be, Mom."

"You know, all those little fights we had over the years . . . I think they helped bind us together. I miss them. Do I make any sense?"

Laurel nodded, wondering if her mother was also talking about the two of them. "I wondered why I hadn't heard from you," she said. "Is that why you haven't called me? You're too depressed?"

"I've also been feeling guilty. I just couldn't talk—face a lot of issues about Anyuka."

"So you fought. Maybe you cared enough about each other to be honest."

Emotion caught in Jessica's throat. Was Laurie, sounding old beyond her age, talking about them as well?

After their conversation Jessica pulled aside the living room curtains, and light streamed in. She was astonished at the bright day, the cloudless sky. She could see straight across to the far hills of New Jersey, watch cars that looked like Matchbox toys climb distant roads. Life went on. The sun warmed the world, even though her *anyuka* was dead.

JESSICA SAT AT Ricky's piano, absentmindedly picking out notes with one finger. Through the window she could see the graceful arcs of glittering lights on the Triborough Bridge. She was thinking about Laurie.

"You must be feeling better, Jess," Ricky remarked. "What *is* that tune?"

Jessica shrugged her shoulders. "I had a civilized conversation with

Laurie today. Would you believe it? And now I have a brand-new dilemma." She turned around to face Ricky, who was sitting at her drafting table. "Marianne just called to tell me she found Kevin's poem in an obscure anthology. It was written by one William Griffith."

"Tell her!"

Jessica turned back to the piano and played the same notes over and over. "I will. I know I have to . . ."

"That old show tune, it's driving me crazy. Where did you hear it, Jess?"

"It's the tune that Kevin Glade is always humming." Jessica picked out the notes again as Ricky sang.

"Something, something . . . Kokomo, Indiana."

Jessica stared at Ricky.

"Young kids don't know show tunes," Jessica said. "All they listen to is loud rock."

"It's an *old* song. *Way* before Kevin's time," Ricky said.

"Where do you suppose he heard it?" Ricky asked.

Jessica pushed back the piano bench and stood up. "He heard it where he grew up. Of *course.* That's why there were no records of him in Putney, Vermont."

Ricky smacked her head. "You're right, you must be." She snatched the cordless phone from her desk and thrust it at Jessica. "Kokomo information," she instructed.

"Here we go again," Jessica said.

BETSY WAS HAPPY she had picked the women-only class on human sexuality. After just two weeks she was beginning to think she wasn't to blame for what Kevin had done. Today Ms. Henderson's lecture was reinforcing the message her mother had tried to give her when she started dating Kevin. It was reassuring to hear it officially.

"Don't feel guilty if you're not ready. There's too much pressure on a young girl to have sex. And we're all different, our hormone levels are different. Physically we develop at different rates. And some girls are psychologically ready years later than their friends."

"What if I'm ready too early?" Dorie asked.

The class laughed.

Betsy raised her hand. Her face felt hot.

"What if a guy gets the wrong idea? What if he tells you you led him on? What if you went part of the way and then you stopped?"

"You have a right to say stop anywhere along the way. Even up to the last moment. *No* is *no*!" Ms. Henderson said.

"We just necked . . . that's all," Betsy blurted out.

"That's nothin'," from Dorie.

"If a guy got you all aroused and didn't perform, would you have the right to force him?" asked Ms. Henderson.

The class laughed.

"Physically and mentally a boy can stop at any time without any harm to him. He may be disappointed, but that's as far as the ill effects go. If he forces you, it's date rape. It's a crime, just like any other rape."

An uncharacteristic silence fell over the room. Ms. Henderson looked into the faces of her students. "If it's happened to you . . . a crime has been committed. The guilt is *not* yours."

Betsy thought she heard a collective sigh. Obviously there were others keeping dirty little secrets. She so much wanted to tell someone hers. Then maybe she could really get on with her life.

UNLOCKING HER DOOR, Kevin followed her in. He's literally breathing down my neck, she thought.

What she mostly thought about lately was Alan Levine—even at the funeral while Kevin held her hand in a tight grip. She wished in a way it wasn't so, but after last night with Alan . . . Well, it was so easy, relaxed. He'd helped her with her paper, they'd had dinner together, talked. No hassles, no pressure. And she'd been elated she'd finally turned in her paper.

She dropped her grocery bag on her desk. "I've got some sandwich stuff, Kevin. Don't have time for lunch—or dinner," she explained. "French," she added.

"I brought you a present," he said, handing her a small stuffed dog and a card.

On the envelope he had drawn a red heart pierced with an arrow and dripping blood. God, she thought, grow *up.*

"Thanks, Kev . . ." She dropped the gifts on the dresser.

"Where were you last night, Laurie? I waited for you for hours."

"You shouldn't have, Kevin. I was working on my paper, and then I showed it to a friend in my bio class. I turned it in today." She hurried on, not wanting to see his reaction. "And tonight I'm cramming for a make-up exam—*en Francaise,*" she said weakly.

"I was up all night worrying. . . . At least I'll know where you are tonight."

She stood there, a ways from him, without removing her coat, hoping he would leave. She looked at his unshaved face, noted that his hair, always perfectly groomed, was mangy. His leather jacket was buttoned askew.

"Kevin, you okay?"

"The funeral. It brought back memories. I've been thinking about dying again—"

"Again?"

"I've been feeling so alone."

His words, which once she had believed, sounded false. Was it because she was preoccupied with her own sadness? "I know this may not be the best time to say it, but I need some space, Kevin. I need to get myself together. My grades have been in the gutter and—"

Kevin grabbed her hand. "I thought everything was okay between us."

His palm felt clammy, Laurel wanted to yank free. But at the same time she didn't want to hurt him. He was, after all, trying so hard.

Just then the phone rang, and she had her excuse to pull away.

"Mini! Hi. Sorry I missed you . . . love to . . ." She eyed Kevin nervously as she spoke. "I—I'll call you back," irritated at herself for feeling inhibited with Kevin looking on. Before she could break off, he turned and left, shoulders hunched, head down. At least she didn't call after him.

While making a date with Mini, Laurel eyed the present Kevin had brought her and dropped it into a dresser drawer. All of Kevin's presents now seemed more tacky than touching. Unhappily she fingered the envelope, and when she hung up the phone she tore it open. He'd printed a poem on the unlined paper.

Shadow

I was happy
Under a stone,
Never once minded
Being Alone.

Dark though it was
And cramped and hushed,
I never minded
Being crushed.

I never minded
Being me,
Till the stone shuddered,
And set me free.

Scrawled underneath was, "Don't leave me, Laurel."

"I DON'T REALLY want to hear it, Mom."

Whatever happened to trusting each other to disagree? thought Jessica. "But the poem Kevin wrote—"

"Mom. You don't know everything."

"I'm not *young* enough to know everything."

"Touché, Mom, but—"

"Oscar Wilde said it first."

Jessica ended the conversation on an upbeat. She could afford to. She was going to Kevin's hometown to nail him, and then Laurel would hear what she had to say, like it or not.

"OH, JESS," TOM said, "I called to talk to *you,* to find out how *you* are. I don't want to hear about Kevin's poems."

"But he stole them, Tom. Plagiarized—"

"So the kid's an artist, not a writer. And he's desperate to impress."

"His drawings are—perfect, mechanical, all veins and parts like the inner workings of a clock. They have no beauty . . . no soul."

"Jess, my love, he's also obviously devoted to Laurel. Did you see him at the funeral? And now with your mom gone, it will be tough on both of you. I'm glad Laurie has someone at school to lean on—"

Before she could answer that, the line to Brazil crackled and went dead.

"Great," Jessica said, putting down the phone. The telephone company just saved us from a knockdown, drag-out about Kevin. Tom was so rational and, she was convinced, so wrong about Kevin Glade.

She was leaving for Kokomo in the morning. For all she knew, Kevin had a record, was a . . . what? He had gotten into Cornell, hadn't he? Doubt crept in. Could Tom be right about him?

But that morning, by placing a few strategic calls, she had confirmed her guess about Kevin. He had attended school in Kokomo all the way from kindergarten through high school.

She wished she could tell Anyuka about her plans. Before nightfall tomorrow, Kevin Glade, pretend pianist, false poet, Orphan of the Year, would be exposed. She could almost hear Anyuka's words wishing her well. *"Bon voyage, draga* Jessica. Happy hunting."

MCKENZIE BROUGHT HIS steaming coffee cup into Sandy's office and plopped himself in her chair while she filed reports in a metal cabinet. "Hate paperwork," he mumbled, sipping his coffee. Sandy's empty mug was set on the desk, and McKenzie eyed the last chocolate-covered donut in the open paper bag. "Are you sure you don't want this donut?"

"Uh-uh," she said, filing away her last report.

"So what's up, Ungar? You've been holding out on me."

Sandy looked up and smiled. She rolled the file drawer shut. "Wilkerson invited me out to dinner."

"The D.A. No kidding?"

"What do you think?"

"Lunch, it's business. Dinner, pleasure."

Sandy looked uncomfortable as she sat in the visitor's chair near her desk.

"How'd that happen? I didn't know he had the hots for you."

"I went to see him. To get him to drop the April Meadows charge against the serial. Maybe he wants to discuss it."

McKenzie laughed. "Sure, Sandy."

"He hasn't reacted to my request. But if he retains the charge, I just might believe it; he won't go with anything he can't prosecute. Anyway, I've got a lot on my mind these days."

"Romance."

"Ha-ha."

"Juggling two guys. Which is the lucky one?"

"Give me a break. I don't know them. Do you?"

McKenzie looked surprised. "You want *my* opinion?"

"You did such a good job on Dan, I might listen up."

McKenzie smiled. "Thanks, Ungar. You helped shape him up into one good cop . . ."

"So, who gets your vote, the D.A. or Martin?"

"I go for Martin. He's a square and a wiseass, but he's a nice guy who'll treat you good. The D.A. is too old for you." He shrugged. "Depends on what you're looking for, I guess."

"Someone who treats me good," she said quickly.

"Been married before?"

"To someone who didn't."

"I thought you were a tough broad."

"Oh, I am. I was brought up to be tough, we lived in a tough area. But if I ever have a kid, I'll bring her up to have the good life, not the bad."

"It's a tough world out there, they say."

"Tell me about it."

"Let me know how you make out with the D.A.," McKenzie said, reaching for the last donut on his way out.

THE LATEST POEM proved it, Laurel thought. Kevin was teetering on a high wire, and if she made a false move, he just might tumble over. She pictured the gorge at Cascadilla.

Thank God he doesn't know about Alan, she thought.

Chapter Nineteen

SIGNS FOR FERTILIZER, insecticides, and John Deere tractors had abounded on the highway. The long, flat stretch from the airport to Kokomo was straight middle-America, and more exotic to Jessica than Rome or Paris.

But Kevin's high school looked, except for the lack of trees and the scraggly ivy, like any in a New York suburb. She hurried between the white pillars and climbed the curved central staircase. She disliked preying on the trust of good people, but she had to get into the school, had to talk with someone who knew Kevin. She had a two o'clock meeting with the coach, who had also been Kevin's history teacher and adviser.

A bell rang and she was caught in the tide of students, but no one jostled her as she made her way upstairs. No raucous laughter or shrill voices assailed her ears; students changed classes in an orderly march. Sleaze and deception would really stand out in this heartland, she thought.

Dick Delilo waited at his classroom door. He looked more like a history teacher than a coach, Jessica thought, though he was husky and well over six feet. His salt-and-pepper hair and horn-rimmed glasses gave him a scholarly air.

He greeted her and extended a hand smudged with chalk dust.

"I appreciate so much your taking the time, Mr. Delilo—for Kevin's sake. As I explained, he's going through a difficult time—having some personal problems. If you can give me some insights into his high school years, it will be helpful. I was out of the country when he was growing up."

"Anything I can do for Kevin. But I'm afraid I'll be proctoring an exam for a sick colleague in a couple of minutes."

"I just wondered if there were *any* signs of something wrong back then."

"I never saw a single problem with Kevin. But I'll give you a quick rundown. In a nutshell, Kevin was a hero in our school. The Most Likely to Succeed, editor of the literary magazine, captain of the football team . . . you name it."

"Football? He never even mentioned football. He's not the type."

"I know. He isn't a hulk. And he wore glasses off the field. But he's smart, fast, and aggressive."

"But he's an art major. . . ."

"Kevin can do anything. Played the piano, even sang in the musical comedies. You can be real proud of Kevin. He was one of my favorites. Popular with the students *and* the teachers."

"He refuses to talk about his high school years."

"Well, I'm sure something was going on in his head. Maybe he put too much pressure on himself after his folks died. You can be sure we were shocked when he disappeared."

"What?"

"I mean, when he took off to become a ski bum. He could have gone to any Ivy League college. I'm glad he's got himself to Cornell. He should have no trouble academically." He glanced at his watch. "And I'm glad to meet a relative of Kevin's. I knew his parents, of course. It was a terrible tragedy."

"Yes, yes, it was," Jessica said, wanting to change the topic. "About the yearbook. Kevin seems not to have one."

"I haven't forgotten. I spoke to Mrs. Mooney, the yearbook adviser, and she'll send you a copy when she digs it up. But it occurred to me after we spoke on the phone, Kevin won't be in it. He was absent a lot his senior year. I remember reminding him to go to the studio for a makeup photo, but he never did. Understandable, of course. Losing both parents at seventeen. I guess after the plane crash he never quite got it together. And just before graduation. What a nightmare."

Jessica could barely concentrate on Delilo's next words. Plane crash! Senior year? She tried to hide her excitement.

"If there's nothing else . . ." He glanced at his watch again.

"No, no. Sorry to have kept you. I was in town for a meeting, so I thought I would . . ." She put out her hand.

"My pleasure," he said, giving her hand a vigorous shake. "Say hello to Kevin. I know he'll pull through. He's a terrific kid."

WHENEVER BETSY HAD recalled the scene in the past, it had been through a veil. But now the lens she was peering through brought it into sharp focus. Just after dinner she told her parents what Kevin had done that August.

It had been a hot night. Betsy was asleep in her bed. A creak of the window, hands lifting the sash, an indistinct face in the moonlight. Before she could turn on the lamp, Kevin was beside her bed, his face pressed close to hers, his angry eyes on her.

"Kevin, get out!" she whispered. He mashed his wet lips on her mouth, put his hand in her nightgown, feeling her breast. "My parents are downstairs—"

Fear paralyzed her. Fingers clamped her jaw shut. He was breathing heavily, unzipping himself, prying her legs apart with his legs. She felt his penis trying to push into her.

"A sweet good-bye, my sweet."

She bit his finger, shoved him against the night table, sending a ceramic lamp crashing to the floor.

At the sound of her father's voice Kevin bolted to the window. A knock on the door, she pulled up her sheet, and Kevin slipped out as the door opened. A beam of light from the hall revealed the shattered lamp.

"Sorry, Dad." The words rushed out. "I must have had a nightmare and woke up too fast." She was glad he couldn't see her face clearly. Her cheeks burned, her body felt hot, as though fear and shame had suffused it. She could still feel Kevin's hand on her breast, his penis between her thighs. She looked into her father's face. She wanted to tell him but couldn't.

"No big deal," her dad said.

Her mom appeared at the door. "I'm not feeling too good," she said. Her mom sat beside her on the bed, felt her warm forehead.

Kevin was leaving for Cornell in the morning! *Everyone* admired Kevin, trusted him. Maybe she'd led him on, she would later think. Maybe it was at least partly her fault.

"Why didn't you *tell* us? Why?" her mother said. Her father hid his head in his hands.

"He didn't actually . . . rape me—"

"I'll kill him, I'll—"

"I wanted to be rid of him. I was too ashamed to have it out in the open."

"You could've told *us,"* Nicole said. She held Betsy's hands against her cheek.

"Could I, Mom? You always were worried about him. *Poor Kevin."*

"Oh, my God. I'm so sorry, baby."

"It's not your fault, Mom."

Her dad kept shaking his head, still not wanting to believe, to face up to what could no longer be denied about perfect Kevin. "What fools we were," he said.

Her mother stared at them. "Well, what do we do now?"

"BITE DOWN ON his lower lip until your teeth meet," Sandy read. Will it gross women out? She wondered. She was editing a section on rape in "The Action Manual for Citizens" she was writing for the department. She put her pencil down and snagged a potato chip from the bag on her desk. In twenty minutes she would hurry home to dress for her date with Wilkerson.

Dan McKenzie poked his head through the open door. "Are you busy? There's someone here—from New York—wants to see a female cop."

"Send her in." Sandy gathered her papers and stuffed them into a folder as she gave the well-dressed woman who walked in the once-over. Expensive business suit, understated gold jewelry, patent pumps. FBI agent? She stuffed the bag of chips into her desk.

"Detective Ungar," she said, standing up, extending her hand.

"Jessica Lewisohn."

"Law enforcement?"

Jessica laughed. "If you call checking up on your daughter's boyfriend in that category."

Sandy sat down and motioned Jessica to a chair. "Must be pretty serious if you came all this way," Sandy said. "What's the problem?"

"I think my daughter's boyfriend is a con man. He's a liar, and he's after something. He's after my daughter, but not in any *normal* way. I just checked with his old high school. It's weird. His teachers apparently loved him, his marks were excellent, and he's got an unblemished record." Jessica shrugged her shoulders. "So far you must think I'm another neurotic, overly possessive mother. Well, I plead guilty to some of that. But it doesn't change what I feel and know about him."

"Go on, Mrs. Lewisohn. I'm listening."

"I figured as long as I'm here, I'll find out if he has a record. Something no one knows about."

"Trouble is," Sandy said, "I can't do a search because you think he's up to no good. If, say, he *stole* something from you, now that would be grounds for a computer check." She cocked her head, waiting for her suggestion to sink in.

"Well . . . he lied about a *ring.* Yes, the ring. He stole an opal ring!"

Sandy nodded. "Right! What's his name?"

"Kevin Glade."

Sandy picked up the phone. "Dan. Run a check on Glade, Kevin. See if he's got a sheet."

Jessica paced restlessly while Sandy took two phone calls. She stopped in front of a bulletin board on the wall. Notices and posters were stapled and tacked there helter-skelter. A girl whose picture hung there bore an eerie resemblance to Laurel. Jessica felt a lump in her stomach when she read the word "Murdered" stamped across the photo.

Sandy noted the change in Jessica's expression. "What's up?" she asked when she'd hung up.

"That picture. She looks like my daughter. What happened to her?"

"Killed by a serial. Or maybe her boyfriend."

Jessica's throat closed up. "So young . . ."

"The boyfriend, a Billy Owens, was a Lorna Barrett freak—" Sandy stopped herself from relating the gruesome details.

Dan walked in, a wide smile on his face. "Got a fax from the D.A.," he said, waving a sheet of paper. He laid it on Sandy's desk.

"Delayed at work. Meet me at the Red River Grill. 7 P.M. Okay?" She read it without changing her expression. She looked up at Dan. "Kevin Glade?"

"Squeaky clean. Zero, zip, and zilch."

Jessica took a deep breath. She didn't know whether to be relieved or disappointed.

"Go with your gut," Sandy said. "And keep an eye on your daughter."

So Kevin was Mr. Clean, his parents upstanding citizens. Then why had he lied—claimed they had died in a car crash when he was five years old when they had died in a plane crash when he was a high school senior?

Jessica adjusted her seat belt as the plane ascended. She had requested a window seat but was too preoccupied to watch the scenery. She fixed her pillow, leaned back, and covered her legs with a green airline-issue blanket. Kevin had lied about his parents' deaths, about his age, the Putney School, his hometown, his murdered "Aunt Tina," Betsy's poem and now the poem "Autumn Song."

She pictured his smooth, handsome face, the unnaturally dark hair. Did he use touch-up? Why, at his age? She heard his humming, the drumming of his long fingernails on tabletops—to cover his nervousness, to drown out the echo of his lies? And yet, according to Mr. Delilo, Kevin played the piano. People who played piano didn't have long nails.

Even though her visit to the police had yielded nothing on Kevin, she shuddered at the thought of the murdered girl in the poster—a younger version of Laurel.

What am I missing? What are we *all* missing? she asked herself over and over.

The lush pink and vermilion flower petals in the Georgia O'Keeffe poster above Laurel's bed looked to her like labia. Maybe that's why Kevin hates it, she thought as she held an edge that dangled crookedly. She righted it, stuck a thumb tack into it, and banged the tack with a shoe. She secured the two other loose edges, climbed down from her bed and appraised her work with satisfaction.

When the phone rang, she ignored it and continued gathering the mound of laundry on her bed and crammed it into a pillowcase. She picked up smaller clumps of discarded clothing from around the room and dropped them into a nylon laundry bag she'd retrieved while vacuuming under the bed.

Still the phone rang, and she finally held her ears until it stopped. "He's not your responsibility," Alan had reminded her last night.

Angrily she dumped the contents of her wastepaper basket along with beer bottles and soda cans into a large plastic bag. Finally she retrieved a mug from the window ledge and raised the window to air out the room.

"Damn!" she said aloud, staring at the silent phone. It had rung insistently three times in the past two hours. She was sure it was Kevin's latest tactic, his reaction to her having stopped their nine o'clock dates. What should she do? She couldn't avoid him forever. And the constant ringing of the phone was driving her crazy. She would have to think of a way to tell him her feelings. And soon.

She threw her sneakers and a pair of boots into the bottom of the closet and hung up the clean clothes that were strewn around. She grabbed a damp towel from her desk chair and hung it on a hook inside the closet door, lifted her book bag off the floor and heaved it onto her desk. Was it still some kind of love, or pity, that she felt for Kevin? She was so confused. Was it right to see Alan tonight? Why not? Why should she feel like a criminal or something, sneaking off to see him, or Mini and Doug? Kevin had a hold on her, present or absent.

She stepped back and surveyed her room. It hadn't been this neat all year. She lifted the window higher and stared out. It was growing dark, and she could see a luminous full moon. The stark quiet and the occasional footfall on the path across the way unnerved her. It was a clear, sharp night, and she looked into the shadows, as though trying to make out a hidden figure.

She shut the window and dropped the blind. And once she'd adjusted the slats to repel imaginary inquisitive eyes, she turned on all the lights and then the stereo, full blast.

KEVIN, INCREASINGLY AGITATED, trudged toward Laurie's dorm. Where the hell was she? In spite of the book bag conspicuously slung over his shoulder, he had no plans to work. Instead, he had checked the library for Laurel and then moved past Alan's place on Stewart Avenue, trying to find her. All evening, when she should have been home, her phone had gone unanswered. He had just tried again from the campus store.

He approached her dorm. He had to find out for sure where she was. Maybe he'd go in and take a look at her diary. He passed her window and suddenly stopped short. Light was visible through the closed blinds. She was home!

He ducked into the doorway. Was Alan with her?

The door opened and a couple emerged. Kevin moved quickly inside and headed for Laurel's room. Attuned to the sound of footsteps on the stairs, or a door opening, he pressed his head against her door, listening for Alan's voice. He heard voices, the stereo. He strained to hear as long as he could stand it. Suddenly the knob turned. He hurried to the staircase and crouched behind it in the shadows. Her door opened and closed. He held his breath until her key turned in the lock. The outer door slammed, and as he hurried past, he heard rock music blaring behind her door.

He followed her—too close—thinking she had already made the turn at the corner, to the car lot. But she walked straight ahead. And he knew where to. He stood still and watched her. In moments she was out of sight. No books, no car. He turned to look back at her window. She'd left the light on, and he could hear the radio.

WILKERSON ORDERED A martini, and Sandy thought of a Jack Daniel's neat but settled on white wine as she faced him across the white tablecloth. Her empty, nervous stomach might rebel against hard booze, she thought.

She caught her reflection in the mirrored wall across from her and approved of the compromise she had made between the sexy black outfit and the tailored suit. She was wearing a short wool skirt, silk blouse, and a leather vest. Her hair was loose and had fallen into place when she brushed it.

She couldn't help wondering if the D.A. was just buttering her up because he knew April Meadows was her domain and was about to indict Jukes for April's murder. Had she made a fool of herself by dressing for a date?

Wilkerson broke into her internal monologue: "So I hear you're a feminist."

He looked a bit stiff and uncomfortable too, Sandy thought. And his remark seemed like an opening line he might have practiced.

"A feminist is a person who believes women should be equal to men."

Wilkerson laughed. "Low aspirations!"

The knot in her stomach began to unwind.

The waiter brought the menus and their drinks, and after Wilkerson made some suggestions they both decided on lobster tails.

"You're a regular here?"

"I used to be, before my wife died."

"Oh, I'm sorry. When . . . ?"

"Two years ago—cancer."

"I didn't know you'd been married."

"Seven years. What about you? Ever marry?"

Sandy nodded, hesitated, and then risked a confidence. "To a rat. In college. Once burned . . ."

"That bad?"

"He was an addict and abusive."

"I'd never have imagined you in that kind of relationship."

"Why not? Because I'm not a wimp? Remember, I was a kid. But I've also seen a lot of strong women who wound up in an abusive relationship. They didn't *choose* it. That's the shrinks laying more blame on the women. I don't buy it."

"Interesting." He sampled his drink. "Is that why you're so involved in the April Meadows murder?"

She picked up her glass. "I guess it plays a part. Never connected it before. Of course, it's the kind of case you want to solve, regardless." She took a sip of wine. "Have you decided on the case yet?"

"She's all yours. I just removed her murder from the Jukes indictment. Your presentation convinced me."

Sandy looked pleased. "Thanks," she said, and lifted her glass toward him.

"You're welcome," he said, and added: "Looks like you've got a killer loose in your neck of the woods."

* * *

"HAVE YOU SEEN Kevin lately?" Mini asked. "He looks like Humphrey Bogart after a bad night."

"I hope Laurie's left that ghoul at home," Doug said. "He's got her veins in his teeth."

"I told her we wanted to talk, that we were taking a quick break between practice rounds."

"Did you tell her not to bring Count Dracula?"

Mini poked Doug as she spotted Laurie heading toward them in the nearly deserted dining hall. "You think she's clueless?" Mini whispered.

They jumped up to greet her. She leaned across the table, and they both kissed her on the cheek.

"Should we get something to eat?" Laurie asked, noting that the employees were beginning to put the food away. "I'm starved," she said as Mini and Doug sat down.

"Sure," Mini said, but made no move to get up.

Laurel reluctantly took a seat. "I haven't seen you in ages. I've missed you both. And debate. I guess it's in my blood."

"We haven't heard from *you* in ages," Doug said.

"That's true," Laurel said. "I've been busy."

Mini and Doug exchanged glances.

"That's feeble, Laurie," Doug finally said.

"We've been friends for too long not to level with each other," Mini put in. "I have a serious question to ask you, Laurie. Do you still want to be friends? The truth, no bullshit."

"Of course I do!"

Doug looked her in the eye. "Promise you will not repeat this to Kevin."

"Okay . . ."

"For sure?"

Laurie nodded. "I promise."

"Okay, here it is. Kevin told us to keep away from you. That you didn't want us to bother you anymore. It was like a threat. If it's true—okay. If not, I think you should know."

"Never! I never . . . it's a lie." Laurie's face reddened, and fury, not hunger, churned in her stomach.

* * *

NICOLE BROUGHT A tray with a glass of milk and home-baked brownies into Betsy's room and set them down on the bed. "Finished your homework?"

Betsy nodded and cleared her books away, making space for her mother to sit down next to her.

"I'm glad we convinced Dad to calm down," Betsy said. "I wanted to talk to you alone."

Nicole watched her daughter as she ate the brownies and washed them down with the milk. Still only a child, really, she thought.

"Did I hear Dad go off to teach his course?"

Nicole nodded. "Why *didn't* you tell us about Kevin, babe?"

"I didn't want to disappoint you, Mom. I didn't want you to think I was a nerd. I knew it was important to you, my having a boyfriend, to be social . . ."

"I pushed my own daughter . . . like some stage mother. Of course, I thought it was for your own good. And Kevin *seemed* so ideal."

"At first it *was* okay. But I was in way over my head with him. And I didn't know how to dig myself out. And he was leaving for college—"

"Are you *sure* you don't want to go to the police? Your dad and I will back you one hundred percent!"

"I know, Mom. I'm sure. Try to make Dad understand. It was almost two years ago."

"When that woman from New York came to see me, you told me everything was okay. I wish you'd spoken up then."

"But you didn't tell me she was suspicious. You only told me about the poem. And I was so glad to be rid of him, I didn't care."

"My God, I feel so guilty about that woman. She sensed her daughter was in danger, and I didn't believe her! Betsy, honey, I want to warn her. Is it okay with you?"

"Do it! This second!"

Nicole nodded and dialed information. But in response to her request a recording came on, and her heart sank as she heard the message. "The number for Jessica Lewisohn has been changed. At the request of the customer the new number is unlisted."

Chapter Twenty

KEVIN UNLOCKED LAUREL'S door knowing it was a suicidal act if he got caught. But he couldn't stop himself. If not her, at least her private things—the carelessly flung underwear on the bed, the uncapped toothpaste on the bathroom sink. It was delicious to be alone with them, with the details of her.

The room, though, was neat, which felt like a personal insult. He was always ragging on her to clean up her act. Just yesterday this place had looked a mess. But the change wasn't for him . . . it was for Alan.

He went to her top dresser drawer and rummaged for her diary. At any moment she might be back—with Alan. It was a ten-minute walk from Alan's place, five if they drove. His fingers crawled through her undies. Her diary was gone. He tried the desk drawers, the night table. He lingered past the danger point, even poking through the trash. He was tempting fate, his usual control eroding. Before he finally tore himself away, he eyed the print he so detested, now carefully righted, on the wall.

He locked the door. His head felt dizzyingly light. He knew the only antidote to his misery was to get Laurie back. For good, and no matter how.

"WHAT'S THE MATTER?" Alan asked, an arm around Laurel's shoulder as they sat on his lumpy living room couch. "Was my spaghetti that bad?"

Laurel finished the last of the red wine in her glass. "No. No . . . all that wine in the sauce and . . ." She looked into her empty glass and tilted it.

"The secret of my success as a chef. Is it me?" he asked.

Laurel touched his hand as he put her glass on the giant cable spool that served as a coffee table. "Oh, no. *No.*"

"You're awfully quiet tonight. School or your mother? If it's neither, there's only one person left."

"Yes. Kevin. I just found out he's been pressuring Doug and Mini. No, not pressuring—*threatening*!"

"What do you mean? How?"

"He actually told them to keep away from me. That I didn't want them to *bother* me!"

"Wow!"

"I probably shouldn't be here—"

"Wait a minute. Why *are* you here?"

"Because I want to be."

He kissed her on the lips. She kissed him back, then drew away.

"Things haven't been good with Kevin for a long time. But being with you made me realize how good I feel when I'm away from him. I've got to make a decision, and I can't keep putting it off. I've got to tell him."

KEVIN LEANED AGAINST the storage shed, an unlit cigarette in his mouth—his excuse for loitering in the dark outside Alan's house, getting a light. It was getting colder. He hadn't expected to be posted by the shed this long. He had arrived before Laurie, watched as she was buzzed in. He had even recognized them in the window upstairs.

For hours he had huddled in the shadows waiting for her. His foot fell asleep, but he didn't shift his position. He was mesmerized by the lighted window.

Now the light in the window went out and the apartment went black. He knew it—she was sleeping with that wimp. His mind flooded with images: a bloody claw stuck in a disembodied throat, a skull cracked open.

The cold wind bit into his consciousness. He stamped his foot to start the blood circulating, blinked away the images. He stepped out into the open. Alan's car was parked just ten feet from where he stood. For now he would have to settle for a minor disaster, remove a spark plug or mess with the ignition fuse so the car wouldn't start. But it was too risky to lift the hood if he didn't know exactly what he was doing. Maybe he'd pour sugar into the gas tank, ruin the motor. Alan was a geek, a loser. Totally fucking his wheels was only a start.

Suddenly Kevin spotted a glinting, jagged object lying on the ground, a piece of broken glass from a shattered beer bottle that had caught the moonlight. He looked around. Two dudes were passing by across the street. He walked toward the car and dropped his keys near a back wheel. Then choosing the largest, most lethal-looking slice of glass, he wedged it between the front of the wheel and the ground. When the car rolled forward, the glass would slash the tire.

He wished he could wield that piece of glass on Alan's throat.

NICOLE WAS NESTLED in her husband Nat's arms.

"Betsy won't go to the police," she said. "She says she has nothing to gain and—"

"Revenge," Nat said.

"That's not like you."

"It's easy being a liberal when it's not your daughter."

"Chances are, since she wasn't actually raped they wouldn't do a thing to the—"

"Scumbag."

"What worries me now is that woman's daughter." She searched her memory. "Laurel was her name." Nicole adjusted her nightgown and sat up. "You're the creative one. Help me figure out a way to find her new telephone number."

"Ask the police. Tell them what he did. They have access to unlisted numbers, for sure."

"I'd be telling them what happened. Of course, it would be confidential . . ."

"Hey, if her number has recently been changed, the old number is in the current phone book with her address."

"Brilliant, Nat. We can write to her, tell her to call *us.*"

KEVIN HARDLY REMEMBERED walking home or unlocking his door. What he was feeling was too much like the rage after April had rejected him. He knew he had to shut his mind down. But the image of April lying on the floor began to seep in. A red-out was coming on him again.

He knew he was shot for the night—and the next day. There would be no classes, no phone calls, no visitors. He saw himself as a wounded soldier lying in shock in his foxhole, waiting for the enemy, wondering if the burning flesh he felt was really his.

LAUREL PICKED UP the phone. "I was just on my way out for breakfast," she said after hearing her mother's voice. She had just stopped off in her room to change and pick up her books and was in a hurry. The rear tire on Alan's car had developed a flat when he started to drive her home, and she had been forced to walk back to her dorm.

Alan . . . she decided to give her mother a present for a change. "Guess what, Mom? I met a new guy! *And* he's *Jewish!*"

Jessica wasn't sure if she was putting her on. She'd restrain her enthusiasm and get right to the subject of her call. "Glad to hear it, hon, but what about Kevin?"

Silence, then: "Kevin or no Kevin, I've got a right to see whoever I please," she said, as if talking to herself.

Jessica opened her mouth to speak but was afraid she would shout hooray. Approval could be the kiss of death.

"Earth to mother. Are you there, Mom?"

"Yes, right here. Who's the new guy?"

"His name is Alan. He has short hair, wears Docks and Brooks Brothers clothes. Your basic perfect person. A mother's dream come true."

"Really?" Jessica tried not to betray her pleasure.

"You would love it, wouldn't you, if I dumped Kevin and brought preppie Alan Levine home?"

Be careful, Jessica told herself, you're on thin ice. "He may be Jewish, but is he a doctor?"

Laurel laughed. "No, he'll be a poor schoolteacher."

Now was the time to strike, Jessica decided. "I called early because I couldn't sleep all night."

"Uh-oh," Laurel said.

"There's something I haven't told you about Kevin." She rushed on, afraid Laurel would cut her off. "I know you really cared about him, but there's something you should know." He's a four-flusher, a

Rozsi expression, she wanted to say, but she kept it to herself. "The poem—the one about autumn?"

"Yes?"

"It's not his poem. It was written by William Griffith!" It was on the tip of her tongue to tell Laurel everything, starting with Betsy's Vermont poem. But Laurel cut in on her thought.

"You couldn't wait to tell me."

"No, Laurie—"

"*Thanks* a lot, Mom. Thanks for checking up on him." She slammed down the phone, rushed to her desk, and found the poem Kevin had supposedly written just for her. As she read it, she knew it was too good to be his, realizing she'd been a fool not to have suspected before.

VAIL WAS TWO days behind him and so was his life as a ski bum, Kevin Glade thought as he lowered the sound of the Spin Doctors blasting away on his car stereo. Sure, he was nervous about going back to his hometown. But the real estate deal had forced him to grow up, deal with his life. A fast closing on his house was just his style, gave him no time for regrets. He tried to picture the house where he'd spent his childhood: his own room, the backyard, the living room, the stone fireplace— A shrill sound cut in.

As soon as he heard the siren, he knew he had screwed up big time. Especially since he'd lost his wallet, or had been pickpocketed in the gas station at his last pit stop. He put the brakes on, wishing he'd used cruise control. Figured he'd hit a speed trap once he'd finally allowed himself to let out his Porsche. And he was almost home. Ex-home: Kokomo, Indiana.

Finally he was able to slow down enough to pull over and was immediately sorry he had worn the T-shirt that said "Fuck Censorship," and that he looked like a derelict because without cash or plastic money he'd had to sleep in his car all night. He took a fast check in the mirror, at his day-old beard and his messed-up hair. He wished he'd had worn his expensive leather jacket instead of the cracked and worn one that he liked better.

A trooper was beside his window. Another mistake. He should have jumped out and made it to the police car before the trooper got out. His pals always did that, but his father never budged. When the cops saw the M.D. on his license, he was treated with instant respect, deference.

"Doin' over eighty, buddy," the trooper said. He looked around in the car. "License, registration," he said.

"Just lost my wallet, sir."

"Sure, buddy." The trooper waved his partner over.

Kevin had some hope. His partner looked young and eager. But trooper number one spoke.

"Step out of the car. Prepare for a frisk and a car search. You will be brought before a judge. If you are arraigned and unable to post bond, you will be arrested and locked up until bond is posted."

He had caught many other fools in this speed trap, Kevin thought as he got out of the car. A way to make money for the county. Just cool it and call your lawyer, and you'll be on your way, he told himself.

"Do a check for a stolen vehicle," the trooper said to his young partner. "And . . . what's your name?"

"Kevin Glade, sir."

The trooper nodded to his partner, who hightailed it to the police car.

"Turn around."

Kevin faced the car, put his hands up on the top as he'd seen in the movies.

"Got any drugs or weapons?"

"No, sir," Kevin answered, surprised to hear his voice quaver.

JESSICA TURNED THE key in the police lock, twisted the knob, and pushed the door open. Rozsi's living room greeted her as if nothing had changed. There was hardly even any dust on the furniture.

It was the first time she had set foot in the apartment since the police had unsealed it. She walked gingerly into the foyer, as if she were disturbing someone, trespassing. She almost expected her Anyuka to step out from the bathroom shower. "Jessica, *draga eletem*!" What an unexpected surprise! But there was no Anyuka, only her apartment, giving off an air of expectation.

Jessica walked into the silence, headed for the living room, and turned on the radio to console herself with music her mother listened to. The sounds of Rubenstein playing Chopin . . . it was almost as if her mother's spirit inhabited the room.

Then she saw it, the sculpture and the gift box on the coffee table. She tried to fight tears as she walked closer. She picked up the Hanukkah card. The sculpture was Rozsi's last present to her. She turned on the switch to light the fluorescent flowers, darkened the room, and cried to the étude she knew Rozsi would have enjoyed.

AFTER TROOPER NUMBER one—Parker, his name tag read—had instructed trooper number two, Lucas, to radio for a tow truck, Kevin knew it was futile to argue anymore.

He sat in silence in the backseat of the police car for the ride to the government center, where they filed the paperwork. The judge, in a courtroom as small as an office, took three minutes to set bail at five hundred dollars, then disappeared before Kevin could get out a word of protest or extenuation.

"When can I call my lawyer?" he asked for the third time as they headed to the jailhouse, a ten-mile ride through unfamiliar countryside.

"In due time," Parker said in his phlegmatic voice. As they pulled into the lot, Kevin's spirits sank at the sight of the huge cinder-block building, the barbed wire, and the inmates throwing a ball in the yard.

The troopers left him behind in a large, open area surrounded by cells. In full view of prisoners he was forced to strip to his underwear to allow the guard to check his body for scars. He put on a green top and pants that looked like surgery garb. No amount of reasoning with himself that everything would be okay was working. He checked the time when they confiscated his watch. Three hours had elapsed since he had been stopped for speeding. And no one on earth knew where he was.

"I'd like to make my phone call now," he told the guard who was walking him to a cell.

The guard opened a cell door and, as soon as Kevin stepped inside, locked it. "Your name?"

"Glade. Kevin Glade."

"I'll be sure to make a note of it," he said, and walked off out of sight.

JESSICA LUGGED A suitcase that was packed with photo albums, silver candlesticks, and her father's stamp collection to the elevator. Jamie had advised her to remove all of Rozsi's treasures before the drug addicts were on to her empty apartment. She nervously clutched the coat pocket where she had stashed Rozsi's wedding rings, engagement watch, and the pearls her father had given her on their twentieth anniversary.

She hurried to her double-parked car, unticketed today, grateful she didn't have to flag down a cab here.

At home on Riverside Drive, she was ashamed at her relief at being greeted by the doorman, who parked her car and handed her suitcase to the elevator operator. In her living room, she sipped a glass of sherry and listened to another Rubenstein rendition of Chopin, still broadcast on QXR, and began to relax. She sorted through Rozsi's familiar Art Deco jewelry, and before long she was leafing through an old album, reminiscing.

When the phone rang, she checked the clock. She had been absorbed for over an hour. It must be Tom, she thought. He liked to call after ten.

But it was Nora, the head nurse at the psych institute.

"I hope it's not too late, Jess, but I had a hell of a time getting your number."

"Nora, I'm sorry. I should have sent you—"

"No sweat. It just delayed me. And I've been so busy. Anyway, it's good news. Crazy Ed Polley is back inside. Ward's Island. He coked up and stopped taking medication. Tried to push a little girl into traffic. He's been off the streets for two weeks and should be there at least two more years."

A cold tingling up her spine. "He's been in two weeks? Are you *sure?*"

"Absolutely."

"But he's been calling me since then. He called the night my mother died!"

"I'm sorry, Jess. I didn't know about your mother."

Jessica barely heard her. "Nora, are you sure? I've been getting calls in the middle of the night—just a few days . . ."

"Ed Polley's out of commission. He's in isolation. No way he's calling after hours."

Jessica was too stunned, and scared, for the moment, to realize who the mysterious caller was.

KEVIN GLADE GLANCED at the packet the guard had handed him, at the stubby round-handled toothbrush and the booklet outlining prisoners' rights. He backed against the side wall of the crowded cell, arms crossed, trying to give off a "don't-fuck-with-me" message. Chances were, most of these people were petty thieves and small-time drug dealers. "What're ya in for?" was the main topic of conversation. An old con tried to hit him up for two hundred dollars to make his bail. Some enterprising prisoner had scrounged a sheet—there were none on the four cots—and hung it from a ceiling vent to cover the toilet in the middle of the back wall, but none of the sixteen men seemed eager to use the facility.

A prisoner in an orange prison uniform, cuffed and chained at the ankles, was thrust into the cell. He snarled. He tried to muscle the guards away, and tension mounted. "When am I gonna go upstairs?" yelled one man to the guard.

"I want upstairs," echoed another.

Upstairs were the permanent, better cells. Two more guards ran in as the agitation spread. Those in for the night didn't care to spend it with an angry con on his way to a serious pen. The men shrank against the walls, giving the con in orange space.

"When do I get to make my call?" Kevin called out to a guard.

"You been booked?" the guard asked.

"Yes!"

"What's your name?"

"Glade. Kevin."

The guard took in the scene, now apparently under control, and joined the other guards as they moved out. "Okay, Glade. I'll be back."

* * *

"TOM, I'VE BEEN waiting for you to call! I was just about to dial your number when the phone rang."

"Your line was busy, Jess. What's the matter?"

"I just came from Anyuka's apartment—an hour ago. I saw it without her for the first time."

"I'm sorry I'm not there with you, Jess. I know how hard it is. Can you hold out until Christmas?"

"There's more, Tom. Nora called. Ed Polley's back in the psycho ward."

"Good."

"No, not good. He's been there for two weeks, and I've had calls *since* then. The night Anyuka died. It's not Ed Polley calling me, terrorizing me. It's *Kevin*! I should have known. *It's Kevin.*"

"IT'S AFTER MIDNIGHT!"

"I know. Sorry, Eric."

"It's okay, Kevin. Hey, what are lawyers for? Don't answer that."

"I've been in this jail over eight hours. I feel like I'm in another country. Another planet."

"I'll come and get you."

"Just send me the 5 c's and—make it a thou. No, two. And a car."

"No problem."

"And Eric?"

"Yeah?"

"Just one more thing. We're gonna sue their asses!"

Chapter Twenty-One

"BILLY, IS THAT you, Billy?"

"It's me, Mom!"

"Happy birthday, son."

He cut the connection. He knew the police could trace calls if they had enough time.

AS THE LINE inched forward at the post office, Nicole wondered if her letter to Jessica had been strong enough. And, of course, her English was still imperfect. She reread the letter.

> Dear Jessica Lewisohn,
>
> I am sorry to tell you that you were only too correct about Kevin. He tried to attack my daughter sexually. Only yesterday Betsy revealed to us what Kevin had done to her. The incident happened last June.
>
> I am certain that you will abide by our wishes to keep this information confidential. I am writing as one mother to another to warn you and your daughter. For personal reasons Betsy has made the decision not to press charges.
>
> Please call me when this letter arrives. We are very much concerned about Laurel.

Nicole nervously posted the letter via overnight mail. I hope I'm not too late, she thought, wanting to kick herself for not taking Jessica seriously. But young Kevin had been such a gentleman . . . She still couldn't picture him . . . She couldn't even complete the thought.

* * *

Dear Kevin,

I've been putting this off because I do care for you. But I'm just not happy anymore. Remember the day at the lake when we first met? Let's not spoil what we've had. . . .

Laurel threw the pen down on the desk, snapped her diary shut. "Don't be a chickenshit," she said aloud. "Tell him yourself, tell him the truth and make a clean break." For both our sakes. What am I afraid of? Kevin could be scary sometimes, but lately he wasn't bothering her. In a way he seemed more to be pitied than feared.

He had seen it in the window of a jeweler in Ithaca. And every time he passed it, he had an image of Laurel in a white lace wedding gown and wearing the ring. He was standing beside her in a tux, and as her hand extended he placed a wedding band on her finger. Till death do us part, he thought as he entered the shop.

"She still loves me," he whispered aloud, carefully replacing the diary on Laurel's desk. He felt in his pocket for the ring. Should he leave it for her? No, a foolish thought. He would wait outside her room, take her out to that new fancy restaurant in Ithaca, and after a candlelit dinner present it to her, convince her how happy he would make her for the rest of her life.

He quickly left her room, locked the door, and sat on the cold steps of the building. He put his head in his hands. *"Alan is a good friend."* He said the words over and over as he sat outside. They were the words in her diary. And the book was out in the open, easy prey today. Only *friends*? Hadn't she spent the night? Alan was dangerous whether he was sleeping with her or not. He had to remove him from the playing field.

Laurel had gone to talk to Kevin, who wasn't home but, she discovered, was camped out by her doorstep. Her annoyance all but collapsed at the pathetic sight of him as he meekly followed her into her room.

She wished she could tell him that she was on to him about what he'd said to Mini and Doug, but she'd given her word. She would start with the poem.

"My mother called me today, Kevin. She's found out some things about you. . . ."

Kevin said nothing, didn't move.

She took a sheet of paper from her desk and held it out to him. "Does the name William Griffith mean anything to you? *He* wrote 'Autumn Song,' Kevin. Not you."

Still silence.

"And who wrote this poem?" She read: " 'I never minded being me, 'til the stone shuddered and set me free.' Was it the same poet who wrote all your other poems?"

"I'm *sorry.*" He took the paper in both hands and crunched it against his chest. "I didn't think he would mind a fellow sufferer borrowing his words. He's dead, Laurie. The poems are in the public domain—"

"That's not the point, Kevin."

She sat down on the bed and watched as he tore the page into pieces and held them over the wastebasket, then let them flutter to the bottom.

"Guilty as charged," he said quietly, his shoulders hunched. "I guess I'd do anything to keep you, Laurie, to try to tell you how much I love you."

Laurel felt herself beginning to relent until she remembered his threat to Doug and Mini.

"Kevin, it's not just the poems. You know that. We're not happy together." She watched him closely, looking for some sign that this might go better than she had dared hope. What he did next was at once typical and unexpected.

He knelt abruptly by the bed. "Don't make your decision now, Laurie. Please. Not while you're angry with me. It's not fair to either of us—"

"Kevin, *stop* it. We're not right for each other anymore."

"Give me one more chance." He put his head in his hands. "I don't know what I'd do without you, Laurie. I'll kill myself if you—"

"Kevin, that's crazy talk."

"Just one more chance. One more weekend. That's all I ask." He clutched her skirt. "Please, Laurie."

She pulled away from him and paced the room.

"I don't want to be alone this weekend," he said, following her. He wished he could tell her the truth—that it was his birthday—but he had lied and told her it was next month. "You promised we would go away this weekend. Don't you remember that?"

"We *talked* about going. . . ."

"I counted on it."

"What's so important about *this* weekend?"

"It's . . . I have something I want to show you."

"Kevin, I'm sorry, but—"

"Don't you have *any* feelings for me?"

"Of course I do. But they're not the same . . ."

Alan! He knew it. Rage was building. I've got to get her away, show her the ring. He spoke slowly, his hand twitching in his pocket, feeling for the ring.

"Do you have other plans?" His mind raced to come up with a way to get her to Hartewoods. Suddenly, it came to him. "I have tickets to the Stones concert! I wanted to surprise you, when we got to Hartewoods. It's right nearby at the Middletown Arena. We could spend the night at the cabin—"

"The show is sold out, Kevin. How could you—?"

"I've had the tickets since August. I bought them for you as soon as they went on sale. I know how much you love the Stones. Don't you want to go?"

"I'd *love* to, but—"

"We'll be back by Sunday. It's probably their last tour." He kept his voice steady. "We'll say farewell to the Stones. And if it's really over between us, well, it'll be our good-bye too." He loved that last touch. It should do the trick.

"Kevin . . ."

"We'll remember all the good times, just have a fun weekend. Just one weekend out of your life, Laurie."

"Just friends?"

"Just friends. I promise."

When Kevin saw the expression on Laurie's face, he knew he had won.

* * *

As soon as he got back to his dorm, he punched a Manhattan beeper number. It was his connection in Manhattan.

"It's me, man. Upstate. I need a favor."

"Oh, yeah? Whacha need?"

"Two tickets to the Stones gig."

His connection laughed.

"It's for my girl. . . ."

"Naturally, it'll cost you." He laughed again. "No *problema,* man. I got an address up there for a pickup. An' good luck with the chick, bro."

"Hometown boy comes back. Bozos pick him up for speeding, slap him in a cell, and don't allow him to make a call for eight hours. He's got long hair, granny glasses, and looks like a hippie. On top of that he's driving a Porsche!" McKenzie waved the legal papers in the air above Sandy's desk as he spoke.

"So the presumption is, it's stolen. But they could have checked out his story."

"Now he's suing." McKenzie dropped the papers on her desk.

"And the boys upstairs are in a sweat, right?" she said.

"You got it."

Sandy took a look at the papers. "I'll handle it," she said.

"Why should you get involved? It's Commissioner Lovett's headache."

Sandy clearly remembered Jessica Lewisohn, that worried mother from New York. What an opportunity to meet the boyfriend in the flesh, she thought.

Sandy took the papers and stood. "I'll tell you later. I have a special interest in Kevin Glade."

The sounds of laughter and a full orchestra greeted Jessica when she opened the door to the darkened theater. In her haste she had forgotten about the matinee performance of *Pinafore.* She needed Ricky now, and when she heard Little Buttercup singing one of Jessica's favorite songs, she realized it was only the first act.

She took a sharp right, stepped over the velvet rope and up the steps leading to the balcony, and made her way to the lighting booth. She opened the door cautiously. Ricky was on headset calling cues to the show. Stefan and Dennis, the tech directors, stood at the window, watching the stage. They turned to smile and whisper hello. Dennis pulled out a seat for her, and she sat down as Ricky held up a finger. "Stand by," she said into the headset. "Follow-spot cue seventeen on Buttercup—and *go.*"

"What's up?" Ricky whispered.

"It's Kevin! *He's* been making the phone calls." Jessica didn't waste any words. She knew Ricky might have only seconds before the next cue. "And I can't reach Laurel. I'm going up to Cornell. I was hoping—"

Ricky stared hard at the stage and spoke into the headset. "We need more front light on the poop deck. Let's get channel twenty-one up to fifty percent." She looked up at Jessica during the applause and raised her eyebrows.

"Hoping you could drive with me up to Cornell."

A long solo allowed Ricky to turn to Jessica. "That important?"

"I feel it is. Something is wrong and I'm scared."

"I'll go with you."

Ricky turned back to the stage and called out, "Let's get channel thirty-one through thirty-three up to full on this cue." She paused. "No, back to fifty percent." She held up her finger to Jessica and checked out the lighting on stage, then looked up at Stefan and Dennis. "These guys will cover in the second act." She smiled at them. "Right, folks?"

"To the rescue," Dennis said.

"Stand by," Ricky called. "Cue twenty-seven and *go.*"

Jessica threw them a kiss and ran down the stairs as the audience laughed at still another light-hearted line written by Mr. Gilbert for Mr. Sullivan.

KEVIN GLADE EYEBALLED Sandy and leaned back in his chair. He wore button-downs, a pair of chinos, and tasseled shoes. "I have no arrest record."

"I'm well aware of it," Sandy responded. Of course, he'd never know she'd checked him out because of Jessica. And lucky too, because in all the panic to get him to back down, the paperwork on his arrest had not come through.

"You did your homework."

Sandy was sitting on the edge of Commissioner Lovett's desk, wondering whether she was being too informal. The commissioner had hastily vacated his swivel chair when she offered to handle Kevin. "This needs the woman's touch," he said, happy to be relieved of the job.

"I keep on top of things," Sandy responded. "Believe it or not, there are some of us actually interested in justice. And I know there are abuses that need to be corrected."

Kevin sat up and nodded.

"Prison guards are not our most enlightened citizens." She paused, gauging his reaction. "You didn't come with your lawyer, and I appreciate that."

"I'm not here to make money. I just want the *system* changed."

"And I'm here to help do it. The commissioner doesn't want it to happen again. I'm on your side. Most cops are. The few who like to bust your chops need a wake-up call."

"That's all I want."

"Tell me about yourself," Sandy said quickly, hoping to get his mind off the topic and to get some sense of him. "I hear this is your hometown."

"Was . . . I'm here to sell my house. I've been putting it off—coming back."

"And this welcome-home incident didn't help any. I know you're thinking we should concentrate on serious crimes."

"I get the local paper and I read about April Meadows. She went to my school. I never knew her." He shook his head in disbelief. "And now a serial killer."

"I know we look bad, but we're doing our best, and that's the truth. The commissioner authorized me to set up a special committee to look into this situation and fix it. We want to save our muscle for the real crooks."

"I think we're on the same side." Kevin shook his head. "When I was growing up, this was a safe town."

"Are your parents still living here?"

"They died in a plane crash."

"I'm sorry."

Kevin glanced at his watch and stood up.

Sandy extended her hand. "We'll be in touch. I'll let you know how things develop, every step of the way."

"Thanks." He shook her hand.

"My pleasure," Sandy said. And she meant it.

If only Sandy knew he wasn't Laurel Lewisohn's boyfriend. She was interviewing the wrong individual. Billy Owens was in New York impersonating Kevin Glade.

"Your mother wants to speak to you, Laurel. Aren't you ever in your dorm?"

"I don't want to talk to her right now, Dad."

"Anyuka's apartment was just unsealed by the police and your mother found a sculpture. Something special Anyuka was working on. A surprise for your mom she must have finished the day she died. It made her very sad."

"Oh, Dad." She had a catch in her voice. "I'm going through a lot myself right now. I'm breaking off with Kevin. But I need to do it in my own way."

"She told me about it. It's your call, honey. But she's got some notion that Kevin was making those middle-of-the-night calls."

"*That* is just too far out. I'm leaving for Hartewoods, Dad—with Kevin. A sort of last time together. I made it clear to him and he *seems* to understand. Please, Dad, don't tell Mom."

Punishing Mom for being right? he wondered.

Kevin unscrewed the cap to the gas tank in Alan's car. He poured what he figured were two cups of sugar into the tank, remembering how he had offered to wait for Laurel while she packed a bag, how she had tried to get rid of him for a while, and he knew why.

"I need to take care of a couple of things. I won't be long," she said into the intercom.

"Sure, no sweat," he said, screwing the lid back on the tank.

* * *

SHE RUSHED TO the phone and dialed Alan. She waited for the beep and identified herself. "Decided to handle my problem in what I hope is the right way. Spending the weekend with Kevin, after all, but strictly platonic. We're seeing the Stones. Three more days and it will be over." Quickly she signed off, grabbed her bag, and rushed out to meet Kevin.

Chapter Twenty-Two

SHOTS ECHOED OFF the lake as Laurel turned in to the winding, wooded driveway.

"Hunting season?" asked Kevin.

"Uh-huh. Deer, bear, rabbits."

They got out of the car and walked up the narrow steps to the front door.

"My dad taught us to hunt. Even made us vests from the deer hides." Laurel took the key from above the door and opened it into a dark, cold house. She shivered as she led the way, picking up a flashlight from the kitchen table. She shone it on the wall, searching for the panel box of circuit breakers. "But that was ages ago. We haven't hunted for years." The rifle was under the bed in the guest room gathering dust. Without considering, she stopped short of mentioning it.

Kevin moved back at a skittering sound. "What was that?"

"Mice," Laurel said. She played a beam of light against the cobwebbed corners along the floorboards. "They move in when we move out. You get used to them."

"You have bears here?" Kevin asked, peering through the screened porch into the woods, relieved that Laurel had found the light switch.

"And bats and beavers and snapping turtles." After they dropped their parkas and bags on the living room floor, Kevin bent over the logs and lit a match. A mouse raced across the stones of the fireplace.

"Ouch," he said as the flame burned his fingertip. He struck another match, set the wood aflame, and glanced at Laurel's face in the firelight. When the fire roared, his bones warmed and his skin burned pleasantly. He felt the diamond ring in his pocket glow like a magical coal. Soon he would toast his love and claim her for his own. Really his own. She had no notion yet of his intentions. Well, the engagement ring would prove it.

Laurel pulled off her Shetland sweater and stretched. I'm always happy in Hartewoods. I love every inch of it, every stone in the road. She walked over to where he was sitting close to the fire. "Come on, I'll take you to the lake, show you the trees the beavers gnawed down."

"No, thanks. It's almost pitch black outside—"

"Except for the moon!" Laurel laughed in the teasing way she'd had when they first met. She was feeling so good. She turned off the lights and sat down beside him. She shone the flashlight under her chin, which eerily distorted her face. "Did you play scary games when you were a kid?"

" 'So,' Stefan asked, 'do you have the shotgun?' And Dennis said, 'Yes! It's time to shoot!' " Ricky paused for breath. "We were standing on Broadway and the street was crowded and people were ready to hit the pavement. You should have seen those scared faces. Stefan had the shotgun mike, get it? And Dennis had the camera."

Jessica gave a very halfhearted laugh as she relaxed her grip on the steering wheel. She spotted a red-tailed hawk, but she didn't bother to point it out to Ricky. She had Laurel on her mind.

Ricky dropped the cheerful act. "What if he did make those calls? And we agree it's not a sure thing. Why would he hurt Laurie? He *wants* her."

"She's breaking it off with him."

"She hasn't done it yet. You said yourself she wasn't definite. She could be at a picnic or something. Or visiting a friend. It's a weekend. . . ."

"I know, I know." Be home, be home, Jessica thought. Be safe and sound. "But only when I see her will I stop worrying."

Ricky reached for the car phone. "Should I try her again?"

"We're almost there." She pulled off the highway and drove up the curving hills heading to Cornell. "If he made those phone calls, he's got a lot of hate in him."

"What's your excuse for being here—when you find her?"

"We're up here for you to do the lighting in—what's the name of the theater we're stopping at before we go back?"

"Salt City Theater. In Syracuse."

"Plausible?"

"Plausible. Say it's an emergency. The electrician died. Of shock."

Jessica didn't smile. They rode in silence awhile. A few minutes later, Jessica pulled into the lot behind Laurel's dorm.

They hurried to the front door, and Jessica rang the bell.

"Gone!" she said, ringing fiercely. She checked out Laurel's window from where she stood. The blind is well named, Jessica thought. I can't see a damned thing.

"I HAVE SOMETHING to show you." Kevin poured her another glass of wine. "It's very special, for a very special occasion. Forget the games."

He reached into his pocket and held out a small package wrapped in gold foil. "I think Rozsi would want me in the family, she was a terrific artist. I don't pretend to be in her league, but I try. I'm really psyched on that fluorescent sculpture—it's so cool . . ."

Laurel's hand trembled on the box. How did he know about the sculpture? Had he been in Rozsi's apartment? Had he made those calls to her mom? The thoughts were too awful, far-fetched. Except were they really? She remembered how Mini and Doug had asked her not to reveal she knew about Kevin's threat to them. Yes, that's how they'd put it—a threat.

She looked into Kevin's eyes. They showed nothing.

"BUSY," JESSICA SAID as she hung up. She nervously tapped the car phone. She glanced at Ricky, seated beside her. "Well, since he's at home, shall we pay Kevin a surprise visit?"

"Sure thing, surprise is the number one strategy in attacking the enemy."

Jessica backed out of the lot, checked the campus map, and headed toward Kevin's dorm.

LAUREL GUESSED AT what was in the box, but she had to open it. A diamond ring. He had totally ignored their deal, gone against it. This was supposed to be their last weekend—he'd lied again. Her mother was right. There was something very wrong with Kevin.

"Do you like it?" he asked.

She couldn't speak.

"Were you leading me on?" An accusation.

"Of course not," she said, trying to mask her fear.

"I figured it out, Laurel. You just didn't realize how serious I was. That's why you want to break up. You want a *commitment.*" He clasped his hands together. "*Marry* me, Laurel. You know I love you—"

"Kevin, I don't know what to say. I . . ." She tried to think fast, to keep fear from overwhelming her. But if he *had* been in Rozsi's apartment the night she died . . .

Her eyes moved involuntarily toward the door.

"What's the matter?"

She looked at the ring and carefully chose her words. "Kevin, it's the most beautiful ring I've ever seen."

The phone rang.

"Don't answer it!" he commanded.

"Okay," she said, grateful her voice hadn't betrayed her.

"Tonight will be our wedding night."

"YOU JUST CAUGHT me on my way out, Mrs. Lewisohn. I came back to the dorm because I forgot something," Stevie said. He looked apologetically at Jessica and Ricky, who were standing in the middle of the room. "Sorry I can't stay, but if you want to wait for Kevin—"

"Thanks," Jessica said quickly. "We'd like to. If you don't mind."

"Not at all. I have a banquet at the Hilton and I'm late. I'm a hotel major, not a guest. Gotta rush." He grabbed his coat from the chair and opened the door, then paused a moment, looking puzzled. "Kevin left a note that he'd be away for the weekend. Well, I hope he shows up for you." Before he closed the door he stuck his head into the room. "Nice to meet you both. Just shut the door, it's on lock."

"I don't get it, Jess," Ricky said when he was gone. "Why'd you tell him we had an appointment with Kevin?" She dropped into a chair.

Jessica paced as she talked, her eyes darting around the room. "I didn't know he'd be away. But what an opportunity! He won't be interrupting us while we search his room—"

"Search his room?"

"I had to think of an excuse for us to stay after Stevie left. I *have* to find out about Kevin. What better way than by looking through his stuff?"

"What if Stevie tells him we were here?"

"Good question. I'll just have to think of something."

She stopped pacing to look at the walls. "Are those drawings of Laurel bizarre?"

"I don't know, Jess. They're pretty good."

"But so many of them . . ."

Ricky jumped up at the sound of footsteps passing the door. "Let's not waste any time, Jess. I don't want to be caught here if Stevie comes back for his gloves."

"Right."

"I'll take the closet," Ricky said.

"I'll check his desk." Jessica felt Laurel's eyes looking down at her as she tried to pull open his drawer. What she saw when she opened it left her stunned.

LAUREL TRIED TO pry his fingers from her shoulders. "Don't scare me like that, Kevin." He tried to kiss her, but it was too much for her to pretend, and she turned her head aside. "Please, Kevin. This isn't what we agreed on." How foolish, *stupid* that sounded to her now.

He shoved her away, nearly toppling her. "You're waiting for Alan? That's why the phone was ringing." How did he know about Alan? Kevin had been following her, had learned his name.

"No, Kevin," she said, backing farther away from him, toward the door. "Alan's only a friend. Really. He wouldn't call me here," she said, praying she was wrong, that it *was* Alan trying to call her, worried about her with Kevin.

She heard distant sounds of gunfire and realized she was all alone with Kevin. Hartewoods was a summer community, and any hunters tracking animals in the woods were far from the house.

"I'm—I'm going to the drugstore. I need something—you know, women's things."

He dangled her keys in front of her face.

"Give them to me, Kevin." She reached for them, but he snapped them away.

"All right, I'll walk."

Kevin went to the door and held it shut.

"This isn't funny, Kevin."

His back was against the door now, and he pulled her toward him, held her tightly, and covered her face with kisses. "I'll make you love me," he whispered. "I'll make it easier for you to love me than to leave me, Lorna."

Lorna? Who was Lorna?

LORNA BARRETT'S FACE stared at Jessica from the open desk drawer. She picked through glossy magazine shots, yellowing newspaper clippings, and a video. The resemblance was unmistakable—to her own Laurel, and Betsy Wilcox . . . *and* to the dead girl in Indiana! "Oh, my God. The boy who killed that girl was a Lorna Barrett freak. All three girls could have been sisters."

Ricky heard the dead tone in Jessica's voice and looked up in alarm.

Jessica rummaged madly through the drawer, finding a pair of glasses and an old book of poems. She could barely turn to the dog-eared pages. Yes! The poems he had given Laurel; all stolen from this book.

She held up the glasses. They were clear, as she suspected. With trembling fingers, trying not to panic, she folded them and returned them to the drawer.

"Oh, Ricky," she said, "it's worse than I could have ever imagined. Kevin . . . *he's really Billy Owens. He killed April Meadows.*"

Chapter Twenty-Three

WHO WAS LORNA? she wondered. A slip of the tongue? Laurel tried to maneuver him away from the door, but he only pressed his back more firmly against it and gripped her tighter. She was trapped. If she moved, he pressed his fingers more painfully into her flesh.

"Kevin, you're *hurting* me."

Silence.

She let her body go limp under his iron clasp, hoping he would relax his grip. But he only closed his eyes, seemed in some kind of a trance. He squeezed her arm with his right hand and with his left hand caressed her throat. He ran his fingers down toward her breasts. "Lorna . . ." he repeated.

She didn't trust herself to breathe. She watched his eyes as his fingers continued downward into the curves of her breast—and stopped. She forced herself to shut her eyes.

Was this a game he was playing? Was he teasing her, the way a cat teases a mouse with its paw? And then when it tries to escape goes in for the kill?

"NO ONE WILL believe me, but Kevin Glade is Billy Owens!"

"Don't get hysterical, Jess. You can't be sure," Ricky said.

"I *am* sure. Don't you see it? I told you he was a liar. God, I never imagined he was a murderer!"

"Calm down—"

"Where is Laurel? Where's my baby?"

"Have you tried her friends?"

"Mini and Doug were my last hope. What can I do, Ricky?"

"Let's drive around, we'll look for her."

"We're wasting time!" Jessica grabbed her purse and dug for a tissue. She pulled out her filoFAX, quickly found a number, and dialed as she dried her eyes. "The police—Sandy Ungar. I'll call her," Jessica said as she held the receiver to her ear.

Finally a voice. "Dan McKenzie, State Police."

"Detective Ungar, please. This is an emergency!"

"Can I help you? Detective Ungar isn't in."

"My daughter's in terrible danger. The killer of April . . . of April Meadows—*he's with my daughter. He's Billy Owens.*"

"Your name?"

"Jessica Lewisohn. You've got to find him!"

"I'll take the information—"

"The information is that Kevin Glade is Billy Owens. I've suspected him all along. He's a liar. Just tell Detective Ungar he has pictures of Lorna Barrett."

"What?"

"She'll understand."

"I'll pass on this information, ma'am."

"Can't you arrest him?"

"He's only wanted for questioning. Is there something else you can tell us?"

Jessica thought of the glasses, the poems, the pictures of Lorna Barrett. All disconnected and meaningless to anyone but Sandy. "I don't have time, I've got to find my daughter. Tell Detective Ungar, give her these numbers." Jessica read the numbers off the phone and added her cellular number, then hung up.

She looked at Ricky, tears in her eyes. "He thinks I'm a kook. We've got to find her ourselves."

AT THE DOOR to her apartment complex, just as Sandy was about to thank Lloyd Martin for dinner, and what turned out to be a shorter than expected evening of dancing, he took her into his arms and kissed her, full on the lips and like he meant it. And she felt comfortable about it, just as she had when they were on the dance floor. And, surprise, he ran down the steps before she could say a word, waved at the bottom of the stairs before closing the outside door. Whatever happened to brash, aggressive Chief of Detectives Lloyd Martin? One kiss. A bit shy away from the office? Or was he just trying to make an impression? If her heart rate was any measure of his success, he was making mucho points.

She smiled as she unlocked her door and kicked off her shoes. She enjoyed having two men pursue her. My heart is saying Lloyd Martin, and my head is saying the D.A., she thought. Before she turned on the light, she could see the answering machine blinking a message. She was in no mood for another police emergency. Lloyd's beeper had interrupted their date. Still, she dutifully pressed Play.

"Hi, Sandy. Don't know if this means diddly, but a Jessica Lewisohn wants you to call her in upstate New York." He read off the numbers. "She's over the edge, thinks her daughter is in some serious danger. Says Kevin Glade is Billy Owens. Enjoy the rest of the weekend. No rest for the weary. You-know-who, over and out."

HEARING JESSICA'S PANICKY voice, Sandy was glad she hadn't wasted a moment in calling.

"You can relax, Jessica," she said. She slipped out of her leather jacket, sat down on the couch and put her feet up on the coffee table. "Kevin Glade is back in town here. And I've met him. He's a terrific guy. You have nothing to worry about—"

"But, Sandy—the pictures of Lorna Barrett, the resemblance between April and—"

"We can't arrest every fan who has the hots for Lorna Barrett, Jessica. Lorna Barrett has thousands of fans."

"I just know he's Billy Owens!"

"I've met Billy Owens. I know what he looks like. I grilled him after April's murder. *Kevin Glade is not Billy.* Trust me. Kevin's an okay young man. And we checked him out, remember?"

"But the calls he made—I don't have proof, but I know it in my gut. And the lies he told me. I'm afraid for my daughter. I don't know where she is."

"Kevin's been *here,* in Indiana, all weekend. I assure you his worst crime is speeding."

"When I see my daughter, I'll be convinced."

Jessica hung up and turned to Ricky. "Kevin's in Indiana, they tell me." She sank into a chair. "Thank God he's nowhere near my daughter."

* * *

ALAN'S PIZZA HAD just been delivered when Laurel's mother called, and he had invited her to come over. Now, as she and her friend sat nervously on the couch, he was conflicted. Laurel wouldn't like it if he revealed she was at Hartewoods with Kevin. But the look on her mother's face, her distraught voice, had to be considered.

"I don't know where she is, Alan, and I'm worried about her. I don't trust Kevin," Jessica said.

Alan nodded but said nothing. As soon as the two women shut the door behind them, he realized he'd selfishly protected himself from Laurel's anger so that he could step in when Kevin was history. But Laurel's mother was right. Kevin *was* a scary dude. And Alan was between a rock and a hard place. Someone was bound to be angry with him whatever he did. So be it, he couldn't just do nothing.

He phoned Hartewoods. When Laurel didn't answer, he headed for his Toyota.

"DON'T WORRY, JESS," Tom said. "She's at Hartewoods with Kevin."

"Kevin!"

"It's probably their last weekend together. They're going to a rock concert and I know you'll love this . . . she's breaking off with him."

"Tom, don't you *understand*? Sandy Ungar just told me he was in Indiana."

"So he's gone back to his hometown to nurse his hurt. That's natural, it makes sense. Didn't the detective tell you he was okay?"

"Yes, but . . . Tom, I'm her mother, and I tell you our daughter is in real danger."

"You always worry about Laurel, honey. It's understandable, your only child . . . but don't you remember all the wild stuff you did in college? You're still alive."

"Sheer luck."

"It wasn't luck. Anyway, kids take calculated risks. It's called growing up."

And sometimes they die, she said to herself.

* * *

Kevin was undressed. Laurel trembled as he removed her clothes. How could she go through with this? But the look in his eyes told her she had no choice. She had to convince him she was still in love with him. That she wanted him. That he had guessed right, that it was commitment she wanted, a diamond ring. She had to find a way to get through this even though the idea of making love to him made her want to gag.

He was moaning as he stripped off her jeans. Now her panties.

The ringing phone broke the silence again. She jerked her body off the carpet and snatched the phone from the desk nearby before he could stop her. He grabbed her around the throat. She fought to remain calm. He was in control. If he believed it, he could afford to let her talk. Her only hope lay at the other end of the line. If it was Alan, Kevin would freak, and Kevin's ear was pressed close to the receiver. She had no choice.

As she opened her mouth to speak, his hand tightened around her neck.

"Hello," she said into the void.

"Laurel, darling . . ."

"Mother!" she said. Kevin relaxed his grip slightly. His head was touching hers as he listened in.

"Thank God you're—"

"This isn't a good time, Mom! I've got to get off."

"Laurel, No! I've got to—"

"Don't *worry,* Mother. I'm buttoning up my overcoat, wearing my galoshes." Strange words under the circumstances. She hung up quickly, before her mother could speak.

Kevin, smiling, gripped her by the shoulders and pulled her down on top of him.

"The prison faxed us the paperwork on Kevin Glade," Dan McKenzie said. He dropped a packet of papers on Sandy's desk. "What's up?"

"I owe it to Jessica Lewisohn. It's the least I can do. If she came all the way from New York to see me, and she's still worried about her daughter . . ." Sandy leafed through the reports as she spoke. "She thinks Kevin is Billy Owens—which obviously he isn't. I know Billy Owens." She looked up. "To tell the truth, I don't know what I'm looking for, Dan. Maybe some sign that this guy *is* dangerous. Maybe Kevin fooled me."

"On the other hand, your instincts are good. And you're experienced." Dan perched on the edge of her desk. "A dude with something to hide wouldn't be pushing an in-your-face lawsuit."

"Here's something!" Sandy handed him a sheet of paper. "His license. It's a Colorado license."

"Vail, Colorado. Didn't somebody say he was a ski bum?"

"Yeah, but he's living in New York state now."

Sandy turned back to the previous page. "Look here! His address is listed as Vail! Wouldn't the prison have picked this up? They were looking to nail him."

"Maybe, maybe not. He gave his home address, not his college address."

Sandy quickly leafed through the remaining papers. "Nothing here," she said, stacking them together. "I don't have much to go on, but I'll do some checking."

"KEVIN! I'M GLAD you haven't left yet," Sandy said.

"I got a slow start. I guess I'm not as anxious to leave home as I thought I was. Any problem?"

"No. Everything's okay as far as the department is concerned. I'm calling about another matter. Did you say you were driving back to *Vail*?"

"That's where I live."

"You're not at Cornell?"

"What gave you that idea?"

Sandy took a breath. "Do you have a relative in this town with your name?"

"I was named for my father, but he's dead. There's no one else. What's this about?"

"I know this sounds bizarre, but I think someone is impersonating you."

"Why?"

"I don't know. Do you know anyone who . . . ?"

Kevin laughed. "Well, come to think of it, I used to have like a shadow, a kid who followed me around like a puppy when I was in high school. He was in middle school at the time. Even dressed like me—imitated my walk. Some people thought he was my brother."

Sandy felt as if a stone had just dropped in her stomach. "What was his name?"

"Billy . . . yeah, Billy Owens."

PRETEND, PRETEND, LAUREL told herself. Give him what he wants; he *wants* to believe you.

Kevin was clutching her, squeezing her arms, thrusting into her, calling out, "Lorna, Lorna." It terrified her. "No one can have you, only me." He intoned the words, digging his fingers farther into her.

Pretend, she thought. Pretend it's someone else. Pretend it's Alan. Maybe he'll fall asleep if he goes on long enough. He often did before. . . .

But how would she escape? She could make a run for it, but he'd only catch up with her. And where would she run to, anyway? She thought of the gun stashed under the bed in the back bedroom. It was her only chance.

"DON'T FAIL ME now," Alan ordered his Toyota as the car lost power trying again to climb the hill. This was the second time it had slowed to a halt. And now as he pulled off to the side of the road, he knew by the sound that it was dead, done for, kaput.

He stood by the side of the road, hoping a trooper would come by. If not, he would trudge to the nearest highway phone and get the car towed.

Cars whizzed by, but none stopped.

"Laurie, I hope you're okay," he said aloud to the stars. " 'Cause it seems I ain't going anywhere tonight."

"PAZZOLINI, HOLLYWOOD P.I.'s work weekends?"

"I work at home, Ungar."

"Glad I got hold of you. I think I've located Billy Owens, but I need tangible proof it's him. I can't just go after him like gangbusters and find out I've got the wrong guy."

"What can I do to help?"

"The letters to Lorna Barrett. Have you got them handy? I need you to look at them."

"No sweat. I'd like him out of the picture myself. Hang on."

Sandy rocked nervously in her chair as she waited.

"Right in front of me."

"Good. See if there's anything distinctive about them. I know you're not a handwriting expert, but anything you pick up might help."

Sandy heard pages rustling.

"Round handwriting. Goes up and down, mostly down. Dots his i's with a circle."

Sandy took notes. "Keep going."

"Lookie here!" He turned the pages. "He ends every letter with a heart. A heart with an arrow and it's dripping blood. Corny but nicely drawn. And his initials are in the heart."

"Every letter?"

"Yup."

"Thanks. I owe you."

She hung up and immediately dialed the number Jessica had left. There was no answer.

JESSICA SHOOK HER head in confusion. Why did Laurel talk to me that way? What she said made no sense. . . .

"Do you want me to drive?" Ricky asked. "You're pretty upset."

Jessica started the motor without answering. "Why was she in such a hurry to get rid of me?"

"Look, she's safe. What did she say?"

" 'Don't worry, Mother. I'm buttoning up my overcoat.' What the hell . . . ?"

And suddenly, abruptly, Jessica backed out of the lot, throwing Ricky forward. She screeched toward the street. "*The danger word!* I'd forgotten. Laurel's in trouble!"

She drove at top speed down the curving hills. Ricky buckled up and held her breath.

"*Button!* The word we agreed on when she was a child. Our secret word." She nearly missed a curve. "If only I'd remembered, I could at least have told her we were on our way."

"Jessica, are you sure?"

"Get the Monticello police right now."

"What will you tell them?"

Jessica floored the gas pedal. She was on the highway, doing ninety. "I'll tell them that a killer has my daughter!"

Chapter Twenty-Four

LAUREL GRABBED HER clothes and covered Kevin with a quilt. "I'm going to the bathroom," she whispered.

Quickly she pulled on her clothes, flushed the toilet, and turned on the shower full blast. Then she moved silently as she could into the bedroom and felt around under the bed in the dark. Finally she pulled out the gun case. But she dropped it on the bed, frightened by the sound of Kevin moving in the living room.

She inched to the door, where she had a partial view. Kevin, a knife in his hand, was on the floor, obviously looking for the telephone cable.

She stepped back into the bedroom and quickly opened the case. She removed the gun, opened the top dresser drawer, found a box of shells and extracted six of them. She pushed one shell into the chamber, trying to be quick and quiet. But it was taking too long—poking the shell into position was harder than she remembered.

She heard footsteps and her name. The heavy rifle shook in her trembling hands, and she quickly shoved the case and then the rifle under the bed—this time within easy reach.

ALAN LOOKED BACK at his beloved Toyota riding behind him on the tow truck. "I had the feeling this was serious," he told the driver. "It was smoking and it had a funny smell."

"Don't sound good," the driver agreed.

"Couldn't start it. Grind, grind, grind. Never happened before."

"Can't tell till Sam takes the engine apart."

"I have a feeling this old car is toast. What do you think?"

"I don't think. I just tow."

* * *

"WE'VE DOUBLE-CHECKED, sir," the head operator told Tom. "The phone is definitely out of order."

"I don't understand. My wife just spoke to my daughter at that number."

"There are no lines down in that area, sir. The trouble seems to be with that particular number."

Tom hung up, trying to convince himself there was really nothing to worry about. Eyeglasses, stolen poems, Lorna Barrett. Nonsense . . .

He paused a moment at his desk. Except Jessica's no fool, and neither am I.

He picked up the phone again. "Hello, Jake. Tom here. I just got a call from my wife. I know it's inconvenient, but I'm taking an early Christmas. My family needs me."

RICKY HELD THE phone to Jessica's ear after she got the state police.

"This is Jessica Lewisohn. I need your help. It's an emergency. My daughter, Laurel, is in our cabin in Hartewoods with her boyfriend, and I believe he's very dangerous. I think he killed a girl in Indiana."

"You *think*? How do you know he's the one . . ."

"I *need* you to check on my daughter, *please.* The evidence I have won't make any sense to you—glasses for show, three poems he stole—"

"What!"

"Look, I don't have time to explain. What's important is that I just talked to my daughter, and she gave me a signal—one she used when she was a little girl—to tell me she's in trouble. *Please* believe me."

"What did she tell you?" the trooper asked.

"She used our secret word."

"Secret word?"

"I know it sounds silly, but she said the word *button*—that was our word."

"Are you sure it wasn't just *a* word . . ."

"She said, 'I'll *button* up my overcoat.' She wears a ski jacket. It's got a zipper!"

"Our cars are all busy now."

Jessica slowed down to make a curve. "Please, I'm on my way, driving as fast as I can, but you can get there faster. Laurel's only eighteen. I know she's in real danger."

"Hartewoods—Route 42 on Lake Road. As soon as we can, Mrs. Lewisohn. We'll check on your daughter."

Would he? Did he believe her?

"WOULD YOU BELIEVE? Some rich dame calls me on a cellular phone to tell me she's breaking the speed limit to get to her daughter in Hartewoods. She thinks the boyfriend might be a killer. And what's her evidence? Seems the girl's boyfriend stole three poems, and something about his glasses."

Trooper Jong looked up from his computer in the office he shared with Trooper Short. Short was his senior, about to retire, and Jong tried to show respect.

"Three poems?" Jong asked. He wanted to finish his work and get home in time to see his kids. He was off duty in fifteen minutes.

"You want me to arrest him for stealing three poems? That's what I should've asked," Short said. "Yeah, assault with intent to steal three poems! Gimme a break, I've got real cases piling up."

Jong looked up again and nodded politely.

"Then the mother—driving at top speed, mind you—asks me to send a car way over to her cabin on Crescent Lake. It's a summer community. What's her kid doing up there, anyway? It's deserted." He didn't wait for a response from Jong. "Probably screwing her little brains out far away from Mom."

"File it and forget it," Jong said. He continued working.

"Secret word, my ass," Short said, heading for his own desk. He threw his notes into the drawer.

Jong looked up. "Secret word?"

"AND IN THE winter the Hartewoods women would wash their faces in the snow because there was no running water. And the nuns from the convent nearby would swing on the rope from the maple tree. They would swing over the lake, the way we did every summer."

Laurel looked down at Kevin. He was fully dressed, and his head was in her lap, cradled in her arms, listening to stories about Hartewoods. She searched her memory for more tales to tell as she stroked Kevin's forehead. Sleep, she thought, with each stroke. *Sleep.*

Kevin closed his eyes, and Laurel peeked at her watch. "Where are you, Mom? Where are you?" But unless her mother sprouted wings, it would be midnight before she got there from the city. And no way to call for help.

Kevin opened his eyes. "One winter weekend," she went on quietly, "we skated on the frozen lake." His eyes closed as she stroked his hair.

Maybe Mom called the police, Laurel thought. God, I hope so.

Kevin seemed to be dozing at last.

"Button, button, button," she repeated silently.

Her hand was on Kevin's brow. It was hot to her touch from the heat of the fire. But her hands became clammy. What if her mom had forgotten their secret word? It was from a long time ago.

She had to save herself, she decided. Her mother might not be coming. She couldn't count on anybody coming. It was up to her.

"DO YOU THINK I'm crazy, Ricky?" Jess asked.

"Even if you're wrong"—Ricky took a deep breath—"press that pedal to the metal!"

Jessica accelerated to a hundred.

"Don't get a cop stopping us."

Jessica slowed to ninety as the phone rang.

Ricky snatched it up. "Detective Ungar," she told Jessica, holding it to her ear.

"Bad news, I'm afraid," Sandy said. "Your daughter's boyfriend is not in Indiana."

Jessica held the wheel tightly and slowed down.

"Why do you say that?"

"I can't vouch for *your* Kevin Glade. It means your intuition may be right. I want to warn you—"

"He's Billy Owens, isn't he!"

"Maybe, maybe not."

"Billy Owens is with my baby! For God's sake, arrest him!"

"I can't arrest him. We have nothing on him, no proof he killed April Meadows. Tell me where your daughter is."

"I'm almost there." Jessica slowed to fifty, then to thirty to make the exit ramp. "I've called the Monticello police."

"Hang on, Jessica. Be careful. Don't do anything crazy. Just tell me, did Kevin sign his name in some unusual manner?"

"Did Billy?"

"Yes."

Jessica passed the police station and accelerated. Only ten more miles. She thought about the poems he wrote, the card. She pictured the nasturtiums, then his signature.

"Hearts. He put his initials in a heart—in red ink. And my daughter's in another."

"He *is* Billy!" Sandy said.

Jessica's arms tingled as they had last year at the cabin when lightning seared a tree and ran up the front steps.

KEVIN'S EYES WERE closed, but Laurel wondered if he was still awake. She spoke quietly, soothingly. "In the summer I sailed, swam the lake, and shot down the slide with my friends." Her voice caught as she remembered her childhood. "I knew every road, every tree, every pebble. I could walk home from my friend's house without a flashlight even when there was no moon."

She looked through the window at the full moon. It illuminated the room and the lake. The lake's smooth surface, undisturbed by even a ripple, seemed to stare at her, its icy belly a hostile stranger.

Kevin's even breathing gave Laurel some hope that he was asleep. As she slowly pulled herself from under him, she gently shifted a pillow to his head. And ever so softly, to see if he was asleep, she whispered, "Room 101. Let's play the game about our worst fears."

Kevin's eyes opened. "What? Okay . . ."

Laurel was shaken, surprised that he was wide awake, but she thought fast. "Your worst fear. I know what it is!"

Kevin eyed her.

"If you really love me, prove it!" she said.

"How?"

"If you can overcome your fear—like the prince in the fairy tale—you can have the princess."

"You'll marry me?"

"I swear it."

"What do I have to do?"

"Come to the water with me."

Laurel shot up, grabbed her jacket, and raced across the living room to the kitchen. She unlocked the porch door and ran outside. She headed for the thickest part of the shrubs, where the blueberry bushes grew toward the lake.

She heard Kevin behind her, crashing through the bushes. She crept along the shore and crouched low, waiting. No sound. Time passed, and now she had no idea where he was. She knew the safest place for her was near the water. She had to make her move. She inched her way along the lake and toward the boathouse. The low, rotting structure hung over the lake.

She looked inside. It was dark, and she could hear water lapping. Bats flew in and out. Flying mice, Laurel thought. Mice—one of Kevin's nightmares he'd told her. But she knew his greatest fear—water! He didn't sail, he didn't swim. There was a canoe. Maybe . . .

She looked behind her. Kevin was probably lost by now. She stepped into the dank boathouse, and as she heard a rattle, a snake slithered into the woods from underfoot. Shuddering, she hid herself along the inside ledge and looked into the murky waist-high water. She could make out her Sunfish and a rowboat stored along the ledge, but the canoe was floating in the shadows. Edging closer, she extended her right foot into the boat to pull it toward her.

An icy hand grabbed her leg and yanked her in. As she saved herself from toppling, she heard Kevin laugh.

Then, before he could stop her, she used the paddle and shoved off, and in seconds they were on the lake, skimming around the bend.

AS JESSICA DROVE over a bump, Ricky grabbed for the dashboard.

"God, Jess, easy, or we'll never get there."

"We're almost there." In turning to miss a large rock, a tire caught a jutting edge, and the car careened toward a tree. Jessica turned the wheel with all her strength as she felt the car going airborne.

When the car landed, Ricky was too shaken to speak.

"You okay?"

Ricky nodded.

Jessica raced down the driveway and braked behind Laurel's car.

"OKAY, KEVIN, YOU won. You beat me here. Now where are my car keys? It's time to go back to school."

Kevin pulled them from his back pocket and held them over the side of the canoe.

Laurel held her breath, resisting the urge to grab for them.

Kevin dropped the keys into the water, and Laurel felt her hopes sinking to the bottom of the lake.

"How do I know you'll keep your word?" Kevin asked.

The canoe was floating idly. Laurel reached for the paddle.

"You'll have to stay with me now—all winter. I can't let you go now."

"What about school?" Her voice sounded pitiful to her.

She began to paddle toward the main road.

"Where are we going!" He grabbed for the paddle, but she hung on.

"You threw my keys away!"

Kevin was standing now. "It's real simple. If I can't have you, no one can."

The canoe rocked. "Stop it, Kevin. Sit down!" She pulled the paddle in. "I told you, if you won the game I'd marry you. I swore I would."

"I don't believe you. I'm not a fool, Laurie."

"Kevin, sit down, please!"

"I won't."

"Why did you come out on the lake? You hate the water."

"To prove to you . . ."

"What?"

"That I'm not a coward."

"Oh, Kevin. You proved it. Let's go back. Back to school."

"Will you marry me there?"

"Yes!"

"Liar!" He lurched forward, and the boat tipped.

Laurel hung on as he fell overboard.

"TROOPER SHORT, DID you get a call from a Jessica Lewisohn?" Sandy asked.

"Sure did. She had some crazy idea that her kid was in danger. My buddy here, Eddie Jong, insisted I follow up. Eddie has kids, and with all the perverts around, *his* wife gave their daughter a special word."

"Did you go to the cabin?"

"Just got back. We played it cool. Didn't go breaking in because of some lame report. Need probable cause, you know. We cut the motor and the lights, and we walked up real quiet to the windows."

"Yes . . ."

"All we saw was teenage sex. And it looked very much like consensual sex."

Trooper Short leaned back in his chair and waved to Jong as he left. "Anything else we can do for you?" he asked Sandy.

"Yes. Get right over there. The boyfriend's name is Billy Owens, and he's wanted for questioning in a homicide."

"No shit!" Short jumped up. "Hang on." He ran after Jong. "Get back in here!" he shouted. He returned to the phone.

"He's a rapist too," Sandy said. "But the victim won't press charges. He's big trouble."

Short felt for the revolver in his holster. "We're on our way."

"So am I. I'm flying out tonight to bust that fucker."

"IT'S LAURIE. I hear her!" Jessica was out of the car and running. "Laurie! I'm coming!" And then to Ricky: "Call 911. Get an ambulance. Call the fire department."

As she stumbled toward the house, she heard voices on the lake, but could see nothing.

"I'll get the rifle," she said, rushing up the steps. She ran into the bedroom, turned on the light, dropped to her knees, and looked under the bed for the guncase. She found the rifle and dragged it out. She stood up and yanked the dresser drawer open, grabbed a handful of shells from the box, stashed them in her pocket, and raced to the living room window that overlooked the lake. All she saw was the moon's reflection glistening on the water.

Then she heard Laurel scream.

"LAUREL!" KEVIN HAD gone under and come up several times, and was thrashing in panic.

He made a desperate grab for the canoe, trying to pull himself up into the boat.

Laurel hesitated a beat, and then smacked his head with the oar. He still held on. Once more she raised the oar and brought it down on his fingers gripping the sides of the canoe. The boat pitched over, throwing her on top of him. They both went down as the canoe drifted away.

JESSICA CAME THROUGH the porch door, lugging the heavy rifle. By the time I load it, I'll lose precious time, she thought. She ran down the path toward the boathouse, wishing she'd turned on the outside lights.

Suddenly she stopped still. She heard rustling in the bushes. A doe, trailed by a fawn, leaped out of the bushes.

Jessica raced into the boathouse. The canoe was gone. Setting the rifle next to an oar, she untied the rowboat and slid it into the water. She stepped into the boat, sat down, grabbed the oars, and rowed as hard as she ever had in her life.

KEVIN CLUTCHED LAUREL, pulling her down with him. He pushed her head farther under until he reached the surface. She tried to fight him off, but he was too strong.

JESSICA SPIED THE overturned canoe. Her brain felt paralyzed, her legs were unsteady. But when she heard sounds of a struggle, she rowed harder. Suddenly she saw Kevin's head, then Laurel's. She headed for her daughter.

Laurel, dazed, her lips blue, coughing water, broke free of Kevin and reached out to her. With all her strength Jessica hauled her daughter into the boat.

Suddenly, the boat rocked wildly. Kevin was trying to climb in. Jessica picked up the rifle and aimed it at him, to scare him off. But she also released the catch, reflexively.

"Billy Owens!" The words exploded from her throat. Abruptly he let go. The boat lurched, and Jessica's ears rang with the sound of the shot. She was stunned. She had thought the rifle empty. She lay the gun down and snatched up the oars.

SHE WAS STANDING in the dining room doorway. Suddenly he heard a click, felt the cold metal of his father's revolver against his temple. He saw the frozen terror in his mother's eyes. He was going to die!

"Help me," Billy Owens cried. But no one heard him. His eyes saw nothing in the dreaded darkness, but he heard a voice.

"She loves me, doesn't she?" *It was his own voice. And at last, he saw clearly the woman in the doorway, the woman in his dream. She was his mother. "I love you," she said sadly. "I've always loved you."*

But as before, she couldn't save him. He could feel her warm breath as she wrapped herself around him, as he disappeared into the depths of the lake.

"MOM, NO . . ." LAUREL said.

Jessica rowed harder. "He can't hurt you now."

"He can't swim." Laurel's teeth were chattering. She could hardly get the words out.

Jessica kept rowing.

"He can't swim. . . ."

Too late. Laurel could see nothing on the lake, not a ripple, only the moon shivering on its smooth surface, and the trail her mother's boat had left behind them.

Epilogue

JESSICA WAS BARELY aware of the lights flashing on the fire engine and two police cars that had come in response to Ricky's call. As she reached the lake's edge, she could see an ambulance and Ricky standing alongside it. Her arms were about to give out. A police officer and two medics pulled them in and rushed Laurel onto a stretcher. Ricky and Jessica climbed inside the ambulance as medics gave Laurel oxygen and covered her with blankets. A young officer rowed out to where Billy had gone under. A spotlight illuminating the water gave it an eerie, unnatural glow.

The ambulance took off, its sirens blaring. Laurel was safe. Jessica knew it was too late for Billy Owens, alias Kevin Glade. And she wasn't sorry.

"LAKES IN THE Catskills are filled with the ghosts of gangsters who were dumped in the thirties," Margo said. "Pittsburgh Phil went down with his slot machine."

"Shhh," Jessica said, tapping her mouth and wincing. She inhaled the unpleasant medicinal air of the hospital room. Laurel slept on. Taking hold of Margo's arm, she escorted her outside, where Sandy Ungar was hurrying toward them.

"I'll hang out with Ricky, get myself some coffee," Margo said, taking off.

"I came as fast as I could," Sandy said. "They recovered Billy Owens's body. Death by drowning . . ."

"The bullet wound?"

"Superficial. You should have no problem."

"Laurel doesn't know about Billy Owens."

"Is she okay?"

"She's sleeping. A little hypothermia, but her tests are good. She was hysterical in the ambulance, but the doctor gave her something. She should wake up soon."

"I'll talk to her."

"Before we see Laurel, I've been wanting to ask you, Sandy—why did you check up on Kevin?"

"A couple of reasons. After you called I thought it over. The poems he plagiarized seemed insignificant, but then I remembered that a poem was taken from April Meadows's bedroom wall. Another thing, you mentioned Laurel was breaking up with Kevin. And I know that seventy-five percent of women who are murdered are killed when they break up a relationship. It seemed like a small thing—to check up."

Jessica peeked into Laurel's room. "She's awake."

Jessica led Sandy into Laurel's room and sat at her bedside as Sandy pulled over a chair.

"How are you, sweetie?" Jessica asked, stroking Laurel's arm. Laurel stared at Sandy's uniform.

"This is Detective Sandy Ungar," Jessica said.

Laurel sat up. "He's dead, isn't he?"

"He drowned," Sandy said.

"He couldn't swim . . ." Laurel looked at Sandy. "The gunshot . . ."

"Your mother's rifle discharged—accidentally. It was only a flesh wound."

"I don't understand why the rifle had a shell in it," Jessica said. "We never store a loaded gun in the house."

"Mom, *I* loaded the gun."

"Why?" Sandy asked.

"I was terrified. He was acting crazy—wouldn't let me out of the house."

"He was a dangerous person," Sandy said. "His real name was Billy Owens. It looks like he killed a fourteen-year-old girl in Indiana almost two years ago. She was his high school sweetheart. Murdered her and ran away—assumed a new identity, Kevin Glade, the name of someone he admired in school. A couple of years earlier he raped a classmate."

"And I felt *sorry* for him . . ."

"Your mother had it right from day one," Sandy said.

Laurel turned to her mother. "Our secret word. You remembered." She took hold of Jessica's hand. "Oh, Mom. I was so dumb. You suspected all along, and I never believed you!"

Jessica planted a kiss on her forehead. Mother's intuition, she thought.

THE SUN HAD just come up, and Patricia Owens opened her front door to invite Kathleen and her child into the house.

"We've met before," she said, staring through puffy eyes. She fiddled with the handkerchief she had kept in her skirt pocket lately to wipe the tears that would unexpectedly run down her face even when she was not thinking about Billy.

"Yes, in the supermarket," Kathleen reminded her.

"You said on the phone it was urgent, that you knew my son." She led them into the living room and gestured to the couch. When they all had sat down, she could hardly help staring at the child.

"Yes, Mrs. Owens. I knew your son." Kathleen took Brendan's hand in hers. "Mrs. Owens, I want you to meet your grandson." Kathleen bent over and said quietly, "This is your grandmother, Brendan."

MARJORIE MEADOWS PUT her head in her hands.

"It's finally over," Gary said as he stroked his wife's hair. "We can at least rest now, knowing no other family will suffer from him."

Marjorie dried her eyes. "Thank you, Sandy, for what you've done."

"I can't take the credit."

"I'd like to meet Jessica," Marjorie said. "Do you think she might join our group?"

"An advocacy group for young women? I'm sure she would. I'll arrange it. Have you found a name yet?"

"S.O.S. Save our Sisters."

"Would you consider being a consultant?" Gary asked.

"Absolutely. Give me a call and we'll work out the details. I've been recommended for the state investigative team."

"Congratulations," Gary said.

"You deserve it," Marjorie added.

Sandy looked at her watch. "I've got a lunch date," she said.

"Meeting someone special?" Marjorie asked.

"Lloyd Martin. He's head of the team. We've been dating." A smile. "He's a smartass, but he seems to be the domestic sort. Wants lots of kids."

They reached the front hall.

"You'd make a good mother," Marjorie said, opening the door.

"I FEEL SO guilty," Kathleen was saying. "If I had told about the rape, April might be alive today. But I was too ashamed and couldn't put my father through a trial. And Brendan, knowing his father was . . ."

"You did the right thing this time—telling Billy's mother. What will you tell Brendan?" Sandy asked.

"I have time to think about it. Maybe that he drowned."

"The truth is, there was no hard evidence that Billy was April's killer. I doubt any prosecutor would take the case if Billy were alive."

Jessica knew it too, Sandy thought. "Billy was a killer, but if he hadn't drowned he'd be free today," she had told Jessica, in case Jessica had any regrets.

But Sandy didn't voice her thoughts today. If Kathleen wanted to protect Brendan by claiming Billy's death was a drowning accident, so be it. Kathleen had a new beau. God knows, she was entitled to a life.

"Why did you choose Lloyd over the D.A.?" Kathleen asked her now.

"He drinks martinis. And he's never heard of Billy Joel."

Kathleen smiled. "My new boyfriend loves Brendan."

Sandy raised her coffee cup. Here's to justice, she thought. "Here's to romance," she said, noting again how terribly young Kathleen was to be a mother. Good luck to her.

JESSICA'S HANDS SHOOK as she opened the envelope. She had found it in Anyuka's bureau drawer. On the face of the envelope was written:

"To Jessica From Anyuka—1955." The year my father died, Jessica thought, unfolding the letter. She brought the letter into the living room and sat in Anyuka's armchair by the phone. She could hear Laurel and Tom in the kitchen fixing tea.

Darling Jessica,

I don't believe in secrets. But one I kept. Your father felt it was wrong to keep this secret, so I compromised. I left this letter so you will know the truth of how your father and I met.

I was sent from my home in Budapest by the Nazis to a labor camp, rounded up with others on a cattle car. I knew the Nazis would kill me. Many of the Jews actually believed the lies they were told, and they were later gassed in Auschwitz. I jumped off when the car slowed down. I was young and had the guts. But an S.S. pig shot at me and hit me once in the back. It was in the forest of Poland, where your father found me and nursed me back to health. He was in the underground, and we spent the war in hiding. We were lucky. We survived.

But a Nazi searching for partisans did not. He came on the spot where we were hiding and he was about to shoot your father. He had his gun aimed at your father while he was asleep. I shot him first. He never saw me. But I saw the surprise in his blue eyes. I often think of his mother. But he was a killer. And I defended our lives.

My darling, *draga,* Jessica, I didn't want to burden you with my sadness. I didn't want the ashes of your ancestors as part of your memory. I wanted my American daughter to have a fresh and free American heart. Excuse me if I did wrong not telling you . . . and if I did wrong to tell you. But the truth is, we both loved you dearly. I hope we gave you a good life. We tried the best we knew how.

Love and kisses, your Anyuka.

Jessica looked around, hating the moment the apartment would be emptied. Anyuka's furniture and treasures had the magic dust of Rozsi on them.

Tom set Jessica's teacup by the phone.

Laurel walked in as Jessica handed Tom the letter, and Laurel and Tom sat on the couch to read it together.

Impulsively, as she waited, Jessica pressed redial on the phone. This was the last call her mother had made. The phone rang.

"My God, my God!" Jessica called out. "It's *our* answering machine. She was trying to call *me* the night she died." Tom and Laurel looked up in shock. "What if she was calling for help? I hung up on her!"

"You thought it was Kevin," Tom said.

"I'll never forgive myself—"

"Blame Kevin. Owens. He's responsible," Tom said.

"Kevin was *here* that night. I know it," Laurel said. "He knew about the sculpture. She finished it the night she died."

"He killed Anyuka!" Jessica said.

"And Matchka," Laurel said. "Anyuka would never have left the window open."

"Unless she was sick and disoriented," Tom said. "Why would he want to hurt Rozsi?"

"I don't know," Jessica said. "I don't understand—"

"Do we know for sure he visited her that night?" Tom asked.

"I saw fresh flowers in a vase the day after she died. At the time I thought Anyuka had bought them herself."

"But why did he bring them?" Tom asked.

"To butter her up. It was typical Kevin," Laurel said. Her voice broke. "I'm to blame for Rozsi and Matchka. . . ."

Jessica sat next to Laurel, who put her arms around her mother. "If I'd listened to you, Rozsi might be alive today." Laurel buried her head in her mom's shoulder.

Jessica smoothed Laurel's hair. "Rozsi was eighty, honey, and had a heart condition. For all we know, Matchka's death was an accident. Maybe your dad is right, Anyuka was ill and opened the window, or Kevin opened the window not realizing Matchka would climb out."

"I gave you such a hard time, Mom. And look what happened."

Jessica hugged her close. "Do you think Rozsi would blame her *draga* Laurika?" Tears rolled down Laurel's cheeks as her mother spoke.

"You're trusting, the way a young person should be. And when you spread your wings, my darling, sometimes they flap in your mother's face."

Laurel laughed as she took a tissue from Jessica, blew her nose, and walked over to Rozsi's sculpture.

"What's my excuse?" Tom asked. "I was so damned sure you were suffering from empty-nest syndrome that I didn't take you seriously,

Jess. I need you to forgive *me* for being such a stubborn ox—as Anyuka would say."

"Too many if-onlys," Jessica said. "If only Betsy's mother had sent the letter a day sooner . . ." Jessica's voice grew softer. "Maybe it was Rozsi's time. Her heart just gave out."

Laurel turned on the lamp. "Just take a look," she said. "The colors are so bright. Just like *nagymama.* Don't you feel she's somehow with us?"

"Inside us. Always. Anyuka will *always* be with us," Jessica said.

The telephone rang and Laurel picked up.

"Oh, my God!" Laurel exclaimed into the phone. "Oh, *Alan,* not your car. I'm really sorry," she said. She talked awhile longer before signing off.

The sparkle had returned to Laurel's eyes for the first time since she'd come home, Jessica noted. She smiled as Laurel sat down beside her to give her a bear hug.

Jessica stared searchingly into Laurel's face.

"Now tell me about this Alan . . ."

Tom and Laurel exchanged looks, then burst into laughter.